Richard Stephen Charnock

Ludus Patronymicus

SALZWASSER
VERLAG

Richard Stephen Charnock

Ludus Patronymicus

1st Edition | ISBN: 978-3-75251-683-8

Place of Publication: Frankfurt am Main, Germany

Year of Publication: 2020

Salzwasser Verlag GmbH, Germany.

Reprint of the original, first published in 1868.

LUDUS PATRONYMICUS;

OR,

THE ETYMOLOGY OF CURIOUS SURNAMES.

LUDUS PATRONYMICUS;

OR,

THE ETYMOLOGY OF CURIOUS SURNAMES.

BY

RICHARD STEPHEN CHARNOCK, PH. DR.,

F.S.A., F.R.G.S., &c.

"Nomen, Numen."
Naso in Ciceronem

LONDON:
TRÜBNER & CO., 60, PATERNOSTER ROW.
1868.

CONTENTS.

AVANT-COURIER.

THE custom of giving nicknames has been common to all nations; but we have many curious surnames that are not nicknames at all. In England and Wales alone the number of names that might be termed odd or curious would scarcely be credited, without first perusing the Registrar-General's List of Peculiar Surnames.* I once showed this List to my etymological friend, Aretchid Kooez, who forthwith sat down, and struck off some passages of his Life in what he calls Patronymic Language.† Gentle and Simple Readers must accept this in part payment of a preface. My quaint friend begins thus :—

I *Wass*‡ *Born In Summersett, Hon* a *Monday, In July, Hat* an *Early Hour* of the *Morning, Howlong Back* I *Forget; Butt Long* since the *Diet* of *Worms And* the *Battle* of *Waterloo. Thayer Wass* a *Comet Hat* the *Time* [*Good Hor Bad Omen?*]. My *Father Wass* a *Weaver And Had* a *Pretty Wife, Hoo Had* a *Small Foot And Hand, And* wore *Herr Hone Hair. Thäer Ware Six Children, Arfin Boys, Arfin Girls* (*Blond*

---

* Selected from the Indexes of Births registered in the quarter ending 31st March, 1831, and of Deaths registered in the corresponding quarter of 1853.

† I shrewdly suspect that friend Kooez must have also dived into Bowditch's work on American Names.

‡ All the words in *Italics* are found as surnames.

And Dark). I Had Ten Cousins, Many Uncles, And Lots of *Quaintances. My Daddy Wass* a *Jolly Fellow, Wass* "fond of *His Friend And Bottle And Got Mellow ;" And, Twice Making His Last Will And Test, Dyde Worth* a *Plum. One Uncle Wass* a *Great Tippler And Dyde* of *Dropsie;* a *Second* a *Gamester,* a *Third* a *Devil* of a *Rake. My Father Wass* a *Jew, One Brother* a *Morman ;* the *Rest Ether Turks Hor Pagans, And Ure Humble Servant* a *Christian. My Elder Brother Wass* a *Tidy Pecker, And (Honour Bright)* didn't *Drink Water, I Can Tell You. Just Look Hat His Bill* of *Fare* for *Frühstück [Breake Fast], Tiffin,* i. e. *Lunch, And Dinner.*

Frühstück.

Tea, Coffee (Au Lait) With Milk, Coldham, Hotham, Eggs And Bacon, Herrings, Haddock, Muffins, Rolls, Bread And Butter, And a *Segar.*

Lunch.

Bitters, Cheese, Butter, Bread, Ham And Chicken, Ale, Porter, Stout, Sherry, Ceider, And a *Pipe.*

Dinner.

[Grace Beevor Meals.]

Pea Soup, Mulloy Kit Tauney, Gravy, Turtle, Hare, Pheasant, Spring, Westerfield White.

Salmon, Turbot Au Béchamel, Codd And Oyster Sauce, Soles, Skate, Smelts, Sprats, White Bate, Trout in *Wine, Plaice, Sturgeon, Grey Mullet With Caper Sauce, Whiting, Perch, Carp, Jack, Eels.*

Roast Beef And Batter Pudding, Mutton With Onion Sauce Orr Capers, Lamb, Veal, Hogsflesh And Apple Sauce, With Cabbages, Greens, Carrots, French Beans, Spinnage, Cow Cumbers, Marrows, Kail, And Peas.

Rabbit, Hare, Leveret, Partridge, Pheasant, Quail, Teal, Snipe, Woodcock, Grouse, Goose, Duck, Duckling, And a *Curry* of *Fowl.*

Jellies, Custards, Ices, Tarts, Seftons, Lemon Pudding, Pies, Apple Charlotte, And Plenty of *Sweets.*

Sallade of *Mustard And Cress, Lettice With* a *Clew* of *Garlick.*

Nuts, Oranges, Olives, Filberts, Apples, Pears, Normandy Pippins, Almonds And Raisins, Plums, Cherries, Dates, Currants, Melons With Sugar Hor Salt.

· *Sherry, Port* (*Curius Old*), *Champagne* (*Clicquot*) *Madeira, Hock, Claret, Cape, Beaune, St. George.*

My *Wife His* a *Darling, Such* a *Duck* of a *Spouse, Butt* Hon my *Soul, How Much Does Not* the *Slybody Cost Mee* for *Herr Wardrobe ! Ive* to *Pay* for *Beads, Ribbons, Robes, Tapes, Tiffany, Cotton, Silks, Cashmeres. By* the *Dickens !* Hat *Christmas, Hime Prest Like* a *Lemon* for *Bonnet, Gown, Shawl, Scarf, Sash, Spencer, Cape, Plume And Feathers ; And Every Winter* for a *Muff, Tippet, And Furss, And* a *Cloak With* a *Hood ; And Now And Then* for *Pearls, Rubies, Emeralds, And Diamonds. Heavens ! Hime Not Ugly,* tho' *Tall, And* my *Head Small; Hime Thin, Slim, And Rather Smallbyhynd.* My *Skin His Dark* [*With* a *Mole Hon* my *Cheek*], *Beard And Whiskers Black, Eyes Brown, Face Round, Neck Short, Skull Thick.* My *Arm His Slight,* my *Hand Nothard, Butt* my *Fist Can Plant* a

Good Blow. The *Hair Hon* my *Noddle His Grey, Butt* my *Knee His Not Bent,* my *Ear Still Sharp. Summ Call Mee Longfellow, Others (Sans Raison), Greathead.* My *Heart His In* the *Right Place, Yet Not Hon* the *Dexter Side. In* the *Early Part* of my *Life* I *Wass* a *Weakly Chap, And Had* a *Deal* of *Maladies; Such* as *Ague, Boils, Fever, Fits, Hiccups, Cramp, Piles, Rash, Rickets, And Once Had* a *Pimple Hon* my *Nose,* a *Bump Hon* my *Head,* a *Whitlow Hon* my *Finger, And Bunyans And Corns Hon* my *Foot, By Gum!* [*Physick* to the *Catts; Heal Ewer Self, Master Pills*]. *Ive* a *Fancy* for *Music, Love Harmony And Melody, Sing Both Treble And Bass, And Carol Like* a *Bird. Buglehorn, Drum, Fiddle, Fife, Harp, Horn, Organ, Hor Tabor, Ar Aul One to Mee.* Ive Been* a *Great Fisher Man, Butt Summ How Hor Other,* I *Always Ketch Cold* in the *Boat* [*Rather Hard Lines*]; I *Like Rowin, Butt Manage Rudder Better Then Oar Hor Skull. Ive Noe Love* for the *Chase;* I *Cant Jump Hedges And Ditches. Why Breake Neck, Legg, Arms, Hor Shoulder Why Knock Down Wheat, Barley, Oats, Ore Even Tares?* [*You Cant Always Cure* the *Scarlet Fever. If You Doe Get Hit, Keep Upp Strength And Spirits, Tak Off Blankets, And Hope* the *Windows*]. *Hime* a *Great Smoker* [*Cant* I *Blow* a *Cloud!*]; *Many* a *Pipe Daily; Near* a *Pound* of *Bird's Eye, Shagg, Hor Returns Every Week. Hon Sunday* I *Tak* my *Segar, Hor,* as *Shum Wouldhave Hit, Weed. Ive Been* a *Great Traveller, And Such* a *Walker! Ive Trodden Many Lands, And Wass Once* a *Pilgrim* to *Calvary, Galilee, Nazareth, Jordan, Jerusalem, And Gath,*

---

* I once heard Kooez sing " *Hime* a *Romer,*" the " *Rover His Free,*" and " *Home, Sweet Home.*"

without *Firman Hor Pass Port. By Jove!* the *Weather Does Not Stop Mee; Hit His Aul* the *Same; Fineweather, Fairweather, Merryweather, Even Foulweather.* I *Delight In Tempest, Snow, Storm, Rain, Shower, Hail, Thaw, Sleet, Frost, Dew, Wind, Fog, Mist, Gale.* I *Wass Always Parshall to Gambling, And Wass Clever, And Had Luck, Hat Hazard, Faro, Skittles, Billiards, Dice, Chess, Butt Wass Not Once* a *Prigg Hor Swindler. By* the *Bye,* a *Short Time Back,* I *Had* a *Law Suit Hat Westminster, Hon Circuit, Hor Hat Sessions [Forget Witch]; Butt Grant You May* have a *Just Cause,* the *Best Counsell [And Pay* a *Heavy Fee],* a *Good Jury [Not* a *Common Jury], And* a *Learned Judge, Hit Does Not Always Follo You Get Justice [Wat Quirks And Tricks!*].* If *Hit Goes Agin You, Wait Till Term, And Try* for a *Rule Nice Eye, Hon Motion, Ore File* a *Bill; Dam,* the *Cost!†* I *Once Went* to *Church, And* the *Parson, In His Sermon, Said,* if *One Wass Just, Had Faith And Trust In* the *Gospel, And Wass* a *Truman, In* the *Cumming World,* i. e., *Paradise, Hor Kingdom* of *Heaven, One Might Bee* a *Perfect Man (Watt Bliss!); Butt* if *One Wass* a *Badman,* after *Getting Off Our Mortal Coil, Thayer Wass* a *Good Chance* of *Going* to the *Devil. Cant Say Hime* a *Croker, Butt Death, Coffins, Churchyards, Graves, Toombs And Monuments Air By Noe Means Pleasant Things.*

Amen, Goodby, Farewell, Byby.

* We certainly have *Our Law* of *Many Colours* and sorts; as *Blacklaw, Whitelaw, Brownlaw, Greenlaw, Shillinglaw, Softlaw.*

† When I got thus far, I exclaimed, in *Lingua Patronymica,* Fie, *Prow Pudor!* But on looking at the orthography and punctuation, I became satisfied that our autobiographer had merely made use of the French peasants' common exclamation, *Dame* = Bless me!

Now, although some of the above surnames really mean what they appear to mean, very many of them, like most of those to be found in the body of the present work, are gross corruptions, and the only way to account for their present form is that there is (as Mr. Ferguson justly observes) a tendency to corrupt towards a meaning. Thus Pettycot will easily become *Pettycoat*; Eyvile *Evil*; Frick *Freak*; Hanaper *Hamper*; Lepard *Leopard*; Manley *Manly*; Hugh *Hue*; Sigar *Segar*; Bradford *Broadfoot*; Kirkbride *Cakebread*; Playford *Playfoot*, &c. &c.

It struck me that a small work on the subject might be acceptable just now, the more especially as it would enable those burdened with objectionable names, instead of assuming others, to discover the proper orthography of their own names. Thus few would probably change their name from Buggin or Simper to Smith, if they thought they were justified in writing Bacon and St. Pierre. The same might be said of such names as Death, Dearth, and Diaper, from D'Aeth, D'Arth, and D'Ypres respectively. Of course some of the suggested derivations are but reasonable guesses; but good guesses are better than none at all, and may often lead to the truth. The title of the work, LUDUS PATRONYMICUS, was suggested by my friend, the Rev. S. F. Creswell, M.A., Head Master of Dartford Grammar School, Kent, and late Scholar of St. John's College, Cambridge, who likewise baptized my VERBA NOMINALIA.

R. S. C.

GRAY'S INN SQUARE,
January, 1868.

WORKS CONSULTED.

Names, Surnames, and Nicknames of the Anglo-Saxons, by J. M. Kemble. London, 1846.

Codex Diplomaticus Aevi Saxonici, by J. M. Kemble. London, 1847.

Northern Mythology, by B. Thorpe. London, 1851.

Grimm's Deutsche Mythologie. Third Edition. Göttingen, 1854.

Förstemann's Altdeutsches Namenbuch. Nordhausen, 1856.

Outzen's Glossarium der Friesischen Sprache. Copenhagen, 1837.

Pott's Personennamen, insbesondere die Familiennamen, und ihre Entstehungsarten, &c. Leipzig, 1853.

Island's Landnamabok, hoc est Liber Originum. Islandiæ, Copenhagen, 1774.

Worsaae's Danes and Norwegians in England, Scotland, and Ireland. London, 1852.

Ueber Deutsche Vornamen und Geschlechts-namen von Tileman Dothias Wiarda. 8vo. Berlin und Stettin, 1800.

Vergleichendes etymologisches Wörterbuch der gothisch teutonischen Mundarten, von Heinrich Meidinger. 4to. Francf., 1833.

Bosworth's Origin of the English and Germanic Languages and Nations. London, 1848.

Latham's Ethnology of the British Islands. London, 1852.

Glossarium Germanicum, by J. G. Wachter. Leipzig, 1737.

English Etymologies, by H. Fox Talbot. London, 1847.

Camden's Remains concerning Britain.

Verstegan's Restitution of Decayed Intelligence in Antiquities concerning our Nation, 1605.

A Dissertation of the Names of Persons, by J. H. Brady. 1822.

Remarks on the Antiquity and Introduction of Surnames into England, Archæologia, vol. xviii. pp. 1057.

Gentleman's Magazine, 1772.

Edinburgh Review for April, 1860.

Patronomatology, an Essay on the Philosophy of Surnames, by Rev. C. W. Bradley, M.A. 8vo. Baltimore, U.S.

Essay on Family Nomenclature, by M. A. Lower, M.A., F.S.A. London, 1849.

Patronymica Britannica, a Dictionary of the Family Names of the United Kingdom, by M. A. Lower. London, 1859.

English Surnames and their place in the Teutonic Family, by Robert Ferguson. London and York, 1858.

Proceedings of the Royal Society of Northern Antiquaries.

Suffolk Surnames, by N. I. Bowditch. London, 1861.

LUDUS PATRONYMICUS.

AGATE. From *at-the-gate*, one living at or near a gate.

AGUE. Mr. Ferguson thinks this name is probably the same as the O. G. Aigua, Aguus, Agio, of which the root may be the O. N. *aga*, exerceo. Mr. Lower derives it from Fr. *aigu*, corresponding with our Sharpe. It may however be same as Agg (U. S. Agg and Agge). The English names Agg, Aggas are from Agatha.

AIR. Mr. Ferguson thinks this name may be from O. H. G. *aro*, *ar*, O. N. *ari*, an eagle. It is rather from Ayr, cap. of Ayrshire, Scotland.

AIRY. Mr. Ferguson compares the names Airy, Air, Arrah with the O. G. Aro and Ara of the seventh century, and the common Scandinavian name Ari, which he derives from O. H. G. *aro*, *ar*, O. N. *ari*, an eagle. Lower says the Cumberland family of Airey consider the name to have been borrowed from an elevated dwelling among the mountains called an eyrie, such designations for residences not being uncommon ; and he says *aery* also signifies a place for the breeding or training of hawks. The name is more probably the same as Harry, Harrie, for Henry ; or it may even be from Harold.

ALABASTER. The same with Arblaster ; from O. E. *alblastere*, a cross-bowman. In the H. R. it is found in Lat. Albales-

B

tarius. "Several of the distinguished archers at the battle of Hastings became tenants in chief under the Conqueror, and are entered in Domesday with the surname of Arbalistarius, or Balistareus or Balistarius. Hence the names Alabaster, Blast, and others " (*Lower*).

ALCOCK. See COCK.

ALEFOUNDER. The ale-founders were ale-tasters or ale-conners. In O. Court Rolls they are called " gestatores cervisi," the term commonly used in the records of Court Leet. Lower classes this term with " ale-draper," and justly calls it a ridiculous designation. There is a beer retailer in London of the name of Alefounder. The last part of the name may be from *fundo*, to pour out.

ALEMAN. From root of Almond, *q. v.* Aleman is the name of a German general.

ALLCARD. The same as the A. S. personal name Alcheard, Cod. Dip. 520 ; perhaps the same as the A. S. name Allward, and the modern names Ailward and Aylward.

ALLCOCK. See COCK.

ALLENGAME. See WALKINGHAME.

ALLPENNY. See HALFPENNY.

ALLWATER. From some local name compounded of "water."

ALMOND. The same as Almund, Ellmund, and the Ælmund of Domesday; from G. *alf-mund*, strong or powerful protector. Ferguson also thinks Almond may be from the A. S. name Alhmund, O. N. Amundr, from *mund*, protection. From Almond we doubtless have the names Almon, Ellman, Holman, Oldman, Element.

ALOOF. From Alf or Alph, for Alfred.

ALUM, *i. q.* ALLUM, ALLOM. The same as Hallam ; from Hallam, the name of parishes co. Derby and York.

ANGER. Some derive this name from *hanger*, a wooded declivity ; but Ainge, Ainger, Anger, Angier, Augier, Aunger (sometimes pronounced Ainger), and Aungier are rather from Anjou, an old prov. of France (now forming dep. Maine-et-Loire, and parts of Sarthe, Mayenne, and Indre-et-Loire), whose cap. was Angers. Aunger and Aungier are in charters found Latinised to Angevinus; and Angevine is found in H. R. with the prefix *Le*.

ANGUISH, *i. q.* ANGWISHE. From some local name compounded of *wich* or *wick*; as Anwick co. Lincoln; or perhaps rather from Angus, the ancient name of co. Forfar, Scotland.

ANVIL. Doubtless from Anneville, name of several villages in Normandy. " The English family (of *Anneville*), according to De Gerville, originated from Anneville-en-Saine, a parish in the arrondissement of Valognes " (*Lower*).

APPLE or APPEL. Ferguson says *happel* is a word used in Silesia for a horse. The name Apple is more probably a diminutive of Hab or Hap, in Hapsburg a nickname for Herbert. Apfel is however a German name. From Hab or Hap we doubtless have the name Happy.

APPLEJOHN. See APJOHN.

ARM. A name which is also found in local surnames; as in Armfield, Armsby, Armsworth, &c. It may be the same as Orme. See WORM, RAM, RUM. Ferguson gives also the name Arms, which he derives from A. S. *arm*, poor.

ARMOUR. Lower says this name is a corruption of armourer; and he gives Armorer as a surname.

ARROW. Ferguson says the names Arrah and Arroh might be derived from the weapon, like Shaft and other similar names; but Arrow is the appellation of a parish co. Warwick, and of a township co. Chester.

ASHMAN. Lower says the forms of this name in the H. R. are Asscheman, Aschman, and Ashman; and in Domesday Assemannus; and he thinks the name equivalent to spearman, *æsc* or *ash* in A. S. poetry being constantly used in the sense of spear, because the staff of a spear was usually made of that wood. I take it that this name is the same as Asman, Osman, Osmon,

Osmund (whence doubtless Houseman, Housman), from *as*, *os*, which in German names signifies excellent (excellens, præstans, egregius). Wachter renders Osmund, vir præstans ; and Oswald, tutor egregius ; and he says *os* is the same as the Welsh *od*.

AUGER, AUGUR, AUGURS. All three are found in the U. S., and the two first in England. Lower says, "Auger, Aucher, a Norman name, whence Fitz-Aucher; also a corruption of Alsager, a place in Cheshire. Archæologia, vol. xix., p. 17." I should rather derive these names from Algar, Elgar (H. R. Algar, Alger ; Domesday, Algar, Ælgar. Algar, name of a bishop of the E. Angles), contracted from the old name Ælfgar, from *ælf-gar*, which might variously translate, very helping, very strong, a help in war.

AUGUR, AUGURS. See Auger.

AUGUST. From Auguste, the Fr. form of Augustus.

B.

BACCHUS. As an English surname, from Backhouse or Bakehouse.

BACON. In H. R. this name is found Bachun, Bacun, and Bacon, and is said to be derived from Bacon, a seigniory in Normandy. Lower says in some instances Bacon may be a corruption of Beacon, and that, from their connection with Bayeux, the Bacons were sometimes Latinised De Bajocis. I consider the name a French diminutive of Bach, from G. *bach*, a brook, rivulet. Hence Bacot, another diminutive. Bacon has been corrupted to Buggin.

BADCOCK. See Cock.

BADGER. Ferguson considers this name the same as the O. G. Patager, from *beado* war, *ger* spear. It is rather from *badger*, an old word for a hawker ; or from Badger, a parish co. Salop.

BADMAN. From A. S. *bæthman*, a bather; perhaps a baptiser. Hence no doubt the names Batman and Bateman, although the two latter may also be from *batman*, a boatman.

BAKE. From Bake, name of an estate in St. German's, Cornwall.

BAKEWELL. From Bakewell, a market town and parish co. Derby. Doubtless compounded of *ville*.

BALAAM. From Bailham, Suffolk; or Balham, Surrey.

BALCOCK. See COCK.

BALM. A corruption of Balsam, or contracted from Balaam, *q. v.* respectively.

BALSAM. From Balsham, in Cambridgeshire, which Fuller characterises as " an eminent village," and the only one in England bearing the name.

BANNISTER, BANISTER, BANNESTER. Perhaps originally *Bainster*, one who kept a bath; from O. Eng. and O. F. *bain*, a bath.

BANTAM. Same as Bentham; from Bentham, a parish in Yorkshire.

BARGE. Lower thinks this name may have been derived from an inn sign. It is more probably the same as Burge ; from Burgh, name of eleven parishes of England. Hence no doubt the name Purge.

BARKER (H. R. Barcarius and Le Barkere). From the old *berkere*, a tanner, bark being used in tanning. The word *barker* now signifies one who strips trees of their bark. Barkary was a law term for a tan-house.

BARNACLE. Ferguson under this name gives " Barnakarl, Barnakel, a surname or a nickname given to a celebrated Norwegian pirate, named Olver, who, setting his face against the then fashionable amusement of tossing children on spears, was christened by his companions, to show their sense of his odd scruples, Barnakarl, baby's old man." The name is more probably from Barnacle, a hamlet co. Warwick.

BARNDOLLAR. See Cashdollar.

BARNFATHER. See Pennyfather.

BARRINGDOLLAR. See Cashdollar.

BARROW, BARROWS. From Barrow, name of parishes and places in at least ten counties in England; from *barrow*, a wood or grove, from A. S. *beara, bearewe*, a grove; or from *barrow*, a hillock or mound of earth intended as a repository for the dead, answering to the *tumulus* of the Latins; from A. S. *beorg* a hill or hillock, *byrgen* a tomb.

BARTER. Lower thinks this name to be from the O. E. *barratour*, one who stirs up strife between the king's subjects, either at law or otherwise. Barter, Barters are both found in the U. S. They may be the same as Batter, Batters, in Battersby, so called from an estate and township co. York. They may also be connected with Butter, *q. v.*

BAT. A nickname for Bartholomew. Hence Batt, Bate, Batts, Bates, Batson, Badkin, Batkin, Badcock, Batcock.

BATCOCK. See Cock.

BATMAN. See Badman.

BEAN. Lower says Bean, Beane are Scotch abbreviations of Benjamin. I should have otherwise derived it from Gael. *beag*, little, young; W. *bechan;* Corn. *bighan, wigan.*

BEDALE. From Bedale, a parish in Yorkshire.

BEDLOCK. See Legg.

BEE. From A. S. *by, bye*, a dwelling, habitation; Sco. *by*, a village, hamlet; Dan. *by*, a city, town, borough. Hence Bradbee, Summerbee, &c.

BEER. Ferguson says Beer is the same as Bear, from A. S. *bar*, a bear, O. N. *bera*, O. H. G. *bero*, D. *beer;* but this name is more probably from Beer-Alston or Beer-Ferris (Ferrers) in Devon, or Beer-Hacket or Beer-Regis in Dorset.

BELCHAMBER, BELLCHAMBERS. A friend assures me he knows of a *William Chambers*, who changed his name to Billchambers, of which he says Bellchambers is a corruption.

BELDAM. From some local name compounded of *ham*, a dwelling. Kennett renders *beldam* a "woman who lives to see a sixth generation descended from her."

BELLOWS. See BILLOWS.

BELOVLY. See LEGG.

BERRY. Berry-Pomeroy is the name of a parish co. Devon, and Berry or Berri is the appellation of one of the old provinces of France. But see BURY and BORROW.

BICHARD. See HAZARD.

BICKERSTAFF. See WAGSTAFF.

BIDGOOD. This name may mean "good or noble in war," or "a good counsellor" (A. S. *beado, beada*, counsellor; G. *god*, good, noble, kind). The A. S. *guth-boda* would mean "a war messenger." The O. N. *bodi* is a messenger, and *gunn, gunnur, gud*, O. H. G. *gund, gunt*, war.

BIGGIN. A common termination of local names in the northern counties and in Scotland, as Dowbiggin, Newbiggin. It means a house of a large size, as opposed to a cottage, a building; from A. S. *byggan*, to build. In Scotland *biggin* is sometimes used to designate small buildings on the banks of rivers, &c., in which night lights are placed to prevent vessels from mistaking their course.

BILKE. Perhaps the same as Bielcke, from Biel, now Bienne, in Switzerland; or a German diminutive of Bill, *i. e.* Will, for William. Bill and Bilo are German names, and Pott gives Bille and Bielke as modern German names.

BILLET. Lower thinks this name a probable corruption of the great baronial name Belet. It would rather seem to be a diminutive of Bill for William. Belet is doubtless a corruption of Bellot, a diminutive of Bel for Isabella.

BILLIARD. See HAZARD.

BILLOWS. Ferguson thinks Billows may be the same as an O. G. Bilo, quoted by Förstemann, and that Pill and Pillow, unless connected with Peel, may be H. G. forms of Bill or Bilo.

Bellew, Pellew, Bellas, Belliss, and Bowles are also surnames. Pellew is said to be of Norman origin, from *bel-eau*, the beautiful water, the designation of some locality [Belleau is the appellation of a parish co. Lincoln]. Bowles has been derived from Bellovesus, a celebrated name mentioned in Liv., Lib. v., cap. 33, said to mean a leader in war (*dux belli*), from O. G. *vel* for *veld*, war. Bowditch says the writer of Britaine's Remains supposes the name Bellows to be a corruption of Bellhouse, and he mentions a History of the Bellows Family by the Rev. Henry W. Bellows, D.D., of New York.

BLACKLOCK. See LEGG.

BLACKMONSTER. "This repulsive name is a corruption of Blanchminster, the White Monastery, the designation of more than one religious house. *Blancmuster* is an ancient alias for the town of Oswestry. The name was commonly Latinised *De Albo Monasterio.*"—*Lower.*

BLADE. The name Blade, Blades, Blaides, Blaydes, Bleyds, found written Bursblades, Buresblades, Bursebred, or Bursebleyd, is said to be of Danish origin. Wilkinson says the family assumed the local name of Burse-blades or Purse-blades, from residing at Burs-blade, near Durham.

BLANKET, BLANKETT. For Blanchett, a diminutive of the name Blank or Blanch; from Fr. *blanc*, white. "Rear-Admiral Blankett was a British officer in the wars against Napoleon" (*Bowditch*). See also Verba Nominalia, under "Blanket."

BLAST. See ALABASTER.

BLAZE. "An ancient personal name borne by St. Blase or Blaise, the patron of the woolcoombers of England," says Lower, quoting Brady's Clavis Calend, 1201. Cf. the Sp. Blas (Gil Blas, Ruy Blas), the It. Biaggio, L. Blasius; probably from Gr. βλαστη, bud, shoot, sprout, blossom; βλαστανω, to sprout, shoot forth, bud.

BLOOD. Ferguson derives this name from O. N. *blaudr*,

bashful, timid. It may be the same name as Lloyd, Floyd, from W. *llwyd*, brown, grey. The name of General Blood appeared in Sporting Life in January, 1867.

BODKIN. Lower says a younger son of the Fitzgeralds of Desmond and Kildare settled in Connaught in the thirteenth century, and obtained, as was not then uncommon, a sobriquet which usurped the place of a surname, and so was handed down. This was Bawdekin, probably from his having affected to dress in the costly material of silk and tissue of gold so popular in that age under the name of *baudkin;* and he says the Bodkins still use the "Croom-a-boo" motto of the Fitzgeralds, but that the Bodekin of the H. R. is probably from a different source. Ferguson thinks Bodkin may be from the English word *bodkin*, which in its earliest use signified a dagger; but he is of opinion that the name is more probably a diminutive of A. S. *boda*, O. N. *bodi*, a messenger, and he gives a Bodecker corresponding with an O. S. Bodic, and a Mod. G. Bodeck, and also an O. G. Bodeken (A. D. 1020). The name Bodkin may also be from *bodykin*, a little man; or, if of Cornish origin, from *bod-kyn*, the head abode or place; or *bod-kein*, the house on the promontory.

BODY, BODDY. The same as Bodda, Boda (Latinised Bodus), probably from A. S. *boda*, O. N. *bodi*, a messenger. See also BODKIN.

BOGIE. See BUGGY.

BOILES. Doubtless from the Irish name Boyle. Hence probably the name Bolus. But see BILLOWS.

BOLD. See BOTTLE.

BOLT. See BOTTLE.

BOLUS. See BOILES.

BONE. Same as Bowne, Boone; and also Bohun, a Norman family that came over with the Conqueror, who derived their name from Bohon, arrond. St. Lo. The Irish name Bohan is found written De Bohn, Bowen, Bone, Boon, Boone.

BONES. See BONUS.

BONUS. The same as Bowness ; from Bowness, a parish co. Cumberland ; or Bowness, a village co. Westmoreland. Hence doubtless the name Bones.

BOOT. This name may be the same as Bott (in H. R. De Botte); from root of Body ; or the same as the surname Booth ; from *booth*, a house or shed built of boards ; from Dan. *bod*, W. *bwth*, Ir. *boith*, *both*, G. *bude*.

BOOTY. Lower says there is a præ-Domesday name Boti; and that Gilbert de Boti was a tenant in chief in co. Warwick. The name is probably from root of Body, *q. v.*

BORROW. From A. S. *burh, burcg*, dative *byrig*, a fort, castle, city, town, court, palace, &c., which is liable to take the form of *ber, berry, borough, brough, bury, bur, burg*. Hence the surnames Berry, Bury.

BOTTLE. From A. S. *botl, bold, bolt*, an abode, dwelling, hall, mansion, house. Hence Pottle, Bolt, and perhaps sometimes Bold.

BOTTOM. From A. S. *botm*, a bottom or valley. Hence the names Bottomley, Higginbottom, Longbottom, Oakenbottom, Othenbottom, Owlerbottom, Pitchbottom, Ramsbottom, Rosebottom, Rowbottom, Shoebottom, Shufflebottom, Sidebottom, Tarbottom, Winterbottom.

BOULTER. Originally one who bolted, *i. e.* sifted or separated bran from flour, an occupation formerly distinct from that of miller. To bolt came afterwards to signify, to examine by sifting, to open or separate the parts of a subject, to find the truth and to discuss or argue, as at Gray's Inn, where cases were privately discussed or *bolted* by the students and barristers.

BOWLES. See BILLOWS.

BOX. From Bock's, *i. e.* son of Bock, or from a local name, as Box, in Wilts.

BOYS. From Fr. *bois*, a wood. Hence De Bosco, Dubois, Dubosc, &c. ; Littleboys, Warboys, Worboys, which Lower thinks to be from Verbois, near Rouen.

BRADBEE. From Bradby, a chapelry co. Derby. See BEE.

BRAMBLE. A probable corruption of Brummel or Brummell; perhaps *i. q.* Broomhall; from Broomhall co. Berks.

BRAND. See BRANDY.

BRANDY. Ferguson seems to think this name, as well as Brand, may be from the Scand. *brandi*, one having a sword, and he mentions Brandi as the name of a Northman in the Landnamabok. Brand, G. Brandt, and Brandy are probably from G. *brand*, famous, renowned (clarus), a word frequently found in German names; as Childebrandus, Hildebrandus, Asprandus, Sigibrandus, Liutprandus.

BREADCAKE and the U. S. names Bredcake and Bridecake are from Bride-kirk, a parish co. Cumberland; and from the inverse, Kirk-bride, we have the name Cakebread.

BRINE. Ferguson cognates this name with Brown, and suggests as a derivation A. S. *bryne*, a burning, which is absurd. Lower, with more reason, says it is an Irish corruption of O'Brien.

BROADFOOT. Most probably the same as Bradford; from Bradford, name of places in cos. Devon, Dorset, Lancaster, Northumberland, Somerset, Stafford, and York.

BRUISE. One of the many forms of Braose or Bruce, R. G. 16.—*Lower.*

BUCKLER. This name, found variously written, Bokeler, Buckeler, Buclier, and Bucler, has been identified with Bacheler and Backeler; and is probably derived from the office of the *Bachelerii Regis*. See Nichol's Topog. and Genealog., Vol. iii., p. 569; Rot. Chart. in Turri Lond., pp. 59 and 102; and Sir Harris Nicholas's Notes to Siege of Carlaverock. The word *bachelor* (Fr. *bachelier*) has been variously derived from *bas-chevalier*, i. e. a knight of a lower order; from *L. baccalaureus*, from *baccâ laureâ*, from being invested with a crown made of laurel berries, or *baculus*, a staff, from the supposition that a staff, by way of distinction, was given into the hands of those who had completed their studies ; or from the old word *batalarius*, one who entered into literary *battles* or disputes.

BUDGET. I. B. Budget has just published a treatise on tobacco, not on finance (*Bowditch*). A diminutive of the name Budge ; or perhaps rather a corruption of Paget, Pagett, Padgett, or Padgedd, a diminutive of the name Page.

BUGG. See BUGGY.

BUGGY. Perhaps from Bugey, a small territory of France, in the old prov. of Bourgogne ; or from Le Bogue, a comm. and town of France, dep. Dordogne. It may also be the same as one of the A. S., O. G., Dan., and Eng. surnames Bucge, Bega, Boge, Bigo, Buggo, Bogi, Bogie, Bogue, Boag, which Ferguson derives from A. S. *begean*, *bigan*, *bogan*, *bugan*, O. N. *beygia*, *biga*, *boga*, *buga*, to bend or stoop.

BUMGARTNER. For Baumgartner, a German name, signifying a tree gardener. ·

BURDEN. From some local name ending in den (A. S. *den*, *dene*, *deorn*, a plain, vale, dale, valley) ; or from Burdon, name of two townships co. Durham.

BURLEY. See LEGG.

BURLINGAME. A U. S. name ; from Burlingham, name of three parishes in Norfolk. But see WALKINGHAME.

BURY. From Bury, name of parishes, towns, &c., cos. Hants, Lancaster, Suffolk, Sussex. But see BORROW.

BUSS. Lower says that in the south of England this is a common nickname of Barnabas.

BUST. A Mrs. Bust, says Bowditch, is buried in Westminster Abbey. I take it to be the same as Buist, which Lower renders thick and gross, and the German Beust, name of the Austrian statesman.

BUSTARD. See HAZARD.

BUTTER. In the U. S. there are both Butter and Butters. Butter Crambe, Butterlaw, Butterleigh, Butterley, Buttermere, Butterton, Butterwick, Butterworth, are local names in England.

There is also Booterstown (in some documents Ballybotter, Ballyboother, Butterstown, and Boterstone) near Dublin, which some say was originally Freebooterstown, from its being the resort of these picturesque desperadoes. Lower says Boterus and Botorus are found as personal names in Domesday ; but the name Butter may be from G. *bude*, a house, mansion, habitation, &c. ; or from A. S. *bode*, a messenger; or perhaps rather from G. *bod-her*, a noble or brave leader. Bod is found in several German names ; as Bauto, Maroboduus, Merobaudes, Genebaudes.

BUTTON. This is doubtless a local name. The pedigree of the Hampshire family is found written De Button, and Lower says it was sometimes spelt Bitton, and may be derived from the parish of Bitton co. Gloucester ; and that in Sussex Burton is often pronounced Button.

BUZZARD. See HAZARD.

C.

CABLE. This name is probably the same as Cabbell, in H. R. Cabel, and perhaps with Caple or Capel (in charters Latinised *De Capella*).

CAKEBREAD. See BREADCAKE.

CALF. From *calvus*, bald. Hence Calvin or Chauvin, Chauve, and perhaps Shave.

CANT. From G. *kante*, a corner, edge, coast.

CANTER. Same as Chanter and Cantor, no doubt a precentor or chanter in a church ; from A. S. *cantere*, a singer.

CANTON. Lower renders this name a territorial division or district (Fr). Canton is the appellation of four townships in the U. S., and is found as a U. S. surname.

CANTWELL. From some local ending in *ville*.

CARD. Lower considers this the same as Caird, which Jamieson renders a gipsy, a travelling tinker, a sturdy beggar.

CARELESS. A corruption of Carlos, or its original, Carolus.

CARRIAGE. See COURAGE.

CASE. See CHEESE.

CASEMENT. See CASHMAN.

CASH. 1. From Cash in Strathmiglo co. Fife. 2. From Mac Cash; or Mac Cosh, Mac Uais. The barony of Moygoish, in Westmeath, derived its name from Hy-Mac Uais. [There was a Colla Uais, "Colla the noble or well descended."] We have also the Gaelic names Coish and Coysh; whence perhaps the name Gush.

CASHDOLLAR, Barndollar, Barringdollar, Markthaler, and Thaler. All found as U. S. names. Bowditch seems to derive them from G. *thaler*, a dollar, but they are rather from some local name compounded of G. *thal*, a valley. Markthaler would therefore signify "one from the Markthal."

CASHMAN. From O. G. *gast-mund*, a powerful man (*gast*, potens); or from *geis-mund*, a strong man (*gesus*, vir fortis). Cf. the old German names Adalgis, Gisericus, Vitigis, Wetgisus, &c. It may also be from some Scotch name commencing with Mac. If the name be of German origin, we may have from it Cheeseman and Casement. But see CHEESEMAN.

CASHMERE. This name and Cashmer are both found in the U. S. They are probably from some English local name ending in *mere* or *more*, from A. S. *mære*, a lake, pool, marsh; or *môr*, waste land, a moor.

CAT. From Catherine.

CATTLE. This may be a diminutive of the surname Cat, for Catherine; or from the Irish name Cahill or Cathail; from *cathal*, valour.

CAUDLE. A corruption of Caudwell, from Cauldwell co. Derby.

CHAFF. Probably from Fr. *chauve*, bald.—*Lower*.

CHAMPAGNE. From the province of Champagne, in France.

CHANCE. Originally Chancé, *i. q.* Chauncy, perhaps from Chaunceaux, a comm. and town of France, dep. Côte d'Or.

CHARTER. Lower thinks this name may be derived from the town of Chartres, in France. But qu. from Chartre, a comm. and town dep. Sarthe.

CHATAWAY, var. Chattaway, Cattaway. Doubtless the same as Hathaway, Hathway, Hadaway, Haduwic; probably from O. G., *hat*, high, lofty; *hath*, *had*, *chad*, war; *wig*, strong, warlike, a soldier, warrior, hero. Hence the old names Ollovico, Litavicus, Merovigus, Ludovicus.

CHATTING. A patronymic of the name Chad, or from some local name compounded of *ing*, a meadow. Chatt and Chatto are surnames, and Chat Moss is the appellation of a district in Lancashire.

CHECK. See CHICK.

CHEEK. See CHICK.

CHEESE. Ferguson ranks Cheese, Chase, and Case with Cissa (Chissa), king of the S. Saxons, and the Friesic Tsjisse (Chisse), a name in use at the present day; from O. S. *ciasan, ciesen, ciosan*, A. S. *cysan, ceosan*, O. Fries *kiasa*, O. N. *kiosa*, to choose; and he thinks Cissa may mean "one chosen or elected." The name Chese is found in H. R.

CHEESEMAN. Lower does not give this name, but "Cheeseman, a maker of or dealer in cheese, Le Cheseman, Le Chesemaker, H. R., analogous to the modern butter-man." He gives also Cheesewright and Cheesemonger. The latter is no doubt a modern name, but Cheesewright may be compounded of *chaise*, a chair. I find also in Ferguson, Chisman and Chismon, and am disposed to derive Cheeseman from O. G. *geis-mund*, a strong man. See CASHMAN.

CHEESEWRIGHT. See CHEESEMAN.

CHERRY. Lower says this name is of Fr. Huguenot origin, and said to be descended from the family of De Cheries, seigneurs of Brauvel, Beauval, &c., in Normandy; that Chéris is the name of a place near Avranches; and that the name is Latinised De Ceraso. There is, however, a parish called Cherry-Hinton co. Cambridge. But see SHERRY.

CHESSMAN. See CHEESMAN.

CHEW. From Chew Magna,. a parish in Somerset. There are also Chewstoke and Chewton-Mendip in the same county. Lower suggests also Cheux, a village near Caen, in Normandy.

CHICK. This name may be the same as the French name Chicque (Gascon Chicot) and the Spanish name Chico; from *chico*, little, small. Hence no doubt Check, Cheek, and, as a diminutive, the name Chicken. See also Verba Nominalia, under " Chic."

CHICKEN. See CHICK.

CHILD (in H. R. Le Child). This name corresponds with the German family names Hild, Hilt, and the Danish female Christian name Hilda (appellation of one of the maidens of Odin). In A. S. names (as in Brunechild, Hildegard, Hiltrut, Adilhilt, Reginhilt) *child*, *hilde*, &c., are from A. S. *cild*, an infant. In German names (as Childeric, Childebert, Hildebrand, Hiltebolt) *child*, *hild*, means a warrior (*bellator*, *præliator*), from *held*, id. Hence doubtless the name Child. In some names *child*, *hild*, means war; hence *hiltiman*, a warrior, and the surnames Chillman, Killman, and perhaps sometimes Hillman. In some names *child*, *hild*, is from *alt*, noble : hence Hiltiwin, nobilis bellator ; Hiltegunt, nobilis virago ; although according to Wachter the latter, as a Francic name, may also translate virgo bellatrix, or vira belli.

CHILDREN. Ferguson thinks this name corresponds with an O. G. Childeruna for Hilderuna. Both the latter might translate " noble friend." See CHILD.

CHILLMAN. See CHILD.

CHIN. From Duchene, *i. q.* Duchesne, Du Cane, Du Quesne, " of the oak," " one living near an oak."

CHIP, CHIPP, *i. q.* CHEAPE. From some place so called ;

from A. S. *ceap*, a bargain, sale, business, price ; from *ceapian*, to bargain, chaffer, trade ; whence Cheapside, Chipping Barnet, Chipping Norton, Eastcheap, &c. ; hence Chipman, Chapman (A. S. *ceápman*).

CHIPMAN. See CHIP.

CHISEL. Ferguson seems to think Chisel, Chessal, and Kissel diminutives of Cheese, Case, Cissa, Kiss, *q.v.* There are two parishes (great and little) named Chishall in Essex ; and Chiselhampton, Chiselhurst, Chisleborough, Chisledon are local names in England.

CLASS. See GLASS.

CLAYARD See HAZARD.

CLEVERLY. See LEGG.

CLINKARD. See HAZARD.

CLOAK. If of Cornish origin, from *clog*, a steep rock, or *cleggo*, a rock, cliff, downfall. Clogg may be the same name. Ferguson thinks Cloak and Cloke are from O. N. *klókr*, prudent, and Clogg from the Mod. Dan. form *klog*.

CLOGG. See CLOAK.

CLOTHIER. See LEATHER.

CLOUD. From the Gaelic name McCloud, a corruption of MacLeod. Hence perhaps the name Clout.

CLOUT. See CLOUD.

COAL, *i.q.* COLE, from Nicol or Nichol. Cole is the appellation of places in cos. Somerset and Wilts.

COAT. From A. S. *cot, cote, cyte* (G. *koth*, D. *kot*, W. *cwt*), a small house or hut. Hence Middlecoat, Peticoat, Pettycoat, Taylecoate, Topcoat, Wainscoat, Waiscot, Wescott, Westcoat.

COCK. This may sometimes refer to the bird (Fr. Le Coq), but in composition it is no doubt mostly used in a diminutive sense ; thus Alcock or Allcock (Hal for Henry) ; Badcock, Batcock (Bartholomew) ; Balcock (Baldwin) ; Glasscock (Nicholas) ; Hiscock, Hitchcock (Isaac) ; Lovecock, Maycock, Mycock (Michael); Slocock, Woolcock.

c

COCKLE. A diminutive of the name Cock. Another diminutive is Cockett (Fr. Cochet), and of patronymics are Cocks, Cox, Cocking.

COFFEE. Lower thinks the names Coffee, Coaffee, Coffey may be local, or of common origin with Coffin, Caffin, &c., the root being Lat. *calvus*, bald. Ferguson says, " Coffee I take to be the same as Coifi, the name of a converted heathen priest who, on the reception of Christianity by the people of Northumbria, undertook the demolition of the ancient fanes. It has been asserted that this is not an Anglo-Saxon but a Cymric name, and that it denotes in Welsh a Druid, but Mr. Kemble has shown that it is an adjective formed from *cóf*, strenuous, and means the bold or active one." I take it to be the Irish name O'Cobhthaidh or O'Coffey; from *cobhthach*, victorious, which O'Reilly says is the proper name of a man. Murragh O'Cobhthaidh was Bishop of Derry and Raphoe, and lived A. D. 1173. For the latter see Annals of the Four Masters.

COFFIN. The name of one or more medical men. Ferguson thinks this name may be corrupted from Kolfinn, from O. N. *koilr*, helmeted, and the proper name Finn; or that it was originally Coffing, a patronymic, formed from *cóf*, strenuous. Lower considers it the same as Colvin or Colvinus, who held lands in chief under the Confessor. It may also be the same with Caffin, from Fr. *chauve*, L. *calvus*, bald ; whence Chauvin or Calvin. Coffin and Coffinhal, and Coffinieres or Couffin are found as French surnames, and there is a place called Couvin in Belgium, and Coffinswell is the name of a parish co. Devon.

COIN. See QUEEN.

COLDHAM. From some place compounded of *ham*, a dwelling. In surnames and local names the vocables *cold, gold, wold, wald, wood* are "wood." Cf. the surnames Goldham, Calderon, Goldrun, Waldron.

COLDMAN. See GOLDMAN.

COLLAR. Kollr, Kolli, Koli are the names of several Northmen in the Landnamabok, which Ferguson seems to think may be from O. N. *kollr*, a helmet. I take it that Collar is a corruption of Collard, son of Coll, *i. e.* Nicol.

COLLARBONE. Lower, with reason, suggests that this surname may be from Collingbourne co. Wilts. See also SMALLBONE.

COLLEGE, COLLEDGE. These names have no reference to a University. Lower says, in the north of England any court or group of cottages having a common entrance from the street is called a *college*. The last syllable however may be from *ledge*, a ridge of rocks near the surface of the sea. Cf. Cumberledge, Routledge, &c.

COLLICK. " Mr. Collick was treasurer of the Middlesex Hospital, in England, in 1805 " (*Bowditch*). " Probably," says Lower, " from Colwick co. Nottingham." Ferguson considers Collick a diminutive of Cole, Coley, Colla, and the Northern names Kollr, Koli, Kolli, found in the Landnamabok ; from A. S. *col*, O. N. *kollr*, a helmet ; but this name is rather a diminutive of Coll, for Nichol, from Nicholas.

COLT. Ferguson thinks this may be a H. G. form of Gold. Lower says it appears in the thirteenth century in its present form, and he sees no reason why it should not be derived from the animal, especially as Le Colt is found in H. R. He says further that the Colts of co. Lanark derive from Blaise Coult, a French Huguenot refugee in the sixteenth century. I consider it a corruption of Collett, a diminutive of Coll, from Nicoll.

COMB. From A. S. *comb*, a low place enclosed with hills, a valley (W. *cwm*). Hence Smallcomb.

COMELY. See LEGG.

COMFORT. A Cornish name ; from *cûm-veor*, the great valley.

CONOVER. Name of forty families in the New York Directory ; also found in Ohio. From some local name (perhaps Condover co. Salop), compounded of *over*, a bank ; from

A. S. *ofer*, a margin, brink, bank, shore. Hence the surname Peckover.

CONQUEST. From Le Conquet (L. *Conquestas*), a maritime comm. and town of France, dep. Finistère; or from Conques, a small town of France, dep. Aveyron; or of another, dep. Aude.

COOL. From Coull, a parish of Scotland co. Aberdeen; or Goole co. York; or Cole, name of places cos. Wilts and Somerset; or the same as the surname Cooley, Colley, Cowley; or from Cole, for Nicole, Nicol.

COOT. From Cornish *coit*, *coid*, a wood. Cf. the names Coode, Code, Coad.

CORDEROY. Found Cordaroy, Cordrey, Cordery, Cowderoy, Cowdery, Cowdrey, Cowdray, Cawdrey, Coudray, Coudraie, Coudre, Couldery, Couldrey; from Fr. *coudraie*, a hazel-grove; from *coudre*, from *corylus*, a hazel-tree. Lower says the map of Normandy exhibits many localities called "Le Coudray," and that there is also an estate called Cowdray, near Midhurst, in Sussex; and he mentions a De Coudray in H. R. Cf. the French name Coudrette, signifying a hazel-grove.

CORK, CORKE. According to some, *cork* is a term used by apprentices and workmen for "master." Ferguson seems to think the name Cork may be contracted from Corrick, a diminutive of Core or Cory. It seems that Corc was an ancient Celtic personal name, and may be derived from the city of Cork (formerly Corkan), or from its root, Ir. *corc*, *corcach*, a moor, marsh. The name Corkett, which would seem to be a diminutive of Cork, is a corruption of Caldecott.

COSTARD. See HAZARD.

COSTICK. Perhaps the same with Costeker, and the O. G. name Custica, which Ferguson thinks from G. *kunst*, *kust*, O. N. *konst*, skill, art, science; but it is more probably derived from Constantius or Constantine. Costick may also be from Costock or Cortlingstock, a parish co. Nottingham.

COTTON. Förstemann makes Cot, Cotta, Cotuna, Cuotila as

O. G. names to interchange with *god* or *got;* and Ferguson thinks these correspond with our Cott, Cotton, Cottle. The name Cotton is probably from Cottun, dep. Calvados, or Cotton, name of places in cos. Chester, Stafford, Suffolk, and York. De Cottun and De Cotton are found in H. R.

COUNSELL. From some local name compounded of A. S. *sæl, sel,* a hall or dwelling (O. N. *sel,* a summer shed for cattle). Counsell, Countsell are found as U. S. names.

COUNTERPATCH. Without doubt a corruption of Cumberpatch or Comberbach; from Comberbach, a township in Cheshire.

COURAGE. Corrupted from Coulrake; from the A. S. name Ceolric; or from Coleridge; from Coleridge, name of a hundred and parish co. Devon. Lower thinks Courage may be from Currage, a manor in the parish of Cheveley co. Bucks, and he says that a family of this name settled here after the revocation of the Edict of Nantes. Ferguson compares Courage with the O. G. Gawirich, Goerich, seventh century (O. H. G. *gawi,* Mod. G. *gau,* a country or district).

COWARD. See HAZARD.

COWBRAIN. Lower says this is a known corruption of Colbran, Colbrand, a personal name of great antiquity. Ferguson says Colbrand occurs in a charter of 925, and is probably a Scandinavian name, and he gives two improbable etymologies.

CRACKBONE, CRACKBON. Found as U. S. names. See
• SMALLBONE.

CRAFT. A northern corruption of *croft,* a little close adjoining a house. Cf. the names Calcraft, Horsecraft, &c. It may also sometimes be from A. S. *cræfta,* a craftsman, or the same as the German names Craft, Crafto, Kraft; probably from *kraft,* strength, force, power. Ferguson mentions an O. G. Crafto as the name of a member of a noble family in the twelfth or thirteenth century, and he gives a Ludwig Craft, A. D. 1656.

CRAM. See GRUMBLE and GRAMMAR.

CRAMP. Lower thinks this name may be from Crambe, a parish in Yorkshire. I take it to be the same name as Crump. See CRUMB.

CRAVAT. " Mr. and Mrs. Cravat arrived at Boston in September, 1857 " (*Bowditch*). Doubtless corrupted from the surname Gravatt, Gravett ; probably from the obs. *grava*, a grove or small wood ; *grave*, a wood, thicket, den, cave ; from A. S. *græf*.

CRAVEN. From Craven, a district of Yorkshire; from W. *craeg* a rock, *pen* head.

CREAM. Lower renders Cream " a merchant's booth, a stall in a market. Teut. *kraem*, taberna rerum venalium.—*Jamieson*." But see GRUMBLE.

CRICKET. A diminutive of the name Crick or Creak; or from Cricket, name of two parishes in Somerset.

CRIMP. According to Halliwell, *crimp* in Norfolk is used for a " dealer in coals." But see CRUMB.

CRISP. From Crispin.

CROAK. There are several places in England named Crook or Crock, and others compounded thereof; but the name Croak may mean crooked or bent ; from Fr. *croc*, uncus, Med. L. *croccus* (O. Fr. *croc de fer*, a sort of lance ; *croque*, bâton armé d'un croc ; Eng. *crook*, Arm. *crocq*). Ferguson says Croak is probably from O. N. *krókr* (bent or crooked). Lower renders Crocker (Le Crockere) a maker of crocs, *i. e.* earthen jars ; but Crocker, Croker, and Croaker may be from the same root as Croak. Cf. the names Croake, Croc, Crockett, Crokat, Crook, Crooke, Croke, Crookes, Crooks, and the Fr. Ducrocq.

CROAKER. See CROAK.

CROOK. See CROAK.

CROWFOOT. Doubtless the same as Crawford, Crawfurd, Craufurd, and Craufuird ; from Crawford, name of two parishes in Scotland co. Lanark, and of a parish of England co. Dorset ; also the appellation of eight counties in the U. S., and of a township New York. But see HAZLEFOOT.

CRUMB. Most probably the same as Crome, Croom, Croome, Crum ; from A. S. *crumb, crump, crymbig*, W. *crum*, bending, concave ; Gael. *cròm*, bent or bandy-legged ; G. *krum*, Pl. D. *krom*, crooked, crumped, curvus. Hence doubtless Groom, Groome, Crump, Crimp.

CUBE. See CUBITT.

CUBITT. Jamieson gives Cube, Cubbe, as probable abbreviations of Cuthbert ; hence perhaps Cubitt ; but this name, as well as Cupit, Cupitt, Cobbett, may be a diminutive of Cobb, Copp, Cope, O. G. Cobbo, Coppo, Cuppa (whence perhaps, as patronymics, Cobbing, Copping, Kopping, Coppin, Coppen, Coppinger, Coppens, Copas, Copus, Coppard, and the French Copaux, Coppaz, Copeau, Copel, Copil, Copin, Coppin, Copinot, Coppeaux) ; from A. S. *cop*, O. H. G. *kop*, Mod. G. *kopf*, D. *kop*, the head ; O. Fr. *cope, copeau, coppe, coupeau*, cime, sommet, péage. *Cob* is also a name for the sea-fowl, the sea-cob, and in some parts of England for a spider ; from O. D. *kop*, or *koppe*, retained in *koppespin*, *spinnekop*, a spider. *Cob* is also a close-built strong kind of pony, and *cob, cop* is still used for the top or head.

CUNNING. Most probably the same name as the German König, Eng. King. Cf. A. S. *cyng, cyning*, D. *koning*.

CURTAIN. From some local name, perhaps Kirton, name of places near Ipswich and Boston, in England ; or from Crediton, commonly pronounced Kirton, co. Devon.

CUSHION. A corruption of MacOssian. It is otherwise written Cushin and Cussen, and Anglicised to Cousins, but pronounced Cuzzen. See Ulster Jour. of Archæol. No. 2, and Lower. Ferguson thinks Cushion a corruption of Cushing, a patronymic, of Cuss, perhaps the same with Kusi, surname of a Northman in Ann. Isl.; from O. N. *kusi*, a calf, a diminutive of *kú*, a cow; or that Cuss may be from A. S. *cusc*, pure, clear.

CUSTARD. See HAZARD.

CUTBEARD. A corruption of Cuthbert.

CUTBUSH. See TALBOYS.

CUTLOVE. See LAW.

CUTMUTTON. Ferguson thinks this name may be from Muatin, an O. G. name (*muth*, courage), and *cuth*, known, famous. It is much more likely to be corrupted from some local name. Catmere is the name of a parish co. Berks, and Catmere-ton would easily corrupt to Cutmutton.

CUTTLE. Lower suggests as a derivation Cuthill or Cuttle, a suburb of Prestonpans co. Haddington. The name may also sometimes be a diminutive of Cutt, a nickname of Cuthbert.

D.

DACE, *i. q.* DAYES. From David. Lower however thinks it may come from some continental locality named Ace or Aes with the prefix D'. Hence perhaps the name Dais.

DAILY, DAILEY. See LEGG.

DAIS. See DACE.

DAISY, DAISEY. Lower suggests that Daisy may be from the ancient barony of Aisié (D'Aisié), now Aisier, arrond. Pont Audemer, in Normandy. Dees, or Dease, is an Irish name. The tribe of the Deisigh, called also Desii, gave name to Desies, in Ir. Deise, an ancient territory comprising the greater part of Waterford, with a part of Tipperary. See also Annals of the Four Masters.

DAMPER, *i. q.* DAMPIER. From Dampierre, name of several places in France ; from O. Fr. *dam, dan, don,* lord ; *Pierre,* Peter. Cf. Dammartin, *i. q.* Don Martin, &c., &c.

DAMSON. From Adamson, son of Adam. Ferguson says Damson is the son of Damm ; probably from A. S. *dœma,* a judge. Lower says, " Dame's son, but whether the son of Dame, apparently an old Christian name, or filius dominæ I know not."

DANCE. Doubtless the same as Dence, Dench, from A. S. *Danisca, Denisca,* a Dane.

DANDY. The same as Dendy, found Dendye, Dendy, Dandie, Dandy; thought to be originally D'Awnay or Dawndy, which Lower thinks is the same as D'Aunai ; and he says there are at least seven places called Aunai in Normandy, one of which, Aunai Abbaye, arrond. Vire, was an ancient barony, and from thence probably came the family. The name may also be from Dand, Dandy, familiarly used in Scotland for Andrew.

DANGER. From D'Angers, *i. e.* from Angers, in France, cap. of Anjou. Ferguson thinks it may be an inverse of Gordon, from *Gardene*, signifying " Spear-Danes," or " warlike Danes," which he says is a common epithet applied to that people in A. S. poetry.

DARE. Perhaps originally D'Air; from Air, name of two towns of France, the one dep. Pas-de-Calais, the other dep. Landes ; or from Ayr, in Scotland, cap. co. on the Ayr. It may also be the same name as Dear.

DARK, DARKE. Properly D'Arques. From Arques, a comm. and town of France, dep. Seine-Inf., on the Arques. Lower says William D'Arques or de Arcis was lord of Folkestone co. Kent, temp. William I., having settled in England after the Norman Conquest, and that his ancestors were *vicomtes* of Arques, now a bourg and castle four or five miles from Dieppe in Normandy.

DASH. From D'Ash, or *i. q.* Tash, from At Ash ; from residence near an ash-tree. Hence doubtless the name Dashwood, from D'Ashwood, or At Ashwood. Lower says Dashwood would answer to the old Latinisation De Fraxineto, a twelfth-century surname, with which it is doubtless identical.

DASHWOOD. See DASH.

DATE, DATES. See DEATH.

DAW, DAY. From David.

DAY. See DAW.

DAYFOOT. See HAZLEFOOT.

DAYMAN. Lower says this is a known corruption of Dinan (*i. e.* Dinan, near St. Malo). It may also be the same as Dayment ; perhaps from Dagomund, from O. G. *dag-mund*, a soldier.

DEADMAN. Lower says this is a known corruption of Debenham (co. Suffolk), and that in Sussex it is further corrupted to Deadly.

DEALCHAMBER. A corruption of the name Delachambre or De la Chambre.

DEARLOVE. See Law.

DEARTH. Perhaps from *De Arth*, i. e. from Arth, Switzerland (but see Earth). Bowditch says Mr. Derth figures in the Directory (New York) of 1835; and that Mr. Dearth, of a neighbouring county, after enduring his name for many years, was at last induced to change it, and that a law student at Harvard is named Dearth.

DEATH. Properly D'Aeth, still an English name, and said to be from Aeth, in Flanders. This may refer to Ath, a fortified town of Belgium, prov. Hainault. The name D'ath is found in the U. S. There is a surgeon and also an undertaker named Death. "At the Liverpool Police-court, on Friday, the witnesses and solicitor in two cases bore the ominous names of Death, Debt, and Daggers" (*Morning Star*). One family of the name of H. E. Death, having an objection to the name, changed it to Edeath. The U. S. names Date and Datt and the English name Dates may be derived from Death, D'Aeth, or D'Ath.

DECENT. Perhaps the same as Dasent, which, if not an Irish name, may be from O. G. *degen-send*, a war-messenger (*degen*, ensis, gladius).

DEED, DEEDS. Doubtless for Daid, Daids ; from David, Davids. There is also a Deedy. The Messrs. Deed of Toronto and of Philadelphia (says Bowditch) may be regarded as the representatives of conveyancing.

DEEPROSE. See Diprose.

DEMON. Doubtless from the Fr. name Du Mont. Perhaps sometimes from Dayman, *q. v.*

DEUCE. Probably a corruption of D'Ewes, descended from Des Ewes ; from *des Eaux*, synonym of the English Waters.

DEVIL. Lower mentions a monk named Willelmus cognomento Diabolus ; but he seems to think this name may be from the French De Ville, commonly written Divall, Divoll, Devall, &c., and in records Devol, Devile, Deyvil, &c. I am inclined to think the name to be the same with D'Eyville ; from *de Davidis villa ;* but see Cowell's Interpreter.

DEW. Probably from Eu, in Normandy, commonly called la Ville *d'Eu.—Lower.*

DIAL. Supposed corruption of the Irish Doyle, found in England as Doyle and Doil. According to Mr. Bowditch, there is a Mr. Dial living at Davenport, Iowa.

DIAMOND. In the parish register of Brenchley, co. Kent, there is an entry to the effect that in 1612 " John Diamond, son of John du Mont the Frenchman, was baptised." The elder Du Mont was a Kentish ironmaster, who had settled in that county from France. Inf. H. W. Diamond, M.D., F.S.A.—*Lower.*

DIAPER. From D'Ypres, *i. e.* from Ypres, in Belgium. Hence the figured linen cloth and the towel or napkin so called.

DINE. Found Dyne, but Dine is the most ancient. In H. R. it is De Dine, and it is probably derived from locality ; perhaps from Digne (*Dinia*), a walled town of France, cap. dep. B. Alpes.

DIPROSE. Said to be a corruption of De Préaux ; from Préaux, the name of several places in Normandy. It has been corrupted to Deeprose.

DIVES. Not from the Dives of Scripture, although we certainly have the names Rich, La Rich, Le Riche. It seems to be from Dives, a comm. and town of France, dep. Calvados, on the right bank of a river of the same name. De Dyve and Le Dyve are found in H. R., and Uxor Boselini de Dive was a tenant *in capite* under William the Conqueror, co. Cambridge.

DOE, DOO. From the ancient family of De Ou or D'Eu, from Eu, in Normandy. Hence the surnames Eu, Ew, and Ewe.

DOLL. Ferguson seems to think this name may be from O. N. *döll*, a woman, or A. S. *dolh*, a wound. In H. R. the name is found written Doll, Dolle, De Doll, and is doubtless from Dol, the picturesque town in Bretagne, or from Dole in Franche Comté.

DOLLAR. From Dollar, a town and parish in Clackmannanshire.

DOLPHIN. Ferguson thinks Dolphin the O. N. *dolgfinner*, the Dolfin of early English history. Lower says it is an ancient personal name, and that one Dolfin was a tenant-in-chief in cos. Derby and York at the making of Domesday, and that the family were in Ireland before 1307. It may however be the same as Godolphin.

DONE. Name of a celebrated Cheshire family ; from W. *dwn*, dun, dusky, swarthy. Donne, Dunn, and Done are etymologically connected.

DOUBLE. Same as Doubble, Doubell, Doble, Dobell, De Dobel, and the Norman name Dobbell ; from some local name ending in *ville*.

DOUBLEDAY. See SINGLEDAY.

DOWER. The Prompt. Parv. renders the word *dower* a rabbit's burrow, *cvniculus*. The name is more probably from Dower in Crowan, or Dower Park in St. Kew, both in Cornwall ; from Corn. *dower, dour*, water.

DRAWWATER. Bowditch says Thomas Drawwater, of New Haven, was fined in 1688 for drinking. The name in H. R. is found written Drawater, and is most probably derived from some local name.

DRAY. See DROUGHT.

DRINK. Perhaps the same as the name Dring ; said to be from A. S. *dreng*, a soldier, a strong man. See Lye (A. S. Dict.) Hence perhaps the name Drinkard ; from G. *hart*, strong.

DRINKARD. See DRINK.

DROUGHT. This name may be corrupted from Drewett, Druitt ; perhaps diminutive of Drew, Drewe, Dray ; either from the early personal name Drogo, or from Dreux, in Bretagne. Drewett may also sometimes be a diminutive formed from

Andrew. Lower says Drew, Drewe is a common nickname for Andrew.

DULHUMPHRY. From some French name, with the prefix *De* or *De la*. Onfray and Onfroy, Humphrey are found in Firmin Didot. There are the surnames Umfraville and Amfreville (found Onfreville), *i. e. Hunfredi villa*, the appellation of several places in Normandy.

DULL. Bowditch says there are fourteen families of this name in Philadelphia. It may be from Dull, a large parish co. Perth.

DULLARD. According to Bowditch, there are four families of this name in Philadelphia. See HAZARD.

DULY. See LEGG.

DUNNING. A patronymic of the name Dunn; or the last syllable may be *ing*, a meadow.

E.

EARLY. From Early, in the parish of Sonning, Berks. Hurley is also the name of a villa, near Marlow, same co. But see LEGG.

EARTH. From St. Erth, formerly St. Earth, a parish in Penwith Hundred co. Cornwall; or corrupted from the surname Earith; from Erith co. Kent.

EARWAKER, EARWICKER. Perhaps corrupted from Herwig; from O. G. *er-wig*, strong in war; or *her-wig*, noble or distinguished warrior. Lower however gives Eureuuacre as the name of a tenant in Devon mentioned in Domesday.

EASY. Corrupted from some local name, perhaps Essé, in France, dep. Ille-et-Vilaine; or from St. Issey, in Cornwall. Lower suggests also that it may come, by transposition of letters, from Esay, the old form of Isaiah.

EATWELL. From Etwall, a parish co. Derby; or perhaps rather from the local name Hatfield. See HATFALL.

EAVESTAFF. See WAGSTAFF.

EGG, EGGS. From O. G. *ecke*, the edge or point of a weapon, &c. (*acies, cuspis*); O. N. *egg*, an edge, sword, war, battle; A. S. *ecg*, an edge, or sharpness applied to the mind, also quickness, ability. There is however a De Egge in H. R., co. Salop; and the name may therefore be the same as Hedge, Hague, Haig, Haigh (Haigh, a township of Lancashire); from A. S. *hæg*, Fr. *haie*, a hedge, and that which it encloses, a field or park.

EGGBEER. From Egbert, G. Eggbrecht; from O. G. *eckebrecht*, distinguished for quickness or ability. Cf. Huber, from Hubert. But see EGG.

ELEMENT. Lower says of this name, "Possibly a corruption of Alihermont, a district containing several parishes in the arrondissemont of Dieppe, in Normandy. Alihermont would readily become Alermont, Alémont, Element." I derive it from the same root as the name Almond, *q. v.* Cf. Garment, from Garmund; Raiment, from Raymond.

EMBLEM. From some place compounded of *ham*, a dwelling. Cf. the surname Embleton, also the appellation of parishes, &c., in cos. Cumberland, Durham, and Northumberland.

EMMET, EMMETT. Ferguson says Emes corresponds with A. S. *eam*, an uncle; and Emms, Hems, Emson, and the diminutives Emmens and Emmet, with the old Fries. *em*, of the same meaning. They are more probably from Em or Emm, an abbreviation of Emma or Emily.

ESSENCE. The name of a black man in the U. S. It may come from Assens, a maritime town of Denmark, isl. Fühnen; or from Hessen (Cassel, Darmstadt, Homburg, &c.), in Germany.

EVEN. From Evan; from Ιωαννης, the original of John.

EVENESS. Doubtless the same as the W. name Evans. It may also come from some local name compounded of *ness*, a promontory.

EVERHARD. See VERY.

EVERY. See VERY.

EVIL. The same as Eyvile, Eyvill, which with the prefix *de* occurs in the H. R. See DEVIL.

EWE. See DOE.

EXCELL. Most probably the same as Exall; from Exhall, name of two parishes co. Warwick.

EXPENCE. A corruption of the names Spence or Spens. Lower says *spence* is a yard or enclosure; Jamieson renders *spens*, the place where provisions are kept, and also the clerk of a kitchen; and Lower says, in the latter sense it is employed by Wyntoun, and that Spens is an ancient surname in Scotland. But see SPENCER.

EYE, EYES. From Eye, a town and parish co. Suffolk; or Eye, the name of parishes cos. Hereford and Northampton.

F.

FAGG (in H. R. Fag). See FIG.

FAIL. From Phail, Gaelic for Paul. Hence MACPHAIL.

FAIRCLOTH. A corruption of Fairclough; from Dan. *faar* a sheep, *clough* a cleft in a hill, also a narrow ravine or glen.

FAIRFEATHER. See MERRYWEATHER.

FAIRFIELD. From Fairfield, appellation of places in cos. Derby, Kent, Lancaster, and of eleven local names in the U. S. The name means sheep-field; from Dan. *faar*, a sheep.

FAIRLAMB. Lower thinks this is from some local name ending in *ham*. It may also be from one ending in *lan*. If we could suppose a Scand-Celtic compound (*faar-lan*), the name would mean the sheep enclosure. There is, however, a parish called Farlan, Cumberland.

FAIRPLAY. See PLAYFAIR.

FAIRWEATHER. See MERRYWEATHER.

FALL, also Faw, Faa, a celebrated Gipsy name in the north of England; also found in the London Directory. It is probably from locality, as in H. R. we find De Fall.

FANCY. Doubtless from locality; some think from Vanchi, near Neufchatel, in Normandy.

FAREWELL. From Farewell, a parish co. Stafford, known by the curious designation of Farewell-with-Charley! The last syllable is most probably from *ville*, and the name may mean the "sheep dwelling." See FAIRFIELD.

FARTHING. This may be the same as Farden, and of local origin. "Fardan," says Lower, "occurs as an undertenant in Domesday."

FATHERLY. See LEGG.

FAWN. The same as Fawnes and De Fawnes ; from Fawns, in Northumberland.

FEAR. The same as Fare (Mac Fare), Phear, Phair, Phaire, Phayer, Phairs ; from Gael. *fear*, a man, hero. It may also sometimes be from A. S. *fœger*, fair ; or *fara*, O. N. *fari*, a traveller.

FEARMAN. See PHARAOH.

FEARWEATHER. See MERRYWEATHER.

FEATHER. This name may be from Ice. *fridr*, A. S. *freothe*, *freotho*, liberty, peace, love ; or from G. *frith herr*, a protecting lord ; but I should rather derive from Feodore, *i. e.* Theodore. Ferguson considers Feather the same with Father, G. Vater, corresponding as it does very nearly with a north of England pronunciation, as also with *feder*, one of the A. S. forms. The name Fearby, in Yorkshire, was in Domesday Federbi. Featherstone is the appellation of places in cos. Northumberland, Stafford, and York ; doubtless from the A. S. name Frithestan, whence probably Featherstonhaugh.

FELON. A U. S. name. Most probably a corruption of Fallon, which is also found in the States. Ferguson connects Fallon with Fail, and thinks the latter may be from O. N. *feila*, pudere ; and the former from *feilinn*, pudibundus. Fallon is rather from the Irish name O'Fallon, said to be a corruption of O'Phelan ; from Faolan, whose son Mothea was at Clontarf in 1014. A district in Roscommon was known as O'Fallon's country. O'Connellan gives the O'Faolains or O'Felans, or Whelans, among the Irish chiefs and cláns of Desies.

FEVER. From O. Fr. Lefèvre, "the smith." Cf. the U. S. names Favor, Lefever, Lefevre, Lefebre, Lefavour, Lefavor.

FIFE, var. Fyfe and Fyffe, from co. Fife, Scotland.

FIGG. "A Feg occurs in Yorkshire ante 1086, Domesday, and a Figge in Kent, 31 Edw. III. In the latter county, at a later period, the Figgs, Faggs, and Foggs flourished contemporaneously, and may have had a common origin ; and other kindred forms are Fig, Figes, Figgs, &c."—*Lower.* All these names are through the O. Fr., from L. *fagus*, a beech-tree. Hence also several other French names ; as Fay, De la Fayette, &c.

FILBERT. The same as the O. G. name Filiberthus (Philobertus) ; from *viel brecht*, very renowned (præclarus). Wachter renders *viel* in composition, *weit* and *laut.*

FILL. See FILLPOT.

FILLPOT, PHILPOT. A diminutive of Philp from Philip. Philpot was the name of a gardener at Highgate, Middlesex, and there is a publican at Hammersmith named Phillpott. From the first part of the name are Fill and Filkin, and from the last syllable, Pot, Pott, Potts.

FINCH. See WINCH.

FIPPENY. See PENNY.

FIRKIN. A diminutive of some Christian name, or of the name Phear, or Fear. Ferguson thinks it may be from A. S. *fir-cyn*, race of man, which is absurd.

FISH. From A. S. *fiscere*, a fisher (fisherman). Ferguson says Fisk and Fish signified a salmon-fisher.

FLASHMAN. A corruption of the name Flaxman, a dresser of flax, or a spinner. Lower, under " Flashman," says " *flashes*

D

is a word proverbially applied to flood-gates, and that the flash-man probably had the care of such gates."

FLATMAN. From A. S. *flótmann*, a sailor. "One Floteman was an undertenant in Yorkshire before the compilation of Domesday."

FLOAT. From A. S. *flóta*, a sailor. It may also sometimes be local; for, as Lower says, " an Hampshire family wrote themselves De Flote." La Flotte is the name of a comm. and seaport town of France, dep. Charente-Inf.

FLOCK. Perhaps from Floques, near Eu, in Normandy. Flockton is the name of a place in Yorkshire.

FLOOD, *i.q.* FLOYD, LLOYD. Andrew Borde, in his Boke of Knowledge, makes a Welshman say, "I am a gentylman and come of Brutus blood; my name is Ap Pyce, Ap Davy, Ap Flood."

FLUX. A corruption of Fulkes, Foulkes, Folkes, Fullicks, Faulks, Foalkes, Folkes, Fowkes; from A. S. *folc*, folk; G. *folc*, *volk*, people, nation, perhaps also used in the sense of " renowned." Cf. the G. names Fulco, Folcho, Folca, Folchold, Folcwar, Folcmar, Folcrim, Folcwin, Folcrad, Folcharat, Folchard, Eng. Folkard, Fr. Foucard. Flux might also come from Floques, in Normandy. See FLOCK.

FLY. " A place near Gournay, in Normandy, once famous for its great Abbey. It was anciently called Flagi, Chron. of Battel Abbey, p. 49."—*Lower.*

FOLLY. Doubtless the same as Foley; from the local name Foley, anciently Fowleigh.

FORCE (Fr. De la Force). From *force* (Dan. *fors*, O. N. id.), in the north of England, a waterfall or cascade. Hence the surname Wilberforce, formerly Wilberfosse, from Wilberfoss co. York, named from one Williber, or Williberg.

FORT. From Fr. *fort*, strong, powerful. Cf. the French Le Fort.

FORTUNE. 1. From Fortunatus. 2. From Fortune co. Haddington.

FORTY, FORTYE. From Fuerty, a parish of Ireland, Connaught; or from *forty*, used by the Scottish poet Douglas in the sense of brave. Hence perhaps the name Fortyman.

FORTYMAN. See FORTY.

FOULFOOT. See HAZLEFOOT.

FOULLY. See LEGG.

FOULWEATHER. See MERRYWEATHER.

FOURAPENNY. See PENNY.

FOXWORTHY. A U. S. name. See WORTH.

FREAK. The same as Fricke and Fricker; from H. S. *fricca*, a preacher. According to Dr. Doran, the word *freak*, a whim or fancy, was derived from the caprices of a Dr. Freake, of St. Bartholomew's.

FREELOVE. Lower gives a H. R. name Frelove, and an A. S. name Frealaf. But see LAW.

FREELY. See LEGG.

FRESHFIELD. See FRETWELL.

FRETWELL. From Fritwell, a parish co. Oxon. Camden however thinks it a corruption of the Norman De Fresheville (Latinised De Frisca-villa). From the latter we have Freshville, and perhaps Freshfield.

FRIENDLY. See LEGG.

FRIENDSHIP. A Devonshire name. See HOPE.

FROM. A name found in the U. S.; perhaps from Frome in Somerset, or Froome in Dorset (England).

FROST. 1. From the surname Forest, Forrest. 2. From the German or Swiss name Fürst; from *fürst*, a prince. One Alwin Forst was a tenant in co. Hants before Domesday, and Frosti is the name of a dwarf in the Scandinavian mythology.

FRY. 1. From Humphry. 2. Perhaps sometimes from Cornish *fry*, a promontory; literally a nose.

FUEL, *i. q.* FUGGLE, FOWELL, FOWLE. From A. S. *fugel*, a fowl, bird.

D 2

FULBORN. From Fulbourne co. Cambridge. But see SMALL-
BONE.

FULLALOVE. See LAW.

FULSOM. A U. S. name ; from root of Fulham (Middlesex);
from *fugl's-ham*, the bird's dwelling.

FUNK, FUNKE. Found as U. S. names. They may be
corrupted from Fulnecks, a village of England, co. York, or Ful-
neck or Fulik, a town of Moravia, circ. Prerau.

FUNNELL. Lower thinks this name may be a corruption of
Fontenelle, now St. Wandrille-sur-Seine, in Normandy, an ancient
barony, and the site of a famous monastery, near Carrdebec, and
that the corruption may have taken place thus : Fontenelle,
Fonnell, Funnell.

FURNACE. From Furnace, a village co. Argyle ; or Furness,
a manorial liberty in the north-west part of Lancashire ; or Furnes,
a town of Belgium, prov. W. Flanders. Cf. the surnames Furnice,
Furniss, Fourness, Furnese, Furness, Furniss. There is also a
Furneaux, from Fourneaux-sur-Vire, in Normandy.

G.

GAB. See GABY.

GABLE. See GABY.

GABY. Probably a nickname of Gabriel. Hence no doubt
Gab, Gabb, Gabay, Gable, Gabel, Gabell.

GAILY. See LEGG.

GAIN. From the name Eugaine, which gave appellation to
Colne Eugaine, commonly called Gain's Colne, a parish in Essex ;
doubtless from Enghien in the Pays Bas, anciently Anguien or
Enguien, in Lat. Angia. Gane, Gaines, Gainey are doubtless
from the same root.

GALE. Lower says Gale signifies a Scottish Highlander, but
that the Gaels of Charlton-Kings co. Gloucester, have written

themselves, at various periods, Galle, Gale, Gael, and originally
De Gales. This may either refer to Calais or Wales, which latter,
in Anglo-Norman times, was known as Galles or Gales. In
local compounds the vocable *hall* is often corrupted to *gale*.

GALLIARD. See HAZARD.

GALLON. Bowditch says, "In 1844 one Joseph Galliano
died in Boston, and in our Probate Records he has the alias of
Joseph Gallon, that having been his popular name." Lower
gives the H. R. forms "Galien, Galiûn, Galion, Galun, and
Galeyn." Said Joseph may have been from Galliano, a village
of N. Italy, not far from Como ; but the English name may be
from Gallen, a parish of Ireland, Leinster ; or Galloon, Ulster,
co. Fermanagh ; or Gaillan, Gaillon, two comms. and towns of
France, one dep. Gironde, the other dep. Eure.

GALLOP. See HOPE.

GALLOWS. Perhaps *i. q.* Hallows, from Hallow, a parish in
Worcester, or *i. q.* Callow, from Callow co. Hereford ; or Callow
co. Derby. The A. S. *calo* is bald.

GAMBLE. Lower says, "Gamel occurs both in Domesday
and in the H. R. In the latter 'Fitz Gamel' is also found. A. S.
gamol or *gamel*, old, aged. . . . . Gamblesby, in Cumberland, probably derived its name from a Danish proprietor." Gamla is the
name of a town of Finland. Gamble may however be corrupted
from the name Gumboil, *q. v.*

GAMBLING. Probably of local origin, and doubtless the
same as the H. R. Gamelin, De Gameling. Gamlin-gay is the
name of a parish co. Cambridge.

GAME. See WALKINGHAME.

GAMMON. From Gaelic *ma-ghamuim*, a bear ; from *magh-
ghabhuin*, literally a calf of the plain.

GANDER. Some derive this name from the bird. Grimm
also refers the name of the great Vandal chief Genseric to
gänserich, a gander. Gander is more probably from O. N. *gandr*,
a wolf. Gandr occurs as a surname in the Landnamabok.

GARLICK, *i. q.* the German name Gerlach; from *ger-leich, lich*, warlike.

GARMENT. The same name as Garman, Gorman, Jarman, German, Jermain; from the O. G. name Garmund (O. H. G. Germunt; in the Landnamabok, Geirmundr); from *ger-mund*, a defence in war. Hence, perhaps, by inverson the name Manger.

GEM. A U. S. name. Another form of Jem, nickname for James. From Jem we have, as a diminutive, Jemmett.

GENDER. Perhaps the same as Gander, *q. v.* Ferguson says Gender corresponds with a Mod. G. Genther, compounded of *here*, an army.

GHERKEN, GERKEN. For Jerkin, a diminutive of Jeremiah. Ferguson says Gerken corresponds with a G. Gherken, which he classes with the O. H. G. Gericho, Mod. G. Gericke, Gehrke, Gerke, and derives from A. S. *gár* a spear, O. N. *geir*, O. S. and O. Fries. *ger*.

GIDDY. An ancient Cornish family, formerly written Gedy, Geddey, Gidey, &c. Possibly a nurse name of Gideon.—*Lower*.

GILDERSLEEVES (in U. S. Gildersleeve, in H. R. Gyldenesleve). An Irish name derived from some local name compounded of *sliabh* (pronounced *sleeve*), a mountain, moor.

GILL. A U. S. name. Contracted from Gillet for Willet, a diminutive of Will for William.

GIN. This surname may be from one of the Scottish names Mac Gin, Mac Ginn, Mac Genn, Mac Gane, Mac Geehan, Mac Giehan, Mac Geachan. Lower thinks Ginn, Gin, may be the same as Genn with the G. softened; and he says the latter is Cornish, and is considered to be from the root of Planta-*gen*-ista.

GINGER. From A. S. *gingra*, a younger, disciple; from *ging*, young, tender.

GIRL. Same as Garle, which Ferguson thinks may be another form of Carl. It may also be the same as the O. G. Gerlo, fem. Gerla, which he considers diminutives of Gero and Gera, from *ger*, a spear.

GLASS. 1. From Glass, a parish in cos. Aberdeen and Banff. 2. From Nicholas. Cf. Class and the German Claus; whence Clause, Clausse, Claussen, Classen. 3. From Gael. *glas*, grey, blue, green; found in Ir., W., Armor., and Corn.

GLASSCOCK. See GLASS.

GLAZARD. See HAZARD.

GLISTER. 1. The same as Glaister. 2. For Lister; from the old word *lytster* or *litster*, a dyer; or from *listre*, a person employed to read some portions of the church service. Webster renders " lister," " one who makes a list or roll."

GOAD. See GOAT.

GOAT. From Corn. *goed*, a wood. Hence, perhaps, Goad and Gout.

GODSON. See GOODSON.

GODSPENNY. See PENNY.

GOLD, *i. q.* GOLDE, and the Goldus of Domesday; also Waldie, Waldo; from G. *wald*, a wood, or O. G. *walt*, powerful, governing, ruling; also a prefect.

GOLDHAM. See COLDHAM.

GOLDMAN. From G. *wald-man*, woodman. Hence, by corruption, Coldman. See GOODMAN.

GOLIGHTLY. See LEGG.

GOLLOP. See HOPE. " The Gollops of Strode co. Dorset have a tradition of Danish or Swedish descent from a soldier of fortune who was living in 1465. B. L. G."—*Lower*.

GOOD. For Wood.

GOODAIR. See GOODYEAR.

GOODALE. The same as Woodhall; from Woodhall, name of a parish co. Lincoln, and of places in several counties.

GOODBEER. See GOODYEAR.

GOODBEHERE. See GOODYEAR.

GOODBOYS. From some Fr. local name ending in *bois*, a wood.

GOODCHAP. See GOODCHEAP.

GOODCHEAP (in H. R. Godchep). From some local name ending in *cheap* (See CHIP). Hence Goodchap and Goodsheep.

GOODENOUGH. From some local name, perhaps originally Woodknowe, compounded of *knowe*, a Scotticism equivalent to *knoll*, the top or crown of a hill; but more generally a little round hill or mount, a small elevation of earth; from A. S. *cnoll*, *knöl*, W. *cnol*. Cf. the name Oldknow.

GOODFELLOW. For Woodfellow; from A. S. *wuda-felaw*, a wood companion or follower.

GOODGROOM. See GOODRUM.

GOODHEART. Same as Woodward, an officer of the wood or forest; or from Goddard, Goddart, "one strong in God."

GOODLAKE. Same as the surname Woodley, name of parishes and places in co. Devon, &c. &c. Hence Goodluck.

GOODLUCK. See GOODLAKE.

GOODMAN. 1. The same as Woodman. 2. From the O. G. and A. S. baptismal name Gudmund, "powerful in war."

GOODRAM. See GOODRUM.'

GOODRUM. Ferguson thinks this name may be a corruption of Gothrun or Guthrum; from *guth* war, *ormr* a serpent; and he says Gothrun or Guthrum was the name of the Danish king who was baptised by Alfred. It may also be from G. *wald-ram*, strong or powerful prince; or from Goldrun (Waldron, Calderon); from *wald-run*, a powerful friend. Hence the names Goodram, Goodgroom.

GOODSHEEP. See GOODCHEAP.

GOODSIR. Name of a celebrated Scotch anatomist, lately deceased. It was perhaps originally Woodseer, one who superintends a wood. Cf. Landseer, which Lower renders "one who overlooks or superintends lands for another, a bailiff."

GOODSON. From the parish of Gooderstone, commonly Goodson, co. Norfolk; from *wood* and *ton*. Hence doubtless the name Godson.

GOODWILL. A corruption of Woodville ; perhaps from Woodville, near Burton-on-Trent. See also WOODFALL.

GOODWINE, GOODWIN. 1. From Godwin, Godwine, " beloved of God "=Theophilus. 2. Same as Goldwin, *i. e.* Waldwin, which may translate both " victorious prince," and " powerful friend."

GOODYEAR. Another form of Woodyer, a woodman. This name has been corrupted to Goodair, Goodbeer, and Goodbehere.

GOOSE. From Corn. *gûs*, a wood. It may sometimes be the same with Goss, Gosse, Gass. [There is a Gás in the Landnamabok.] Graff suggests that Goz in O. G. names is another form of Gaud, which is most probably Goth ; to which Försteman refers the O. G. names Gauso, Gozzo, Gossa, Mod. G. Gause and Göss. (See Furguson.) Gas, Gass, Gasse, Cas, Casse may sometimes be from Cassandra ; or even from the Dan. *gasse*, a gander.

GOOSEMAN. Same as Guzman, Gudmund ; from O. G. *guntmund*, A. S. *guth-mund*, a warrior.

GOOSEY. From Goosey, a tithing in the parish of Stanford-in-the-vale, Berks.

GORE. Same as Gower, Goar, Gover ; from Gûyr (Gower), in Wales, signifying " sloping." Archd. Williams translates *gover* a small stream, and the W. *gower* is a croft, close ; and *gofwr*, *govwr*, a strong mound or tower. Verstegan says the name Gower is derived from a kind of cake formerly made for children !

GOTOBED. Mr. Fox Talbot derives this name from O. G. *Gott-bet*, " Pray to God." Lower gives a Gotobedd and a Gotebedde, and thinks the name may have been given as a sobriquet to people more than ordinarily attached to their couch ; and he says a similar collocation of words forming a surname occurs in the H. R. ; viz., Serlo *Go-to-kirke*. The whole name may be from *guth-beada*, a war counsellor ; or the last part from A. S. *boda*, a messenger. It may also be a compound of two names'. Obed is a surname at the present day. Cf. Meyerbeer, from Meyer Beer.

GOUT. See GOAT.

GOWN. For Gowan, from Gael. *gobhainn*, a blacksmith.

GRAIN, GRAINE, GRANE. From Grain in Kent.

GRAMMAR. This may be the same as the ancient name Grimar; perhaps from O. N. *gramr*, *grimr*, fierce, or *gramr*, a king. Cf. the surnames Grimm, Graimm, Graeme, Gream, Gryme, Graham, &c. The W. *grymus* is powerful, strong, nervous; *grym*, force, energy, powerful: the Brit. *grym*, force, energy, power, strength: the Gael. *grim*, *griom*, war, battle; *gruaim*, a gloom, a frown or surly look; *gruama*, surly, stern, morose; *gruaimean*, a surly man, a man with a frowning visage; *groimh*, a grin, a visage, a nickname for one with a grinning countenance. The O. G. *grimm* is rigid, vehement, intense anger, furor, cruelty: G. id. furious, grim: the A. S. *grim*, fierce, rough, ferocious; *gram*, raging, fury; *gremian*, to provoke: the D. *gram*, angry; *grimmen*, to growl: the *Dan. grim*, stern, grim, peevish; *gram*, grudging, hating, peevish.

GRASS. This name means fat, stout; from Fr. *gras*.

GRAVELLY. A U. S. name, same as Graveley; from Graveley, name of parishes cos. Herts and Cambridge. But see also LEGG.

GREENLAW. From Greenlaw co. Berwick. See LAW.

GREENSWORD. See LONGSWORD.

GRIEF. Same as Grieve, Greive; from A. S. *gerefa* (G. *graf*), a bailiff, a reeve.

GRIFFIN. Said to have been early used to designate a Welshman.

> Godefray of Garlekhithe, *and Gryffyn* the *Walshe*.
> Piers Ploughman, ed. Wright, p. 96.

Another orthography of Griffith. Lower says it is a common baptismal name in Wales, and that Domesday shows a Grifin in Cornwall, and in Cheshire a Grifin *Rex*, first a favourite of Edward the Confessor, and afterwards a rebel against him. See also Notes and Queries, 3rd S. xi. 504.

GRIFFINHOOFE. A German name introduced into England

by one of the physicians of Geo. I. Mr. Fox Talbot says one might suppose this to be from the G. *grafen-hof*, implying some person attached to the court of a count, if there had not existed a German family name Greifenklau, or the Griffin's claw; and Lower says, "In mediæval poems, &c., many references to griffins' claws are found. In ' Ruodlieb ' the hero wears, apparently, a hunting horn made of such a talon. ' Pendet et a niveo sibimet *gripis ungula* collo.' " The name probably means the " count's yard or court."

GRILLARD. See HAZARD.

GRIMM. See GRAMMAR.

GRINDALL. A chapelry in Yorkshire.

GROOM. See CRUMB.

GROUSE. There was an O. G. Grauso, of the sixth century, which Förstemann refers to A. S. *greosan*, horrere; but this name is the same with Grose, Gross, implying great, big in stature; from Fr. *gros*, L. *crassus*.

GRUMBLE. A corruption of the old Frankish name Grimbald; from *grim-bald*, fierce and bold; or the same name as the O. H. G. Rumbold, Mod. G. Rumpolt; from *hruom-bold*, famously bold.

GUESS. A corruption of the surname Guest.

GUESSARD. See HAZARD.

GUISE. Erom Guise, a comm. and town of France, dep. Aisne, probably deriving its name from its situation on the Ouse, found anciently written Gusia and Gusgia.

GUM. The same as Gumm, Gomm, the O. G. Goma, a Dan. Gummi in Saxo, a U. S. Gumma [Gommo, Gummoe, Gummow are found in Cornwall]. From A. S. *guma*, Goth. id., O. H. G. *gomo*, O. Eng. obs. *gom*, a man.

GUMBOIL. Corrupted from the O. G. name Gumpold or Gundbold; from *gund-bold*, bold in war. Cf. the old German names Gontharis, Guntharis, Günther, Gundericus, Gundemundus, Guntramnus.

GUMP. Not from *gump*, a vulgar word for a foolish person, a dolt, but from Gump, in St. Agnes, Cornwall; from Cornish *guimp*, *gump*, downhill, in W. *ar gwympo*.

GUN. Same as Gunn. From one of the old German names, Gundbald, Gundebert, Gundric; or from O. G. *gun*, a man (which Wachter derives from *kennen*, to be able). Indeed Wachter thinks that from this *gun* is *gund*, a heroine (*vira, virago*); whence the O. G. names Adelgunda, Cunigunda, Fredegunda, Gundaberga.

GUSH. See CASH.

GUTTER. Corrupted from Gauthier, Gautier, French forms of Walter; from G. *walter*, which Wachter renders "negotiorum gestor." With the Basque affix *es* or *ez*, son, we doubtless have the célebrated Spanish name Gutierrez, whence the English name Gutteres.

H.

HACKSTAFF. See WAGSTAFF.

HADDOCK. This name has been considered the same as the Saxon Hadeca and Hadiko; probable diminutives of Chad, Head, A. S. Hedda, and the O. G. names Haddo, Hadow, Chatto. I take it to be corrupted from Eadwig; from A. S. *ead-wig*, fortunate in war, or *ead-wiga*, prosperous warrior. Hence probably the name Headache.

HAGGARD. Same as Hoggart, Huggard; from *hoog-hart*, a D. G. compound signifying very high or big.

HAIL. Same as Hale; from Cornish *hâl*, *hâle*, a moor; *hâl*, a hill; or *hail*, bountiful; also a river that runs into the sea. There is Hale in Broadoak parish (Cornwall); and Hayle is the name of a seaport and town in Penwith hundred.

HAILSTONE. This is hardly the same name as the Hallstein of the Landnamabok; but is more probably from Helston, in

Cornwall, which Pryce derives from *hal-las-ton*, the hill by a green moor.

HAKE. Same as Haig and Haigh; from Haigh co. Lancaster; from A. S. *hagen*, a hay, hedge, meadow.

HALFPENNY. The names Halfpenny and Twopenny are probably from different roots than the names found under "Penny." Halfpenny is found written Halpeny and Halpeni; and Allpenny and Alpenny are perhaps the same name. They may be corrupted from the surname De Albini, D'Aubignie (whence Daubeney), said to be from Aubigny, in Contentin, Normandy. Twopenny, found Twopeny, may be the same name. There are, however, the French Tubini and Doupenay; and there is also a Dobenny, and a Flemish Tupigni; but some of these may be from Piney or Pigney, in Champagne.

HALSTAFF. See WAGSTAFF.

HAM. From A. S. *hám*, a homestead. Cf. Coldham and Hotham.

HAMPER. Corruption of the name Hanaper, one who held an office of that name. A *Galfridus le Hanaper* occurs in H. R. The Hanaper Office was a place where writs were formerly deposited in coarse baskets called hanapers. See Spelman. The common word hamper is a corruption of *hanaper*.

HANDYSIDE (Handasyd). See SIDE.

HANKPENNY. See PENNY.

HAPPY. See APPLE.

HARDMAN. The same as Hardiman, Hartman (perhaps the inverse of Maynard); from G. *hart-mund*, a strong man.

HAREFOOT. Lower thinks this surname had a figurative reference to swiftness of foot; and he says there is an instance of this application in King Harold Harefoot, and that at the present day the family name *Pié-de-lièvre* exists in France. I consider it same as Harford; from Harford co. Devon; or from the town of Hertford. But see HAZLEFOOT.

HAT. According to Ferguson, Hatt is the oldest hereditary

surname on record. He says it corresponds with the O. G. names Hatto, Heddo, and Chado, signifying "war," and consequently with Haddo, Head, Chad, whence perhaps Shade. It is more likely from the root of *heath*, viz. A. S. *hœth*, D. and G. *heide*, Dan. *hede*.

HATFULL. Corruption of the surname Hatfield; from Hatfield, name of several places in England; from *hœth-feld*, heath field.

HATOFF. This name is probably of Slavonic origin = son of Hat.

HATRED. Same as Outred, the O. G. name Hadarat, and the A. S. personal name Utred or Uhtred; from O. G. *ot-rat*, distinguished in council, or illustrious councillor.

HAZARD. *Ard, art, ert,* the termination of several thousand names, is generally equivalent to "son," and is derived from G. *art*, kind, species, race. Among other names are Bichard, Billiard (Bill), Bustard (Bust), Buzzard, Canard, Caward, Chaffard (Chaff, *i. e.* Chauve), Clayard (Clay), Clinkard, Costard, Covert, Coward (Cow), Custard (Cust), Dullard (Dull), Galliard, Glazard (Glaze), Grillard, Guessard, Hazard, Izzard, Killard, Klinkheart (Klink), Lollard, Mansard, Mustard (Moist, for Moyce, Moyes, *i. e.* Moses), Packard (Pack), Peckard (Peck or Pech), Perchard, Pinchard (Pinch), Pirssard, Pissard, Poignard, Pollard (Pol or Paul), Popard, Punchard (Punch), Ramard (Ram), Rollard, Spillard (Spill), Stoppard, Touchard (Touch), Trenchard (Trench), Windard, Woolard (Wool), Workhard, &c.

HAZLEFOOT or HASLEFOOT. From some local name ending in "ford." Hence Crowfoot, Dayfoot, Foulfoot, Harefoot, Lightfoot, Playfoot [there is also Playford], Proudfoot, Puddifoot Whitefoot.

HEADACHE. See HADDOCK.

HEAL. See HELL.

HEAVEN, HEAVENS. A corruption of Evan, Evans. See EVEN. There is however a German Himmel.

HELL. According to Mr. Bowditch the name Holl in the U. S. is pronounced Hell; and Holle, without prefix, is found in H. R. It may also be the same with Hele; from Hele, Heale, or Heal; a manor in the parish of Bradninch, Devon. Hell however is found as a German name; perhaps from *hell*, clear, bright.

HERITAGE (H. R. Heritag). Doubtless of German origin. See SINGLEDAY.

HEROD. Not the classical name; but the same with Heraud, and an O. G. Herod, which Förstemann derives from *heroti*, principatus. They are probably the same as Harold.

HERRING. This name may be the same as Hering, from some locality compounded of *ing*, a meadow. Hornsey, Middlesex, from the thirteenth to the sixteenth century was called in public records Haringee, Haringhee, or Haringay, signifying the meadow of hares. Pott however gives Herr and Herring as German names; and the root may be O. G. *herrin*, a lady, fem. of *herr*; or from A. S. *here-rinc*, which Dr. Bosworth renders "hostile counsellor;" but which may also mean "war counsellor."

HIGGINBOTTOM. See BOTTOM.

HINDER. A U. S. name. Doubtless the same as the Cornish name Hender; originally Hendower, said to be of Welsh origin; from W. *hen-dwr*, Corn. *hean-dower*, the old water.

HINDERWELL. A parish co. York.

HISCOCK. See COCK.

HITCHCOCK. See COCK.

HOG. Same as Hogg, Hogge, Hugh, Hugo; from D. *hoog*, high.

HOMER. As an English name, not derived from that of the Greek poet. Ferguson thinks it to be from Hamer, according to Grimm, a name under which traces of Thor are still to be found in the popular speech of Germany, and derived, no doubt, from the celebrated hammer or mallet wielded by Thor (from A. S. *hamor*, *homer*, a hammer); or an A. S. form of the O. N. name Heimir; from O. N. *heim*, Eng. *home*, Sco. *hame*. He also says

Homer may correspond with the German name Homeir; probably from *hof-meier*, a farm steward. A more reasonable derivation is from O. Eng. and O. Fr. *hiaumer*, one who fabricates helms, *i. e.* helmets; from A. S. *helma*, a helm.

HONEBONE. See HONEYBUM.

HONEYBUM, HONEYBUN, HONEYBONE. From Honeybourne or Cow-Honeybourne co. Gloucester. Hence Honeybun and Honeybone.

HONEYBUN. See HONEYBUM.

HOOD. A corruption of Wood. Woodward is often pronounced Hoodard.

HOODLESS. Perhaps="wood leas." See LEGG.

HOOK. A corruption of Oak, which explains itself.

HOPE. Name of parishes in cos. Derby, Flint, Hereford, Kent, Salop, York, &c.; and also of two townships in the U. S. Jamieson renders it a sloping hollow between two hills, and Camden, the side of a hill. Ferguson gives A. S. *hopu*, a mound, or O. N. *hóp*, a recess. I find no such word in Saxon. Among other local surnames compounded of *hope* are Friendship, Gallop, Gollop, Lightup, Milsop, Milksop, Peasoop, Pickup, Startup, Stirrop, Stirrup, Trollope, Walkup.

HOPELESS. This name may mean "the hop meadows." But see LEGG.

HORSECRAFT. See CRAFT.

HORSNAILL. Same as Horsnell, which in O. G. might translate either very quick, or as swift as a horse (*ras-schnell*, or *hros-schnell*). Cf. the German names Schnell, Schnelle, Snelgar, and the Eng. Snell, Snelling, Snelson.

HOTHAM. From Hotham, a parish co. York; from *holtham*, the dwelling in the wood. Cf. the surnames Coldham and Ham.

HOUSEHOLD. Same as Oswald. See ASHMAN.

HOUSEMAN. See ASHMAN.

HOVELL. Said to be the same as Havill and Auberville;

from Aubervilliers, a village of France, dep. Seine. Cf. Lower's Pat. Brit.

HOY. Same as Hoey, Mac Hoey, for Mackay, Mac Kay, or Mac-Aiodh, the son of Hugh. It may sometimes be from Hoy, an island and parish of Orkney.

HUE. Same as Hugh, Hugo; from D. *hoog*, high, A. S. *heah*, *hig*, Sw. *hög*. Hence Huett, Hewet, Hewett, Hewitt, &c. &c.

HULL. From Hull co. York; or *hull*, an old word for a hill.

HUM. Same as Hume or Home; from Hume or Home, a parish of Scotland, co. Berwick, which gave title to the once powerful baronial family of Home, remains of whose castle still exist there.

HUMAN. Same as Hughman; from D. *hoog-man*, a tall man, or G. *hoh-mund*, a great man.

HUMBER. Not from the river of this name, but from the personal name Humbert.

HUMBLE. 1. Corrupted from the name Humboldt. 2. From the manor of W. Humble, parish of Mickleham, Surrey. Ferguson derives the old Danish names Humbl or Humbli from O. N. *humall*, the hop plant; and he says our name Humble occurs chiefly in the old Danish districts of England.

HUNGER. From Chipping Ongar co. Essex, or from its root, the A. S. *ing*, a meadow, which in German assumes the form of *ingr*.

HUSSEY is found written De la Hossé or Heuzé, De Hosa, and De Hoese; and according to Stapleton's Rot. Scacc. Norm. was named from *le Hozu*, a fief in the parish of Grand Quevilly, near Rouen; and Lower says there is a place now spelt Heussé, dep. La Manche. The local name is without doubt from the Fr. *houssaie*, a place where much holly grows, a holly grove.

E

I.

ICEMONGER. An ironmonger; from A. S. *isen*, iron, and *monger.—Lower*.

IDLE, IDOL. From Idle, a chapelry co. York, W. R.

IDOL. See IDLE.

IMAGE. See MARRIAGE.

INCH, INCHES. From Inch, name of several parishes and places in Scotland. Inch generally signifies an island, but sometimes level ground contiguous to a river, and is derived from Gael. *innis*, Ir. *inis*, Corn. *ennis*, W. *ynis*, Armor. *enes* and *enesan*, an island; from L. *insula*.

INKPEN. Formerly Ingepen; from Inkpen, a parish co. Berks. Ingpen is doubtless the same surname, and is perhaps the original orthography of the local name. See also PENNY.

IRON, IRONS, HIRONS. From Hieronymus; whence also Jerom, Jerome. Lower thinks Iron, Irons may be from Airan, a village near Caen, in Normandy.

IVORY. Found De Ivery and De Ivri. From the Castle of Ivery in Normandy; so called from its situation on the river Eure or Evre. Hence the family was entitled "Comes de Iberio."

IVY. Same as Ive; corrupted from Ιωαννης, *i. e.* John. Cf. Mac Ivor, from Mac-Ian-Mohr, pron. Mac-Ia-vor, the son of Big John.

IVYLEAF. From root of Yellow, *q. v.*

IZZARD. See HAZARD.

J.

JACKET. A diminutive of Jacques, *i. e.* James.

JELLY. From root of Yellow, *q. v.*

JOLLY. This name has been derived from Julius. But see YELLOW.

JOY. From Johe, found in old records as a contraction of Johanne, Johannes, *i. e.* John. Jouy is, however, the name of many comms. of France, in deps. Eure-et-Loir, Moselle, &c. ; and there is Jouy-sur-Morin, a comm. and village dep. Seine-et-Marne, on the Morin.

JUGG, JUGGS. Same as Jeake, Jeakes, Jex; from Jacques, Fr. for James.

JUMP. A village co. Devon, Roborough Hundred.

JUMPER. From Jeane Pierre. Lower thinks the name means a maker of *jumps*, a short leather coat or boddice formerly worn by women.

JUNE. From the Fr. name Jeune, " young."

K.

KEEL. From Keele, a parish co. Stafford ; or Keal, name of two parishes co. Lincoln.

KEEN, KEENE. 1. Same as Kean, O'Kean, from Gael. *ceann*, head, commander ; Ir. *ceann*, a head, chief, leader, captain. 2. From Kean or Keyne (St.), a parish co. Cornwall.

KEEPING. 1. From Kippen, a parish of Scotland, cos. Perth and Stirling. 2. A patronymic of the name Keep, or compounded of *ing*, a meadow.

KETTLE. From Kettle co. Fife. There are however the surnames Kettel, Ketell, and Kittle. Chetell occurs as a surname in Domesday ; and in H. R. are found Ketel and Ketyl ; and in old writings Catul or Katel.

KEYLOCK. See LEGG.

KILBOY. See KILPATRICK.

KILBRIDE. Name of several parishes of Ireland, the prin-

cipal being cos. Cavan, Meath, and Roscommon. But see KIL-
PATRICK.

KILLARD. See HAZARD.

KILLMAN. A U. S. name. See CHILD.

KILLMARTIN. A U. S. name. Bowditch thinks it a corruption of Gilmartin, "follower of Martin." But see KILPATRICK.

KILLMISTER, KILMASTER, KILLMASTER. Frqm Kil-
minster, near Wick, in Scotland. But see KILPATRICK.

KILMANY. From Kilmany, a parish co. Fife. See KIL-
PATRICK.

KILMASTER, KILLMASTER. See KILMISTER.

KILPATRICK. Name of two parishes of Scotland, cos.
Dumbarton and Stirling; from Gael. *cill* (Ir. id., L. *cella*), a cell,
chapel. Cf. the surnames Kilboy, Kilbride, Killmartin, Kilmany,
Kilmaster, Killmaster, Killmister. .

KISS. This name may be derived from the last syllable of
several names; as from Hotchkiss, Purkiss; for Hodgkins, Perkins.
Ferguson however thinks Case, Chase, Cheese, Choice, and Kiss
may be from different forms of verbs signifying to choose, as the
O. S. *ciasan, ciesen, ciosan,* A. S. *cysan, ceosan,* O. Fries. *kiasa,*
O. N. *kiosa;* and that this is the probable etymon of Cissa
(Chissa), king of the South Saxons, who, according to the A. S.
chronicle, came over to Britain A. D. 477. He says further that
in Friesland, where there is a remarkable twofold coincidence
between the common names of the people, our own names, and
those of our early Saxon invaders, Tsjisse (Chisse) is a name in
use at the present day; and that Cissa may mean "one chosen or
elected."

KITCHEN. A diminutive of Kit, nickname of Christopher.

KITE. 1. From A. S. *cot, cote, cyte,* W. *cwt,* a cot; W. *cut,* a
hovel, shed, &c. 2. From Cornish *coid, coit, cuit, quit, quite,* a
wood.

KNEEBONE. See SMALLBONE.

KNOBLOCK. See LEGG.

KNOCK. From Gael. *cnoc*, a hillock, knoll, eminence, hill. In H. R. we find a De la Knocke.

L.

LACE. Same as Lacy, Lacey, De Laci. A Roger de Laci came over with the Conqueror. The *Itinéraire de la Normandie* mentions a place called Lassi, dep. Calvados (Latinised by Ordericus Vitalis to *Laceium*), which Lower thinks may have been the cradle of this renowned name.

LACK. 1. From A. S. *leag*, a field, place. 2. From Fr. Du Lac, " of the lake." But see LEGG.

LADYMAN. Same as Laidman, which has been rendered— 1. " A man who has the charge of a horse-load or of a pack-horse." 2. The servant belonging to a miln, who has the charge of driving the loads to the owners, as well as of lifting them up (See Jamieson). Lower suggests also Dan. *lade*, a barn ; a barn-man, perhaps equivalent to Grainger. It may also some-times be from G. *lad-man*, for *land-man*, a lieutenant of a dis-trict ; whence *ladscipe*, ducatus ; *hlaford*, dominus, proprie *lad-ward*, præses provinciæ, now *lord*.

LAKE. 1. From A. S. *leag*, a ley, field, place (See LEGG). 2. From Lake, a parish co. Wilts: 3. One living near a Lake. In H. R. the name is found De Lacu, De Lake, De la Lake, Atte Lake.

LAMBKIN. See LAMP.

LAMP. Corruption of the name Lamb, Lambe. It may some-times represent Lampray, Lamprey ; or even Lambert. Hence the diminutives Lambkin and Lampkin.

LAMPREY, LAMPRAY. Not from the fish, but from Lam-pridius, name of a Latin historian of the fourth, and of a Latin poet and scholar of the sixteenth century.

LANCE. This name has been derived from an O. G. Lanzo, Lando, Mod. G. Land; from A. S. and O. N. *land*, id. Lance, Launce, Lancet, Launcelot are more probably from Lawrence.

LANCET. See LANCE.

LARK, LARKE. A diminutive of Lawrence. Hence Larken, Larkin, Larking.

LARKING. See LARK.

LARKWORTHY. See WORTH.

LATE, LAIT. Same as Laity; from Laity, in Leland, Cornwall; from *lait-ty*, the milk-house or dairy. Hence, doubtless, Leuty. Laity is however a French name.

LAVENDER (found Levander). From Fr. *lavandier*, a washerman (L. *lavo*, to wash). Hence the O. Eng. word *launder*, a washer, and the surname Launder.

LAW. From A. S. *hlaw*, a heap, burrow, or small hill. Hence the surnames Low, Lowe, and, among other compounds, Blacklaw, Carlaw, Cutlove, Dearlove, Freelove, Fullalove, Greenlaw, Manlove, Marklove, Newlove, Onslowe (hounds), Pursglove, Purslove, Quicklove, Shillinglaw, Spendlove, Spenlove, Sweetlove, Truelove, Truslove, Wardlaw, Whitelaw, Whitlow, Younglove.

LAWLESS. See LOVELESS.

LAY. See LEGG.

LEAF. From A. S. *leóf*, dear, beloved, precious. Ferguson says there was a Leof, assassin of King Edmund, who sadly belied his name; and that Liúfa and Liufina are respectively male and female names in the Landnamabok. Hence the name Life.

LEANING. Compounded of *ing* a meadow, or *ing* the patronymic. Lean (Gael. Mac Lean) is a surname.

LEARNARD. A corruption of Leonard.

LEARNED, LARNED. Same as Learnard.

LEARY. Corrupted from the Ir. name Laeghaire; from *laidir*, strong, stout, or *laghar*, prong, fork, toe.

LEATHER. Same as Lethar, name of a bishop at the time of Ethelbert. Förstemann refers the O. G. names Leither, Lethar,

Mod. G. Leder, to O. H. G. *leid*, O. S. *léd*, hostile; but these names are more probably from G. *leiter*, leader; or from O. G. *laut-her*, distinguished lord or leader. Hence the O. G. Clothar, and the names Clothier, Luther, and Clotaire.

LEDGER. Same as St. Leger and Ledegar, name of a warlike king of the Saxons in the Nibelungen Lied, which occurs in some local names in A. S. charters, as Ludegárstún and Lutegáreshale, which latter Kemble thinks may be Ludgershall, in Wilts.

LEECH. From A. S. *læce*, a physician. Leach is also a surname, and is the name of a parish co. Chester.

LEGG. From A. S. *leag, legh, leah, lega*, a ley, field, place. Hence the surname Lay and the compounds Belovly, Bedlock, Blacklock, Bully, Burley, Cleverly, Comely, Daily, Duly, Early, Fatherly, Freely, Foully, Friendly, Gaily, Golightly, Gravelly, Hoodless (*leas*), Hopeless (*leas*), Keylock, Knoblock, Lightly, Likely, Lively, Looseley, Loosley, Lovelock, Loveluck, Lovely, Manly, Marlock, Mealy, Mealey, Motley, Onely, Only, Parsley, Purely, Quickly, Ragless (*leas*), Reckless (*leas*), Scratchley, Shamely, Sharpley, Shiplake, Silverlock, Skinley, Softly, Sorely, Timberlake, Truly, Ugly, Weakley, Wedlake, Wedlock, Weekley, Weekly, Whitlegg, Whitelock (A. S. *hwít*, white).

LEGGING. A patronymic of the name Legg. But see WILLING.

LEMON. 1. Same as the G. name Lehman, said from *lehn-mann*, a vassal or feudal tenant. 2. From A. S. *lah-man*, a lawyer (*lah-wita*, id.)

LEOPARD. Same as Leppard, Lepard, and the Italian name Leopardi; from the G. names Leobart, Liebhart, the O. G. Luibhart, Leopard, Leopart, of the seventh century; from *liub-hart*, strong in love.

LETTER, LETTERS. From Letter, an estate in Scotland, near Loch Katrine. Letter is found in other local names; as Letterkenny, in Ireland, co. Donegal; Letterkenny, U. S. Pennsylvania. There is also Letterston co. Pembroke, S. Wales.

LETTICE. From the female name Letitia (Sp. Leticia); from L. *lætitia*, joy, gladness.

LIBERTY. From Liberty, a village co. Fife; also the name of upwards of eight localities in the U. S.

LICENCE. Same as Lysons, in the sixteenth century written Lysans, Leyson, Lison, which Lower thinks may be derived from Lison, dep. Calvados, Normandy.

LIFE. See LEAF.

LIGHTFOOT. The name Martin with the Light Foot is said to have been given to one of the followers of the Saxon hero Hereward, on account of his swiftness; and there is the synonymous Dutch name Ligtvoet; but the modern English name is probably corrupted from the local name Lydford co. Devon.

LIGHTLY. See LEGG.

LIGHTNING (found in R. G.) Doubtless the same as the U. S. Lightnin. The name is said to be from Leighton co. Salop, also the appellation of parishes in Beds and Hunts.

LIGHTUP. See HOPE.

LIGHTWINE. See WINE.

LIKELY. See LEGG.

LILYWHITE. From the local name Litelthwaite, *i. e.* the little thwaite or piece of stubbled ground. Cf. the surnames. Applewhite, Applethwaite.

LIMBER. 1. From Limber, formerly Lymbergh, name of two parishes co. Lincoln. Hence the names Limebeer and Lumber. 2. From Lambert. Cf. Huber, from Hubert, &c., and the U. S. name Limbert.

LIMEBEER. See LIMBEER.

LIMEWEAVER. The first part of this name may be a corruption of *line* or *linen.*

LINCH, LYNCH. Linch is the name of a parish co. Sussex; and *linch* has the following meanings in England, viz. a hamlet (co. Gloucester); a balk of land (Kent); a small hanging wood or thicket (S. Downs); a small step, a narrow steep bank, or footpath (West) ; a small inland cliff, generally one that is wooded (South) ; a ledge, a rectangular projection.

LING. From Ling, name of parishes in Somersetshire and Norfolk.

LINK. Same as Linch, *q. v.*

LIQUORICE, LIQUORISH, LICKORISH. From the Neapolitan name Liquori, which may mean a native of Liguria. Ligorio was the name of a painter and architect of Naples.

LIST. 1. From root of the O. G. names Lista, Listhar; perhaps from A. S. *list*, art, wisdom, science. 2. Connected with Lister, which is probably from the old word *litster*, *lytster*, a dyer. The name of the celebrated musician, Liszt, would seem to be from the Hungarian word *liszt*, flour, but the reason is not obvious.

LITTLEBOY, LITTLEBOYS. From the French name Lillebois, from *bois*, a wood. But see Boys.

LIVELY. See Legg.

LIVING. See Loving.

LOAN. From Loan, a township co. Durham. " A Mr. Loan, of Missouri, is now (1867) an out-and-out radical in the U. S. Congress " (*Bowditch*). But see also Lone.

LOLLARD. See Hazard.

LONE. The Lane family are said to have come over with the Conqueror. The original name was De Lone, then De la Lone, finally Lone and Lane. The name may be from Loon (Laudunum) in Picardy; or from the O. Fr. *loingne*, wood, forest (bûche, morceau de bois); from L. *lignum*. There is still a family named Lone, and also a Loneon, which may be a diminutive.

LONGBOTTOM. See Bottom.

LONGDEN=long valley.

LONGMAID. See Maid.

LONGMAN. This name may be derived from stature; but Longman is also the name of a village co. Banff.

LONGMATE. See Maid.

LONGSTAFF. See Wagstaff.

LONGSWORD. From some local name compounded of *worth*, q. v. Cf. Longworth, Longworthy, Brownsword, Greensword.

LOOSE, LOOS. 1. From Loose, near Staplehurst, Kent. 2. Same as Luce, *q. v.*

LOOSELY, LOOSELEY. From Loseley, a hamlet and manor near Guildford, Surrey. See LEGG.

LOSECAMP (U. S. Loskamp). From some local name compounded of *camp* (Fr. *champ*, L. *campus*); or from Loscomb, a hamlet co. Dorset.

LOVE. Same as Le Love of the H. R. and the French name Le Loup, "the wolf." Hence, as a diminutive, Lovekin.

LOVECOCK. See COCK.

LOVEKIN. See LOVE.

LOVELADY. See TOPLADY.

LOVELESS. This name and Lawless are corrupted from Lovelace.

LOVELOCK. See LEGG.

LOVELUCK. See LEGG.

LOVELY. See LEGG.

LOVER. From Louviers, anciently Lovver, in Normandy.

LOVING. Compounded of *ing*, a meadow, or the same as Living, A. S. Leófing, a patronymic of the name Leóf; from *leóf*, dear, beloved.

LUCE. 1. From Lucius. 2. Perhaps sometimes from the surname Lucy, anciently De Luci; from Luci, a parish of Normandy, arrond. Neufchâtel.

LUCK, LUCKE, LUCKY. 1. From Luke. 2. From Lucca, in Italy. There is however the G. Glück.

LUCKY. See LUCK.

LUMBER. See LIMBER.

LUSH. From Lusk, a parish of Ireland, co. Dublin; or Luss, a parish of Scotland, co. Dumbarton.

M.

MACE. From Macé, an O. Fr. corruption of Matthew. See ROQUEFORT.

MAGGOT. A diminutive of Mag for Margaret.

MAID. From A. S. *mæde, mædewe,* a meadow. Hence Mead, Mudd, and the compounds Longmaid, Longmate, "long-meadow."

MAIDMAN. The same as Maidment; from A. S. *mæd-man,* a hireling (*med,* wages); or, perhaps, rather from *mæd-man,* a meadow man (perhaps a mower). Medeman was an O. G. name of the ninth century.

MAKER. From a parish so named near Plymouth.

MALLARD. 1. From Gael. *maol-ard,* a high promontory; also a bare hill. 2. From Mal for Mary. See HAZARD.

MANGER, *i. q.* MONGER. From A. S. *mancgere,* a merchant of the highest class; or the inverse of German. See GARMENT.

MANGLES. From the O. G. name Managold; from *man-walt,* a powerful man (*walt,* potens, dominans, imperans, præfectus). Cf. Sigivaldus, Dagoaldus, Oswald, Gotwald.

MANHOOD. From the Hundred of Manhood co. Sussex; compounded of *wood.*

MANLOVE. See LAW.

MANLY, MANLEY. From an estate in the parish of Frodsham co. Chester. But see LEGG.

MANNERS. Camden and others derive this name from the village of Mannor, near Lanchester, co. Durham. The name is probably of German origin; perhaps from Mannhardt (whence Maynard); from *man-hart,* a strong or powerful man, or *mund-hart,* powerful protector. Mannersdorf is the name of several market towns of Austria. One of these (in Hungary) is also called Menharsdorf, in Hungarian Menyhard. Mannhartsberg is the name of a wooded mountain range of Austria, which terminates near the Danube.

MANSARD. See HAZARD.

MANTLE, *i. q.* MANTELL; the Domesday Mantel, and the Mauntell of the H. R. Probably from *Maun-dell*, the dale of the Maun, whence the town of Mansfield derived its name.

MANYPENNY. See PENNY.

MARCH. From March co. Cambridge.

MARKLOVE. See LAW.

MARKQUICK (found Mar-quicke). Same as Markwick. From locality. See MARRIAGE.

MARKTHALER. See CASHDOLLAR.

MARLOCK. See LEGG.

MARRIAGE. From some place ending in *wich* or *wick;* from A. S. *wic, wyc,* a dwelling-place, habitation, village, street. Cf. Babbage, Burbage, Image, Markquick, Pillage, Pottage, Prestige, Smallage, Spinnage.

MARTYR. A corruption of Murther, *q. v.*

MARVEL, MARVELL. From Marville, a comm. and town of France, dep. Meuse.

MASH. A corruption of the name Marsh, which explains itself. Hence also Maish, Maishman, Mashman, Marshman.

MATTERFACE. This name has been rendered "modest face;" from A. S. *mathie,* modest. It is rather a corruption of the celebrated Norman surname De Martinvast (found written De Martivas); from the château of Martinvast, near Cherbourg; from G. *fest,* a fortress. Cf. the surname Standfast; from *stein fest,* stone fortress. See also Lower, under "Matterface" and "Martinvast."

MATTOCK. There are the O. G. Madacho, Mod. G. Mädicke and Matticke; but Mattock, Maddick are probably the same as Maddock, Madock, and the Welsh name Madoc; from *mad,* good.

MAUDLIN. A corruption of Magdalen.

MAXIM, *i. q.* MAXUM. Both U. S. names; from some place called Macksham; or from Maxen, a village of Saxony; or St. Maximin, a comm. and town of France, dep. Var.

MAY. In records, Le Mai ; in H. R. Le May. Lower thinks it may be the same as the O. Sco. *maich*, A. S. *mæg*, O. Eng. *mei*, son-in-law, son, or, generally, any relative. May is the name of an islet of Scotland, at the mouth of the Firth of Forth ; and of a rivulet co. Perth ; and of a rivulet of Wales, co. Carnarvon ; and Le May is the appellation of a comm. and village of France, dep. Maine-et-Loire. But May is doubtless generally the same as Mee ; from *mee*, a provincialism for a meadow ; from A. S. *mæde*, *mædewe*. Hence the compound names Mildmay (Mildmé), Youngmay (H. R. Yungemay). Ferguson renders Mildmay "mild maiden ;" and Arthur, "a tender judge." A lady informs me she has known the Christian name May to represent three different female names. It is perhaps most usually from Mary.

MAYCOCK. See COCK.

MAYDENHEAD. From Maidenhead, Berks ; or from some other local name compounded of head ; perhaps the head of some river.

MAYPOWDER. From Maypowder, a parish co. Dorset.

MEAD. See MAID.

MEALY, MEALEY. See LEGG.

MEAN. 1. From St. Meen, a comm. and village of France, dep. Ile-et-Villaine ; or Mehun, a comm. and town dep. Cher. 2. From the Irish name Meehan. It may also sometimes be of Cornish origin ; from *mean*, a stone ; whence Maine, Mayne, Mein ; or, as Lower suggests, from the A. Norm. *mesne*, which Bailey renders "a lord of a manour who holds of a superior lord." Mean, Meene, Meany, Mehan, Meehan, Meehin, Means, and Meins are found in Bowditch.

MEANS. See MEAN.

MEANWELL. From Cornish *mean-wheal*, the stony wheal or work ; or *mean-uhal*, the lower stone. Menwhilly was the name of a place in Cornwall.

MECCA. A local pronunciation of Metcalfe.—*Lower*.

MEDLAR. Medler occurs as a U. S. name ; and Nich. le

Medler is found in H. R. There is also an O. G. Madalhari, and a Mod. G. Madler. Förstemann refers the O. G. names Madalo and Madelint to the Goth. *mathl*, an assembly, deliberation; and Madalhari may be from *mathl-her*, which would translate "a counsellor;" but Le Medler seems to refer to some occupation, and may be derived from G. *mittler*, a mediator; Dan. *midler*, Sw. *medlare* (G. *mittlere*, *mitte*, middle).

MELON. Probably from Mélun (Melodunum), a comm. and town of France, on the Seine. St. Mélon (Mellonus), first bishop of Rouen, was buried at Pontoise in a church which has been dedicated to him. But see MILLION.

MERRY. The name St. Merry is said to have been softened by the French from the personal name Merdericus. Merri is the appellation of a commune, Arrond. Argentan; and there is Mery-sur-Seine dep. Aude; but the name Merry is probably the same as Emery; from Emerick, Emericus; from Almaric, Almaricus (whence the It. Amerigo), O. G. Amalrîch, Amalric, Amalrih, Amelrich, Amilrich, Amuelrich. Almaricus was a name borne by many illustrious persons, as Amalricus, King of the Visigoths, son of Alaric; Amalricus, Archbishop of Narbonne; and Almaricus, Count de Montfort, son of Simon de Montfort, who persecuted the Albigenses. The name seems to be from the Gotho-Teutonic *amal-reich*, immaculate prince, or, as some render it, sine macula potens. Cf. the ancient name Amalfrid, and the female names Amalfrida, Amaloberga, Amalasventa.

MERRYMOWTH. From Marmoutier, a town of France, dep. Bas-Rhin; or from some place at the mouth of a river called the Mer or Mar.

MERRYWEATHER (found Merywedyr). Halliwell says the word *merryweather* was formerly an idiomatic phrase for joy, pleasure, or delight. This name is probably from A. S. *wether*, *wedder*, a ram; Dan. *væder*. Cf. the surnames Fairweather (H. R. Fayrweder), Fearweather, Fineweather, Foulweather, Kieseweather, Starkweather.

MIDDLECOAT. See COAT.

MILDMAY. See MAY.

MILE, *i. q.* MIHILL, for Michael.

MILK. The same as Mellick, the O. G. Milike, Mod. G. Mielecke, Milcke, Milch, which Ferguson takes to be diminutives from the O. G. names Milo, Mila, Mello.

MILKSOP. Same as the U. S. name Milsop. See HOPE.

MILLION. A name occurring in the sixteenth report of the Registrar-General. Lower thinks it may be a corruption of St. Mellion co. Cornwall. It is probably a diminutive of some other surname.

MINNOW. From Fr. *menu*, slender, small, thin.

MISSING. From Messing, a parish of Essex; or Messines (Flem. Meesen), a town of Belgium, W. Flanders. Misson is the name of a parish co. Notts; and Mison and Missen are surnames.

MODE. From the root of Maid or Moth.

MOIST. The same as Moyce, Moyes; from Moses.

MOLE. Not from the Surrey tributary to the Thames, nor the small river of the same name in Devonshire, but from the Welsh name Moel, signifying variously bare, bald, a pile, a conical hill. Cf. the Gael. *maol*, bald, bare, a bald head, a shaved or shorn monk, a servant, also a promontory, a cape.

MOLTEN. From Molton, name of two parishes co. Devon.

MONEY. From Gael. *monadh*, a hill, mountain, moor, an extensive common. Among many other names compounded of *monadh* are Moneymush or Monymush, a parish of Scotland, co. Aberdeen; and Money-Gall and Moneymore, two towns of Ireland; one in Leinster, the other in Ulster. There is however Monnaie, a town of France, dep. Indre-et-Loire; and Lower gives Monnay, dep. Orne; and says, " Hence the De Mony of the H. R. The Le Money of those records is probably plundered from Le Moyne, the Monk." But see MOON.

MONEYPENNY. See PENNY.

MONKEY. 1. The same as Manico, Mannakay, Manchee,

Manchin, the Mod. G. names Mannicke, Mancke, Mannikin, Män-chen, and the O. G. Manniko, Mannikin ; all diminutives of O. G. *mund*, Goth. *manna*, A. S. *man*, *mann*, *mon*, D. *man*, a man. 2. From Monikie, a parish of Scotland, co. Forfar.

MOON. The same with the surname Mohun (found de Moiun), said to be from Myon, found Moon, an ancient barony near St. Lo, in Normandy. According to others, McMahon (whence Mahoney, Mahony, Mahany), Mohan, Mohun, Mohune (by corruption Mooney, Moone, and Moon) are from root of Gammon, *q. v.*

MORROW. A corruption of Mac Murrough ; etymologically connected with the name Murray. The Murrays appear to have settled in the twelfth century in the province of Murref, Moray, or Moravia, comprehending the modern counties of Murray or Elgin, and parts of Inverness and Banff.

MOSS. From Moses.

MOTE. See MOTH.

MOTH. The same as Mott, Motte, Mote, Mouth ; from Fr. *motte*, a hillock. These names must have been originally De la Motte or La Motte, which are not uncommon surnames at the present day. La Mothe is the appellation of several communes and villages of France, especially in deps. Lot, Dordogne, and Deux-Sèvres.

MOTLEY. From some local name compounded of *ley*. See LEGG.

MOUSE. The same as Moyce, Moyes ; corrupted from Moses ; or from the name Maw, Mawe. But see Notes and Queries.

MOUTH. See MOTH.

MUDD. See MAID.

MUDDLE. From some local name compounded of *dale*.

MUFF. From Muff, a parish of Ireland, co. Donegal.

MUFFIN. Corrupted from Mirfin, a surname, and also an ancient personal name ; from W. *morfin* (*mor-ffin*), a sea brink.

MUG. From Mogg, a nickname for Margaret.

MULBERRY. From Mulfra, vulgo Mulberry, in St. Austel,

or Mulfra, in Madron, Cornwall; from *moel vrè*, the bald or bare hill. Indeed the Cornish scholar Pryce makes Mulfra, Mulvera a nom. fam.

MULE. From G. *mühle*, a mill.

MULL. 1. A Lancashire corruption from Molineux, Molyneux. 2. From *mull*, a Scottish word for a cape or headland; from Gael. *maol*. 3. For Moll, a nickname for Mary; also a surname. Mol however was a name of Ethelwold, king of Northumbria, and Mull was the brother of Cædwalha, king of Wessex; and Kemble says the name must be *mule*, a half-breed, and suggests that his mother may have been a British princess.

MULLET, MULLETT. Diminutives of Mull, *q. v.*

MUMMERY. From Montmerry, a village of France, dep. Orne.

MURTHER. Not from the old form of *murder*, but from Merthyr, name of five parishes in Wales, without reckoning Merthyr - Tydvil; or from Merthor co. Cornwall; from W. *merthyr*, a plain, a clear spot.

MUSSELL, MUSSEL. Diminutives of Mus, nickname of Thomas.

MUSTARD. See HAZARD.

MUTTON. The same as Mytton and Mitton; from Mitton, name of a parish of England, cos. Lancaster and York, and of a chapelry co. Worcester. The Mytton family formerly wrote their name De Mutton.

MYCOCK. See COCK.

MYRTLE. From Murtle, a barony of Scotland, co. Aberdeen. Lower thinks it may also sometimes be a corruption of the French surname Martel.

N.

NAP. Nickname for Napoleon. Hence, as a diminutive, Napkin.

F

NAPKIN. See NAP.

NARROWCOAT. Name of two families in Philadelphia. See COAT.

NEAR. Same as Neer; from Neer, a village in the Netherlands.

NECK. Same as Nick.

NEEDLE. A corruption of Neele, Neale, Neal, from the Norman personal name Nigel; from Nigellus, a diminutive of L. *niger*, black.

NEGUS. From Nicks for Nicholas; or corrupted from a local ending in "house." According to Malone, the mixture bearing this name was invented in the reign of Queen Anne, by Colonel Negus.

NEITHERMILL. Same as Nethermill; from Nethermill (lower mill), name of several places in Scotland.

NEQUAM. Not from the L. *nequam*, bad, worthless, good for nothing, nor, as Ferguson suggests, from O. N. *náquamr*, careful, exact, but from some local name (probably Scottish) compounded of *ham*, a habitation. Neckham would easily corrupt to Nequam.

NEST. Corrupted from Agnes. A James Nest occurs in the Registrar-General's List of Names (Agnes, Nes, Nest).

NEWBACK. From *bach*, a brook. See SMALLBACK.

NEWBEGIN. Same as Newbiggin, Newbigging, name of places cos. Durham, Northumberland, and Westmoreland. See BIGGIN.

NEWBONE. A corruption of Newborn.

NEWBORN. From Newbourn co. Suffolk; or Newburn, name of places cos. Northumberland and Fife. See SMALLBONE.

NEWCOMB, NEWCOMBE. From *comb*, a valley; or same as Newcome, Newcomen = stranger. Cf. Newman, Cumming.

NEWLOVE. See LAW.

NICE. From Nice, in France; formerly in North Italy.

NICK. From Nicholas.

NIGHT. Same as Knight, from A. S. *cniht, cneoht,* a boy, youth, attendant, servant.

NIGHTINGALE. Some derive this name from the bird, and there is a French name Le Rossignol. Nightingale Lane, in East Smithfield, London, was, however, formerly Cnihtena Guild Lane, and was so called from the knights' guild. Again, *gale,* in composition of local names, is frequently a corruption of *hall.*

NOTCUTT. A corruption of Northcote; from Northcote co. Devon. Cf. Breadcutt (H. R. De Bredecote), perhaps from Bredicot co. Worcester.

NOTHARD. Same as the German O. G. names Nothart, Nithard, Neidhart; from O. G. *neid-hart,* which may be variously rendered "very honest," "very crafty," "very zealous." See Wachter, under *neid* and *neidhart,* where he renders Nithardus homo valde probus, et ad communem utilitatem natus, &c.

NOTHING. A patronymic of Nott, O. G. Noto, Notho, Not; or from some local name, perhaps originally Northing. Nutfield, Nuthall, Nuthurst, Nutley, Notting Hill, Nottington are local names in England.

NUT, NUTT, NUTTS. The same as Nott, Knot, Knott; from the ancient Scandinavian name Cnut, Knut, Anglicised Canute. Ferguson says Knut derived his name from a wen or tumour on his head, Knott and Nut occur in local names in England. But see NOTHARD.

NUTBROWN. From some local name ending in *bronn=burn,* perhaps Nidbronn; or from Niederbronn, dep. Bas-Rhin.

O.

OAKENBOTTOM. A U. S. name. See BOTTOM.

OAKLEAF. A U. S. name; no doubt from Hockliffe, a parish of England, co. Bedford.

OATS. Ferguson thinks this name to be a pluralism, and he

classes it with Ott, Otte, Otto, and the corresponding German names Otte and Otto. All these names are corrupted from Otto, *i. e.* Octavio. See D. Gilbert's Cornwall, vol iii., p. 318.

ODIUM. A U. S. name ; from Odiham (wood-ham), a market town and parish of England, co. Hants.

OFFER. The same as Offor; from Offord, name of two parishes co. Hunts. Both Offers and Offerd are found in Domesday.

OLDMAN. See ALMOND.

OMEGA. Doubtless a diminutive of some German nickname. Ferguson says Ohme, Omega, and perhaps Home, are the same as the Low G. *ohm*, and its diminutive *oehmke ;* and that corresponding with these are O. G. names Omeko, Omeke, Emico, and Mod. G. Ohm and Ohme. The G. *oheim* is an uncle.

ONION. A corruption of Unwyn or Onwhyn ; from *unwinn*, unconquerable. Lower thinks it is oftener from the Welsh personal name Enion. Onwen is the name of a manumitted serf, Cod. Dip. No. 971 ; and Unwona that of a bishop of Leicester.

ONLY. A U. S. name, the same as Onley (found both in England and the U. S.) ; from Oneley, a hamlet co. Northampton. Hence also the U. S. name Onely. See also LEGG.

ONSLOW. From some local name in England, perhaps Houndslow or Hounslow, Middlesex ; from A. S. *hundes-hlaw*, the hounds' barrow or hill. Cf. Winslow, the hill of battle (*winnes-hlaw*), or the windy tumulus (*windes-hlaw*).

ONYX. A U. S. name. Perhaps the same as the English name Hunkes, said to be a diminutive of Humphrey. Cf. the names Hunnex and Honicke, which Ferguson thinks to be diminutives from the name Hun, Hunn; from *hún*, a giant; whence Grimm traces the name of the Huns.

ORANGE. From Orange, a town of France, dep. Vaucluse, which derived its name from L. Araüsio Cavarum ; from the people called the Cavarii. It was long the capital of a principality, which gave title to the family now on the throne of

Holland. The King of the Netherlands still retains the title of Prince of Orange ; but the town and territory were ceded to Louis XIV. at the peace of Utrecht.

OTHER. See OTTER.

OTHERDAY. A U. S. name. See SINGLEDAY.

OTTER. Same as the well-known Scandivanian name Ottar, which Ferguson renders fear-inspiring. The name is also found written Ohter, Other, Othyr, Ottyr, Oter, and, in Domesday, Otre. " Walter Fitz-Other (says Lower), the celebrated castellan of Windsor, temp. William I., the reputed ancestor of the Fitz-Geralds, Gerards, Windsors, and other great houses, was the son of Otherus, a great landowner under the Confessor. Ingram, in his translation of the Saxon Chronicle, says Otter was originally *oht-here* or *ocht here*, i. e. terror of an army."

OULDBIEF. A U. S. name ; from Elbeuf or Elbœuf, a comm. and town of France, dep. Seine-Inf.

OUTCRY. Corrupted from Outred, Utred, or Uhtred. See HATRED.

OVER. From Over, name of several places, especially in cos. Cambridge and Chester. See also VERY.

P.

PAGAN. From the Norman personal name Paganus ; a peasant or countryman ; one living in a *pagus*, i. e. a village or country town. Hence Pain, Paine, Pane, Pen, Paganellus, Pagnel, Paganel, Paynel ; Fitz-Payne or Fitz-Pen, by corruption Phippen.

PAGE. 1. A boy attending on a great person, rather for show, and as an indication of high rank, than for the performance of menial duties (Fr.) 2. The common and almost only name of a shepherd's servant, whether boy or man ; extensively used in

Suffolk (See Halliwell). 3. A corruption from Peg, the nickname for Margaret. Page is also an old English word for a village.

PAIN. See PAGAN.

PAINTER. The same as Panter; from the old word *panter* or *pantler;* in a family of distinction an officer who kept the bread [*pantler,* Shakspeare]; from *panetier,* L. *panetarius.* "In the court of France the panitier was an officer of high consideration; and in monasteries the paniter would seem to have been charged with the distribution of bread to the poor, no doubt in virtue of his office of chief baker." Proceedings Soc. Antiq. Scot. vol. i. p. 14; Way's Prompt. Parv., p. 381. Hence, by corruption, the surname Panther.

PALFREY. From the name Baldfrid, which Junius renders "audax pace," but which signifies rather a "bold protector" (*bald-frid*). There is an inverse, Fridebald.

PALSY. A U. S. name; most probably corrupted from Paul, whence Paw, Pawle, Pause.

PAMPHLET. Most probably from Pamflete co. Devon; or from Bemfleet, Benfleet, co. Essex; from A. S. *fleot,* an arm of the sea, mouth of a river. The termination *flet,* however, may sometimes be from A. S. *flet,* a dwelling, a habitation, a seat, hall; Su.-Goth. *flet,* domus. Cf. also the O. G. names Elsflet, Gerflat, Gundiflat, Hruodflat, Ratflat, Rihflat, Sigiflat; the O. Goth. names Albofleda, Audofleda, Andefleda; and the A. S. names Aelflaed, Adelfled, Adelfleda, Aethelfleda, Elfleda, and Wynfleda. Meidinger thinks *fleda, flet, flat,* in composition, means *reinlich,* cleanly, neat; from the noun *flath;* whence the N. H. G. *unflath,* schmutz. The Ice. *fliod* is a maiden (Cf. Turner, ii. pp. 37 and 85).

PAN. This name, according to Ferguson, corresponds with an O. G. Panno, which Förstemann makes to be the same as Banno. Pan is more probably another form of Pain, Paine. See PAGAN.

PANE. See PAGAN.

PANTHER. See PAINTER.

PAR. Not from the fish, but from Pierre. See PEAR.

PARADISE. Perhaps the same as the O. G. names Paradeus, Paradeo, Peradeo; from O. H. G. *deo*, *dio*, A. S. *theow*, Goth. *thius*, a servant. But see SINGLEDAY.

PARAMOUR. The same as Parramore, which has been thought to be the Saxon Barmore, O. G. Bermar; from *mar*, illustrious. Parramore is more probably from some English local name compounded of "moor."

PARDON. A name found in France, England, and the United States, and probably derived from some French local name ending in *don*; from Gael. *dùn*, *dùin*, a fort, fortress, town, fortified hill, a hill. It may also be the same with the surname Bardon, from Bardon co. Leicester, or, as Lower says, it may be derived from Parton, a hamlet and township in Cumberland. Parton is also the name of a parish of Scotland, stewartry Kirkcudbright.

PARROT. See PEAR.

PARSON. This name has been derived from A. S. *bar*, a bear; O. H. G. *par*, *pero*. It is the same with Pearson and Person, son of Par, Pear, or Pierre.

PART. The same as Bard, Barth, and the O. G. names Bardo, Pardo, Bartho, Part. But see PEAR and PERT.

PASSENGER. This name is probably of German origin; from *Pass-ingr*, son of Pass, which is a surname.

PATCH. From G. *bach*, a brook, rivulet, or W. *bach*, little, small.

PAUSE. See PALSY.

PAW. See PALSY.

PAYMENT. A very common name in Canada. It would easily corrupt from Beaumont; or even from the name Beeman.

PEACE. The same as Pace, Pacy, Paice, Peacey; from Pacy, in France, dep. Eure, or Pacé, dep. Ille-et-Vilaine.

PEAR. From Pierre, the French form of Peter. Hence the surnames Par, Peer, and, as diminutives, Parret, Parratt, Parrot, &c.; perhaps sometimes, by contraction, Part. Other diminutives and corruptions are Parrell, Barrell; by corruption Pearl.

PEARL. See PEAR.

PEASOOP. See HOPE.

PEAT (variously Peatt, Peet, Peed, Pead). A nurse-name for Peter.

PEBBLE, PEBBLES. U. S. names; from Peebles, a royal burgh, town, and port of Scotland, cap. co. on the Tweed ; or from Peebles, a township of the U. S., Pennsylvannia.

PECKOVER. See CONOVER.

PEER. Same as Pear, *q. v.*

PEG, PEGG, PEGGE. 1. From Peg, the nickname for Margaret (thus Mag, Meg, Peg). 2. From Dan. *pige*, a maid, a young girl. Hence doubtless Pigg, and, as diminutives, Pidgin, Piggin, Piggon, Pigeon, Pidgeon.

PELLET. A diminutive of Pell, the nickname for Peregrine. According to others, Pellet, or rather Pellatt, is a corruption of the baptismal name Hippolyte.

PEN. See PAGAN.

PENNY. This name has been classed with Benn, Benney, Binney, O. G. Benno, Benni, Binne, Mod. G. Behn, Benne, Bihn. It is rather from the W. *pen*, head, chief, end. Hence the names Fippeny, Fourapenny (found Fourapeni), Godspenny, Hankpenny, Manypenny, Moneypenny, Pennycook, Pennycuick, Pennymaker, Pennyman (anciently Pennaman and Peniman), Pennymore, Smalpenny, Tempany, Tenpenny, Thickpenny, Ticklepenny, Turnpenny, Whirlpenny (in H. R. Whirlepeni), Wilderspin, Wimpenny, Winpenny (white). See also ALLPENNY, HALFPENNY, HAPENNY, TWOPENNY, CRAVEN, INKPEN, PENNYFATHER, PENNYFEATHER.

PENNYCOOK, PENNYCUICK. From Penicuick, a parish near Edinburgh.

PENNYCUICK. See PENNYCOOK and PENNY.

PENNYFATHER, PENNYFEATHER, PENEFATHER. (U. S. Penefather.) These names may be from the W. *penffetter*, headstrong, stubborn, obstinate. Hearne however derives the name of a street called Penny-farthing Street from a wealthy family whose name of Penyvadir or Penyfadir he had met with in old registers; and, if so, these names may be derived from locality; perhaps from W. *pen-y-ffed-tir*, the head of the outward land; or *pen-y-mad-dir*, the head of the good land. Lower says the forms of the name Pennyfather in H. R. are Penifader and Penifadir. He gives also a Barnfather and a Bairnsfather, which however he derives from a different source. There is the U. S. name Pennymaker.

PENNYFEATHER. See PENNYFATHER.

PENNYMAKER. A U. S. name. See PENNY.

PENNYMAN. See PENNY.

PENNYMORE. See PENNY.

PERFECT. From Pierrefitte, name of several communes and villages of France, the principal in dep. Meuse, cap. canton, on the Aire (*pierre*, a stone). Cf. the surnames Parfett, Parfit, Parfitt, Perfett, Perfitt.

PERRY. From Pierre. See PEAR.

PERSON. See PARSON.

PERT. From Pert co. Forfar; or Pert, a commune, arrond. Bayeux, Normandy. It may also sometimes be from Perret, a diminutive of Pierre. See PEARL.

PETTIBONE. See SMALLBONE.

PETTYCOAT. See COAT.

PEW. For Pugh, from Ap-Hugh, son of Hugh. See also PIE.

PHARAOH. As an English surname, not derived from the Egyptian name, but from the O. G. name Faro; perhaps from *faren* to travel, A. S. *fara* a traveller. Hence Faramund, a celebrated name among the Francic kings, and the English names Farman and Fearman.

PHEASANT. " In England I have heard of a Miss Partridge, who married a Mr. Pheasant, and her sister married a Mr. Partridge. There was some other bird in the family." This name, as well as Fesant, Fazan, Fazon, are probably from Lepheasant, near

St. Austel; from *le-vissan*, the lower place; or *le-vease*, the outward place.

PHŒNIX. Probably corrupted from Fenwick, "the fenny dwelling," name of places in cos. Northumberland and York. It is quite possible that the name Spinks may be a corruption of Phœnix.

PHYSICK, found Phisicke. From Lefisick in St. Austel, Cornwall. Mr. Bowditch says "Dr. Physic was the first physician of Philadelphia."

PICKLE, PICKLES. From Pickhill, a parish co. York, N. R. Pikel and Pikele occur in H. R.

PICKUP. See HOPE.

PIDDLE. From North Piddle co. Worcester, or Piddle-Hinton co. Dorset.

PIE. The same as Py, Pye, Pugh. See PEW.

PIGEON. See PEG.

PIGFAT. A corruption of Pickford, also a surname, which Lower thinks may be from Pitchford co. Somerset.

PIGG. See PEG.

PILCHARD. A corruption of Pilcher, or=son of Pilch, which is also a surname.

PILL. Same as Peel. From the Celtic *pill*, a stronghold, fortress, secure place. Small towers, usually square, of several stories in height, existing in Scotland, chiefly in the counties bordering upon England, are called Piils. There is the Pile of Foudray, a castle in Furness, Lancashire; Peel Castle, Isle of Man; Pill in Devon; and a parish called Pylle in Somersetshire. In Herefordshire *pill* is used for a small creek, and in co. Somerset for a rock.

PILLOW. See BILLOWS.

PIMPLE. Bowditch gives this as the name of an English family. It may be the same as Penfold; or corrupted from some name ending in *bold*, in A. S. a house or dwelling.

PINCHARD. See HAZARD.

PINCHBACK. Same as Pinchbeck; from Pinchbeck co. Lincoln. An alloy of copper and zinc resembling gold in its appearance, was first brought into notice by a London tradesman of the name of Pinchbeck, who manufactured watches, buckles, and other articles out of it. But see Charnock's Verba Nominalia.

PINDAR. The same as Pinder and Le Pinder, and perhaps Pinner and Pyner; from *pinder*, one whose duty it is to take possession of all stray cattle, and drive them to the pound until they are claimed.

PINFOUND. The same as the Cornish name Penfoune, Penfowne. Tonkin mentions Penfoune as the name of a place in Poundstock. Hals renders *Pen*-fon, now Penfowne in Poundstock, " the head well, spring of water, or fountain;" but it more probably means "the head of the well."

PINK. Corrupted from one of the surnames Pinnock, Pennack, Penneck, Pennick, Pennock, Pinnick, perhaps from the parish of Pinnock co. Cornwall; from *pen-ick*, the head place.

PISSARD. Same as Pirssard. See HAZARD.

PISSE. Probably the same as the name Piesse. Lower says of the latter, "The family came into England soon after the revocation of the edict of Nantes, and bore chiefly the Christian names of Louis and Charles. They have a tradition that the name was derived from the order of knighthood created in 1560 by Pope Pius IV., and called corruptly Pies or Piesse in Bretagne, from which province the Piesses of England are believed to have come."

PISTOL. Halliwell renders the word pistol " a swaggering fellow, perhaps from *pistólfo*, explained by Florio, 'a roguing begger, a cantler, an upright man that liveth by cosenage.' Hence Shakespeare's character of that name." Pistol may be the same as the ancient name Falstolfe, Fastolf, Fastolfe (whence Falstaff), Alt. D. Fastuff; from O. G. *fast-ulf*, strong in help; or the last part of the name may be from O. G. *alp, alf, elf*, which Meidinger renders *stark*, kräftig. Cf. the Alt. D. names Fastrich, Fastwin, and the O. G. name Vastman, which Wachter renders valde celebris. In Luther, Psal. lxxxix. 8, we find " Gott is *fast* mœchtig."

PITCHBOTTOM. See BOTTOM.

PITCHFORD. From Pitchford, a parish co. Salop. Hence the names Pickford and Pitchfork. Pitchford means the ford of the river Pitch, which is doubtless a corruption of its original name.

PITCHFORK. A U. S. name. See PITCHFORD.

PLASTER. No doubt originally *Palaster ;* perhaps one having the charge of a palace (G. *palast*).

PLAYFAIR. Jamieson renders *play-fere, play-fair*, a play-fellow; from *play*, and *fere*, a companion. Playfair is probably from A. S. *leag-fœger*, the fair or white meadow. Cf. the inverse name Fairplay.

PLOT, PLOTT. 1. From *plot*, a portion of flat even ground, also a plantation laid out; from Fr. *plat* (from Gr. πλατυς, L. *latus*), whence the French name Du Plat, and the English name Platt. 2. From Pellet, a diminutive of Pell, for Peregrine; or from Bellot, a diminutive of Bell from Isabel. From Bellot we doubtless have the French name Blot.

PLUM, PLUMB, PLUMBE, PLUME. From *plumpe, plump*, in the North of England, a woody place or clump of trees. Plumb is the name of a township of the U. S., North America, Pennsylvania; and there is Plomb, a commune of Normandy; and La Plume, a commune and town dep. Morbihan.

PLUME. See PLUM.

POIGNARD. See HAZARD.

POODLE. A corruption of Pool, A. S. *pol, pul*, W. *pwll*, L. *palus*. Cf. the Corn. *pen*, which often takes the form of *pedn*.

POPOFF. Probably a Slavonic name; from Pop-ow, son of Pop, a nickname.

PORT. From *port*, a gate, as of a fortified place; a prefix of numerous local names. Lower says Hugo de Port came into

England at the Norman Conquest; but that this name may be the same as the *Ad Portam*, or Atte-Gate of mediæval records. It may also sometimes be corrupted from the name Porret; from Porret, dep. La Manche, in Normandy.

PORTWINE. "A singular corruption of Poitevin, a native of Poitou, in France. So early as the time of Edward I. the corruption had proceeded as far as to Potewyne, a lady called Preciosa Potewyne occurring in H. R."—*Lower.*

POT, POTT, POTTS. See FILLPOT.

POTIPHAR. Not from the Egyptian name Potiphar; but the same as Petifer or Petipher (Potiphur, U. S.); perhaps from A. S. *boda*, O. N. *bodi*, a messenger; A. S. *fara*, O. N. *fari*, a traveller; A. S. *fara*, O. N. *fara*, to fare, travel. "Our Mrs. Potiphur," says Bowditch, "is a nurse, whose bedside deportment has always been exemplary."

POTTAGE. See MARRIAGE.

POTTLE. See BOTTLE.

POWDER. A U. S. name. From Powder Hundred co. Cornwall; from *pou-dar*, the county of the oak.

PRAISE. A name found in the U. S. Same as Price, Pryce, Pryse.

PRAY. In H. R. De la Preye; from Fr. *pré*, a meadow.

PRECIOUS. A corruption of the surname Priesthouse. There is, says Lower, a dwelling called Priesthawes, originally Priesthouse, near Pevensey, co. Sussex.

PRESTIGE, *i. q.* PRESTAGE and PRESTWICK. From Prestwich, a parish in Lancashire. See MARRIAGE.

PRETTY. Found Praty, Pretie, Prettie, and De Prœtis; from L. *pratum*, a meadow. The name is also found in Italy and Spain, and in the latter country the family bear for arms "a green meadow, flowered proper."

PRIAM. A U. S. name; doubtless the same as our English Prime, and the French De la Pryme. It may also be connected with Brim, Breem, which Ferguson thinks from A. S. *breme*, O. E.

brim, renowned, famous.   He gives Brame, corresponding with a Danish name Bram in Saxo, perhaps from Su.-Goth *bram*, splendour, pomp.

PRICE.   A Welsh name, said to be from Ap-Rhys, son of Rhys.   Pryce however renders the Cornish name Penrice, the head of the fleeting ground, and Rhys and Rice would seem to be the same name.

PRIDE.   Found without prefix in H. R.   It may be the same with Priddy, Pridie, Priddey, Priday ; doubtless from Priddy, a parish co. Somerset.

PRIGG, PRIGGE.   From A. S. *burh*, *burcg*, dative *byrig*, a fort, castle, city, town ; or the same as Brigg ; from Brigg (Glandford, Brigg or Bridge) co. Lincoln ; or from the W. Ap-Rigg, son of Rigg, the mediæval orthography of *ridge*.   If connected with the ancient name Prigari, it may be the same as Frick, Fricke, Freek, Freeke, Freak, Fricker, O. G. Fricco, A. S. Freoc, from A. S. *fricca* a preacher, G. *fricker*.

PROUD.   Fuller makes this name a corruption of Prude.   It is more probably the same as Prout, corrupted from the name Provost, the mayor of a royal burgh, the dean or president of a collegiate church.   The Continental names Probst, Proost, Prost would seem to be from the same source.   The It. *prode* is valiant, brave ; the A. S. *prud*, *prut*, C. B. *pridi*, ornatus ; A. S. *præte*, id.; Su.-Goth. *prud*, magnificus, ornatus.

PROUDFIT.   Same as Proudfoot, *q. v.*

PROUDFOOT.   In H. R. Proudfot, Prudfot.   From some local name compounded of " ford ;" perhaps from a place called Pridford or Prydford.   There is a parish called Priddy in Somerset.   But see HAZLEFOOT.

PROUDLOCK.   See LEGG.

PROUDLOVE.   See LAW.

PROUDMAN.   Corrupted from Prudhomme (in H. R. Prodhomme, Prodomme, Prodome, &c.)   Roquefort renders *preudom*, *preud 'homme*, *preudome*, *prodom*, *prodon*, *prudhome :* " homme, sage et prudent, qui a de l'expérience et du savoir, *prudens homo, et non probus dominus.*"

PUDDIFOOT. See Hazlefoot.

PUFF. Same as Pugh. See Pew.

PULL. ' A corruption of the name Pool, Poole. See Poodle.

PULSE, PULS. For Pulls; from Pull for Pool.

PUNCH. From Pontius. Hence, doubtless, as a diminutive the name Puncheon, var. Punshon.

PUNCHARD. See Hazard.

PUNCHEON. See Punch.

PURCHASE. From Purkiss, corrupted from Perkins; from Perkin, a diminutive of Pierre.

PURELY. See Legg.

PURGE. Bowditch gives this as the name of an English family. See Barge.

PURSGLOVE, *i. q.* PURSLOVE, PURSLOW. From Purslow, a hundred co. Salop. The name is doubtless the same with Parslow, which, if I mistake not, is a local name in Essex. See Law.

PUSHING. From some local name compounded of *ing*, a meadow. Bowditch gives both Pushing and Pushee; but the latter is probably corrupted from Pusey.

PUSSY, PUSSEY. Found in the U. S. The same as Pusey, Puzy; from Pewsey or Pusey, a parish co. Wilts; or Pusey, a parish in Berks.

Q.

QUARREL, QUARRELS. Quarrell (H. R. Quarel) may be derived from the O. Eng. word *quarel*, a stone quarry. There is a place called Quarrelton in Scotland, co. Renfrew. Quarrels is perhaps the same name, or it may be from Quarles, which is probably derived from a district in North Greenhoe hundred, co. Norfolk.

QUARTERMAN. The same as Quartermaine and Quatremaine, and the H. R. Quatremayns and Quatremeyns. The origin of this name is doubtful. Four hands form the charge of the shield of the French family of Quatremaine, and there are the French surnames Quatrebarbes, Quatremaire, and Quatremere. The original bearer of the name may have dwelt near a sign-post pointing in four different directions (four hands).

QUEEN. From MacQueen or MacQuin ; Ir. O'Quin, O'Quinn, *i. q.* O'Cuinn, O'Coin, O'Coyne. These names may come from the Ir. *cuinn*, genitive of *conn*, wisdom or sense ; or from *con*, genitive of *cu*, a hound, figuratively applied to a warrior, whence the name Conn or Con. Hence the names Coyne, Coin, Quin, Quinn, Quiney, Quinney.

QUELL. A corruption of Will, or Quill, *q. v.*

QUESTION. McQuestion is found in the U. S., and MacQuiston is a Scotch name. It may be from Wiston, name of a village and parish co. Lanark ; or from the surname Weston, like Quilliams from Williams.

QUHITELAW. A Scottish corruption of Whitelaw; perhaps from Whitelaw, a hill in Roxburgshire. See WHITLOW.

QUICK. From the Cornish *guik*, a village.

QUICKLOVE. See LAW.

QUICKLY. See LEGG.

QUILL, QUIL. For Will, Wil.

QUILT. A name found in the U. S. ; a contraction of Quillet for Willet, Willett, diminutives of Will. See QUILL. Quillé, Quillet, Quilliot, Quillot are found as French names.

QUINCE. A patronymic of Quin, *i. e.* Quins. Quin, anciently Quinchy, is a local name in Ireland, and is often found in composition. There is Quin co. Clare, and Quin in Kildare, and Quince Island co. Cork. But see QUEEN. Lower makes Quince the same with Quincy, in charters Latinised De Quinciato, De Quinci, De Quency.

R.

RABBIT. Same as Rabbitt, Rabett, in H. R. Rabut and Rabbod, mentioned as the name of a "Duke of the Frisians" in Rog. Wend; and Radbod, Redpath, Robert, G. Ratpert, O. G. Ratperth; from *rat-brecht*, distinguished for counsel, or a celebrated counsellor.

RAFFLES. From Raffles, the name of a place in the parish of Mouswald co. Dumfries. That parish contains five old border fortresses; the least dilapidated is that of Raffles. See Gaz. Scot. Raffles Bay is the name of an inlet on the north coast of Coburg peninsula, North Australia, thirteen miles E. Port Essington. A British settlement named Port Raffles, established there in 1827, was abandoned in 1829. See also RULE.

RAGLESS. See LEGG.

RAIMENT. From Raymond, like Garment from Garmund. Raymond is from the G. *ram-mund*, a strong man.

RAIN. 1. From Rain, a parish co. Essex; Rain or Rhain, a town of Upper Bavaria; or Rayne, a parish of Scotland, co. Aberdeen. 2. Perhaps sometimes from Ran, for Randal, Randolph.'

RAINBIRD. A corruption of Rambert, the inverse of Bertram.

RAINBOW. Same as the French name Rainbeaux, *i. q.* Raimboux, Ramboux; *i. q.* Raimbaut, Raimbault; from O. G. *hruom-bald*, famously bold. Rainbold, Rainbolt are found as surnames in the U. S. But see TURNBULL.

RAISIN. From Raisen, name of three parishes co. Lincoln, one of which comprises the town of Market Raisen. Hence perhaps the surnames Rising, Reason, and the U. S. name Reasons. But qu. the French names Rais, Raisin, Raison.

RALLY. A U. S. corruption of the name Raleigh, supposed

to be derived from some obsolete local name (perhaps Raleghe) co. Devon. Raleigh is the name of a parish co. Essex.

RAM. Le Ram is found in H. R.; but this name may sometimes be from O. H. G. *ram*, O. N. *ramr*, strong, vigorous; and perhaps sometimes a nickname of Rambert.

RAMARD. See HAZARD.

RAMBELOW. The same as Rumbellow, Rumbell, Rumball, Rumble, Rumbol, Rumboll, Rimbault; from root of Rainbow, *q. v.*

RAMSBOTTOM. See BOTTOM.

RANSOM, RANSOME. From Ranson, son of Ran, *i. e.* Randolph.

RAP. Same as Rape.

RAPE. A corruption of Rolfe. The name Rape or Rolfe occurs. See RULE.

RASH. Same as the G. Rasch, from *rasch*, quick (O. G. *ras*, *i. q. rad ;* Franc. *rosch*, celer, velox); Dan. *rask*, id., also nimble, ready, brisk, whence the name Rask.

RATHER. A U. S. name. The Boston "Traveller," Oct. 15, 1860, republishes a letter to Col. Rather of Decatur, Alabama, says Bowditch. This name, like Rothery, may be corrupted from Roderic. Lower gives as a surname Ratherham, which he makes a corruption of Rotherham, from Rotherham co. York. But see also RUDDER.

RAW. The name of a township co. Northumberland. But see RULE.

RAWBONE. A corruption of the surname Rathbone; from some local name (perhaps originally Rathbourne) in Ireland.

REACH (*re'ak*). Perhaps from Gael. *reac*, a woman, a damsel; or, if the same name as Riach, then from *riabhach*, brindled greyish, darkish brown, brownish.

READLESS. See LEGG.

READY. From the Scottish name MacReddie, whence Macready.

REAM. From Rheims or Reims, a city of France.

REASON. See RAISIN.

RECKLESS. The same as Ragless. See LEGG.

RECORD. Found written Rickword. The same as Ricord, the name of a distinguished French physician; from G. Reichardt, Eng. Richard.

REDCOCK. See COCK.

REDFOOT. A U. S. name. Corrupted from Radford, the name of places cos. Nottingham, Oxford, and Warwick. See HAZLEFOOT.

REDMAN, *i. q.* REDMOND, REDMUND. From O. G. *rat-mund*, a counsellor. Cf. the O. G. names Ethelred, Cuthred, Folcrat, Herirat, Lantirat, Marcrat.

REDMILE. From Redmile or Redmilne (doubtless signifying red-mill), a parish of England, co. Leicester. Cf. the U. S. name Redmill.

RESTCOME. An American name; compounded of *comb*, a valley. See COMB, NEWCOMB, SMALLCOMB.

REVEL. The same as Rivel; from Curry-Rivel in Somersetshire; or from Revel, formerly Rebel, in Languedoc. Lower says two places in Normandy bear the name of Réville, one near Bernai, the other arrond. Valognes, and that the name Revill (whence he says is Revell) still exists in Normandy. The surnames Reveil, Réveil, Revel, Revil, Révial, Revelat, Revillet, Revilliot, Revelin, Revillon, Revelière are found in the French Directory.

RIBBONS. Corrupted from Reubens.

RICE. The same as the Welsh name Rees. See PRICE.

RICH. Sometimes from Richard.

RICHBELL. This name was no doubt originally Richbold, compounded of *bold*, an abode, dwelling. See BOTTLE.

RICHES. From Richard.

RICKETS, RICKETTS. A corruption of Rickards, Ricards; from Richards.

RICKS. From Richard.

RIDDLE. The same as Riddell, found Rydale, De Rydale, and De Ridale ; from Riddell or Ryedale, in the parish of Lillies-leaf co. Roxburgh. Sir Walter Scott refers to several curious documents which warrant most conclusively the epithet of " Ancient Riddell." See Stat. Ac. of Scotland, vol. iii. p. 27, note.

RIDE. From Ryde, formerly Ride, Isle of Wight.

RIDEOUT. It has been suggested that this name may be from *redoubt*, a military fortification (Fr. *réduit*, It. *riddoto*, Sp. *reduto*), and the names Redout, Ridoubt are found in America; and Ridout, Ridoutt are no doubt the same name. In H. R. it is Ridhut, which may mean red hut or dwelling ; the first syllable may also be from W. *rhyd*, a ford. Again, Redhead would easily corrupt to Redout and Rideout.

RIDING, RIDINGS. From some local name compounded of *ing*, a meadow ; or same as Ridding, from Ridding, a hamlet co. Derby.

RIGHT. Same as Wright, an artificer in wood, in composition = workman.

RIGHTLY. Compounded of *ley*. See LEGG.

RING. Ring, Ringe, Ringa, as ancient names, are from the Su.-Goth. *ring*, an eminent man (vir præstans, eximius), connected with the C. B. *rhen*, satrapa; A. S. *rinc*, a soldier, warrior, a valiant, noble, or honourable man ; Sco. *rink, rync*, a strong man ; O. G. *recke, reche, rink*, a hero, giant; H. G. *hringa*, a prince, governor, which Ihre seems to think are from *reke, recke*, heros, athleta, probably connected with the Su.-Goth. *reiks*, a prince. There were kings of Scandinavia named Sigivid Ring and Hakan Ring, and, says Ihre, Ring is the name of many places in Scandinavia which were formerly the seats of heroes. The Mod. Dan. *ringe*, Sco. *ringa*, is small, little, slight, humble, low. Ring may also sometimes be from *ring*, a circle. Cf. the Italian name Aniello, whence Masaniello, from Thomaso Aniello. Ring is the name of a place near Dungarvan in Ireland.

RINGER. Perhaps from O. G. *ringer*, a wrestler ; from *ringen*, to fight, contend with. Cf. Brider ; from Dan. *bryder*, a wrestler, combatant.

RINGGOLD. A U. S. name ; from Ringwold, a parish of England, co. Kent ; or Ringwood, a market town and parish co. Southampton.

RISING. The O. H. G. *risi, riso*, Mod. H. G. *riese*, O. N. *risi*, Dan. *rise*, Sw. *rese*, is a giant, and *ing*, son or descendant ; but this name is most probably the same as Raisin, *q. v.* "One B. Rising, who had for several years before held a commission in her Majesty's army, was in January, 1867, elevated to the curacy of Newport. Reising is a U. S. name."

ROACH. From Fr. *roche*, a rock.

ROB, ROBB. See ROBIN.

ROBE. See ROBIN.

ROBIN. A diminutive of Rob, from Robert. Hence Rob, Robb, Robe, Rope.

ROLL. See RULE.

ROLLS. See RULE.

ROOF. See RULE.

ROPE. See ROBIN and RUBY.

ROSE. See RUSE.

ROSEBOTTOM. See BOTTOM.

ROSEWHARM. A name found in Bowditch. A corruption of the Cornish name Roswarne ; from Roswarne, an estate in the parish of Camborne.

ROTTEN. From Rodden, a parish co. Somerset. Rotten, Rotton, Rodden, Roddam, Roden are found as U. S. names.

ROUGH. See RULE.

ROUGHEAD. Same as the French name Ruffet. But see RULE.

ROWBOTTOM. See BOTTOM.

RUBY. Same as Roby, Robie, Robe, Robb, Rubb, Rope, Roop, from Robert.

RUDDER. The same as the German names Roadhar, Rüder (whence Rüdersdorf), Roder; from O. G. *rat-herr*, noble counsellor; or *rat-her*, eminent in council, or simply a counsellor.

RUE. From the French name De la Rue, *i. e.* from the street.

RUFF, RUF. See RULE.

RUFFLE, RUFFELL. See RULE.

RULE. Nisbet derives this name from St. Regulus, who brought the relics of St. Andrew to Scotland. It is more probably the same with the A. N. Raoul, in H. R. Ruel; corrupted from Randolph or Radolph. Hence Ralph, Rolph, Rape, Rough, Ruff, Roof, Raw, Roll, Rolls, and, as a diminutive, Ruffle. Ruet, Ruf, Ruffe, Ruffel, Ruffet, Ruffey, Ruffin are found as French names.

RUM. Förstemann derives this name from O. G. *hruom*, fame. Ferguson thinks it may be from O. N. *rumr*, a giant, one who might truly be called "a rum customer." But see RAM and WORMS.

RUMAGE. See MARRIAGE.

RUMBALL. See RAMBELOW.

RUMBELL. See RAMBELOW.

RUMBELLOW. See RAMBELOW.

RUMBLE. See RAMBELOW.

RUMMER. The same as the O. G. names Rumheri, Rhumhar; from *hruom-herr*, distinguished lord. It may also sometimes be the same as Rimmer, Rimer, or Rhymer. Rummer, Rimmer, Rymer, Rymers are found as U. S. names.

RUSE. Same as Rouse and Roux = red; or same as Rose, from Cornish *rose*, *rôs*, a valley.

RUSHOUT. The name of a British M. P. (1857). James Rushout was created a baronet at the Restoration of Charles II. An ancestor of the Rushouts was Thibaut Rushaut, a noble English knight. The name may be derived from some Dutch or Flemish local name ending in *hout*, signifying wood, timber. Cf. the Flemish Turnhout and the English local names Bagshot, Oakshot, compounded of *holt*, a wood or grove. Rushout or Rushaut may also be a corruption of the French name Rousset, Roussell, Russell, diminutives of Roux.

RUST. A corruption of the French name Rousset. (See RUSHOUT). Rust or Rusth is the appellation of a town of West Hungary.

S.

SACK, SACKS, SACHS. From Isaac, Isaacs. Cf. the names Sacchi, Sacchini, Sacchetti. But see SEX.

SALE, SALES. This name is found written De la Sale, De Salle, De Aula, De la Saule, De Halle, Saul, and Halle, and is derived from A. S. *sel, sele,* a hall, Fr. *salle.*

SALL. A U. S. name. Perhaps sometimes from Sall, a parish co. Norfolk; and at other times from Fr. *salle,* a hall. See SALE.

SALMON. 1. From Solomon. 2. From Saleman. "The manor of Salmons in Cáterham co. Surrey is known to have belonged, temp. Edward III., to Roger Saleman " (Brayley's Surrey, iv. 189). The name Saleman might signify both a saleman and an attendant or keeper of a hall.

SALT. From the village of Salt co. Stafford. In 1166 the name is written Selte. In the reign of Henry III. Jvo de Saut held one knight's fee in Saut, of the Barony of Stafford. Subsequently, Hugh de Salt held Salt of Philip de Chetwynd. From this tenure, and from resemblance of the arms, it is probable that Salt was a cadet of Chetwynd. In the Visitations of Staffordshire there are pedigrees of this family, from whom descend Thomas Salt, Esq., jun., M. P. for Stafford, and William Salt, Esq., F.S.A. (See Lower.) The name may also sometimes be the same as Salt or Sault, from the Barony of Salt co. Kildare, so named from the district called *De Saltu Salmonis,* " the salmon's leap."

SAMPLE. From St. Paul, St. Pol. Cf. the name Sampol.

SAND, SANDS. The vocable *sand* is found in composition of

many localities, but the surnames Sand, Sands may mean a messenger, one sent ; from G. *senden*, Goth. *sandjan*, A. S. *sendan*, Franc. et Alam. *senten*, to send ; G. *sende*, missio, dimissio. Hence, doubtless, Sandeman, Sandman, Sentman, and the U. S. name Sendfirst, which may mean a princely messenger, or ambassador. Cf. the German compounds *chur-fürst*, elector ; *vier-fürst*, tetrarcha.

SANDELL. Perhaps the same as Sandall ; from Sandall, name of a parish (Kirk), and of a township (Long), co. York, West Riding.

SANDMAN. See SAND.

SANDY. This name has no connection with the Sandi of the Yorkshire Domesday, which has been derived from *sand*, a messenger. It is the same as Sandie, corrupted from Alexander. It may sometimes be from Sandy (with Gritford), a parish co. Beds.

SATTENSHALL. Bowditch says that a person of this name arrived in Boston in an English steamer in September, 1857. The last part of the name is derived from *hall*.

SAUL, SAULL. Perhaps sometimes from Saul, a parish co. Gloucester, or Saul co. Down, Ulster, Ireland. But see SALE.

SAVEALL, SHAVEALL. Corrupted from Saville.

SAW. From Saul, like Raw from Raoul or Ralph. Cf. Saw, Sawkins, with Raw, Rawkins.

SAYWELL. A corruption of Saville, Savile, Savil.

SCAFFOLD. A name found in Lower's Appendix. It probably means sheep-fold (A. S. *sceaf*, G. *schaf*, a sheep).

SCAMP. From a French or Belgian local name ending in *camp* (L. *campus*). Scampton is the name of a parish co. Lincoln. See also LOSECAMP.

SCANDAL. From some local name compounded of *dale*.

SCAREDEVIL. A name found in the U. S. Corrupted from the name Scardeville, which Lower thinks may be from Ecardenville (perhaps originally Escardenville), dep. Ewe, Normandy.

SCATTERGOOD. (H. R. Schatregod.) From some local name ending in "wood."

SCHOOLCRAFT. A U. S. name. From *croft*, a little close. See CRAFT.

SCOLDING. Formed like Winning, *q. v.*

SCORE. From A. S. *score*, a shoer.

SCUFFLE. From some local name compounded of *ley*, a meadow.

SCURRY. The same as Scurrah and Scurr; probably from the Ir. name O'Scurry, or O'Sgurra, one of the chiefs given by O'Dugan on the six Sodhans. The Sodhan is a large territory in the barony of Tiaquin, which was made into six divisions, called the six Sodhans. The name Sgurra may be from the Ir. *scor*, a champion, or *sgeir*, a rock in the sea, a cliff, shelf; or *sgeireach*, rocky.

SEABORN. From some local name compounded of *bourn*. (See SMALLBONE.) There is however a Seyburn, and Ferguson thinks these names may be from the Scandinavian name Sœbiörn (sea-bear).

SEABRIGHT. Same as Sebright, corrupted from Sibert, Siebert, Sigibert, from O. G. *sig-brecht*, distinguished in victory. See SIP

SEACOCK. See COCK. This name may some day corrupt into Seacook.

SEAFART. A U. S. name. The same as Seffert, Seyffert, Seyfried, corresponding with the G. Seyffart, Siefert, Seefried, from Siegfred, or Sigefred, name of an A. S. bishop of Chichester, which Ferguson renders "peace of victory;" but, with more reason, from G. *sig-frith*, victorious protector.

SEAGOOD. From some local name compounded of *wood*.

SEAL, SEALE. From Seal, name of parishes cos. Kent, Leicester, Surrey, and Sussex; from A. S. *sel*, a seat, hall, manor-house, mansion.

SEAQUILL. From some local name compounded of *ville*. It

may have been Segville or Sigville. We have several local names compounded of *seg*, *sig*, from *sig*, *sige*, victory.

SEARCH. Same as the U. S. names Serch and Sarch; perhaps corrupted from the name Sergius. Cf. Searchfield, the last syllable of which is *ville*.

SEAS. From Seez, a comm. and town of France, dep. Orne.

SEASONGOOD. Formed like Seagood, *q. v.*

SEE. Same as Sea; from residence near the sea. "Atte Sea, as a family name, is very common in medieval records" (*Lower*).

SEGAR. From A. S. *sigra*, O. N. *sigarr*, a conqueror; O. N. *sigr*, A. S. *sige*, O. G. *sieg*, Franc. et Alam. *sigo*, victory, Hence the surname Sugar. Cf. Sigo, Sigi, Sager, Siggœr, Siggeir, Sigar, Seager, Seeger, Seaker, Secker, Saggers, Siggers, and the compounds Sigiwin, Sigismund, Sigmund, Sigofrid, &c.

SELF, SELFE. "The name Sewlf (sea-wolf) occurs in a charter of Canute, and it is probably the same as the Saulf in the Domesday of Derbyshire, where it is in the Scandinavian form. Hence may be our Salve, Self, Selves."—*Ferguson*.

SEND. From Send (with Ripley), a parish co. Surrey; or Send, a chapelry co. Wilts. It may also sometimes be another orthography of Sand, *q. v.*

SENDALL. A U. S. name. Perhaps the same as Sandell, *q. v.*

SENDFIRST. A U. S. name. See SAND.

SENTANCE. From some local name, perhaps St. Anne's. St. Anne is the name of a mountain of France, dep. Orne; of a maritime village, Guadeloupe; of another village in Martinique; of some parishes in the West Indies; and of one in the island of Alderney; of a river of Lower Canada, and of a lake in British North America.

SEQUIN. Not from the coin, but the same as Segwin, Siggins, from *sig-win*, victorious warrior.

SERMON, SURMAN, SURMON. Found as U. S. names. Perhaps from Saargemünd (Fr. Sarreguemines), a commune and town of France, dep. Moselle. These names would also corrupt from the ancient names Sigmund, Sigmundr. See SEGAR.

SESSIONS. The same as Sissons and Sisson; from Soissons, a town of France, dep. Aisne. Lower however derives Sisson, Sissons from Siston, a parish co. Gloucester. Sizun is the name of a town of France, dep. Finistère.

SETON. From Seaton or Seton co. Haddington; and perhaps sometimes from Seaton, name of parishes cos. Cumberland, Devon, Durham, Northumberland, Rutland, York, &c. Seaton is also a surname.

SETTLE. From Settle, a market town and chapelry co. York, West Riding.

SEX. From A. S. Seaxa, a Saxon. Cf. the names Six, Sax.

SHADDOCK. See SHADE.

SHADE. (There is a German Schade.) The same as Chad or Ceadda; whence probably, as diminutives, Shaddock and Shattock. *Hath, had, chad* signifies war.

SHAKSPEARE. Variously Shakespeare, Shakespear, Shakespere, Shakespeyre, Shakyspere, Schakespeire, Schakspere, Shaxper, and Chacksper. "Concerning its etymology," says Lower, "there can be no doubt. 'The custome, first παλλειν, to *vibrate* the speare before they used it, to try the strength of it, was so constantly kept, that εγχεσπαλος, a Shake-speare, came at length to be an ordinary word, both in Homer and other poets, to signifie a soldier' (Francis Rous, Archæologia Attica, 1637). The Bard's contemporaries evidently understood the name in that sense. . . . Our family nomenclature presents us with several analogies, as Break*speare*, Win*spear*, *Shake*shaft, *Shake*launce, Hackstaff, Briselance, and Bruselance, Wagstaffe, Bickerstaffe, Hurlbat, Draweswerde (Drawsword), Cutlemace ('cut the club or mace'), Hackblock," &c. I have elsewhere (cf. Notes and Queries, vols. ix. and x.) stated that Shakespere might be a corruption of Sigisbert, which would translate "renowned for victory" (*sige*, victory); in answer to which Mr. Ferguson seemed to think that the name might be from Sicisper, Sigispero, or Sigiper, which he would translate "victorious bear" (perhaps rather "victorious man"). My suggestion would seem probable from the fact that the name Shakeshaft might be from *sigishaft*, *sighaft*, used by the Franks for "victorious;" or from *sigis-haved*, "head of victory," "victorious leader." I am however disposed to think that the latter name is merely a corruption of Shakestaff; and, as I have shown elsewhere, most names compounded of *staff* are derived from A. S. *sted*, a place. On further consideration, I am inclined to doubt my former derivation of the name Shakespeare, although it would easily corrupt from Sigisbert, by contraction of the first vocable, and by dropping of the final t. I agree with another correspondent of Notes and Queries in tracing the name to *Jaques Pierre*. In French, Italian, and German, surnames are frequently made up of two names. Cf. the French' names Jeangirard, Jeangrand, Jeanguemin, Jeanjacquet, Jeanjean, Jeanmaire; Pierrehumbert; the Italian Gianpietri, Zampieri; and the German Meyerbeer, whose brother was Michael Beer. The nearest names to *Jacques Pierre* that I have been able to find are, *James Peters*, *Jacques* Henri Bernardin de Saint *Pierre*, and *Petrus Jacobus*.

SHALLY. Same as Shalley and Shanley, *i. q.* Shelley; from Shenley, name of a parish cos. Suffolk and Essex, and of a township co. York, W. R. See SKINLEY.

SHAMELY. A U. S. name. See LEGG.

SHARPLESS. From Sharples, a township co. Lancaster. See LEGG.

SHARPLEY. See LEGG.

SHATTER. From Chartres, a town of France, dep. Eure-et-Loir; or La Chatre, dep. Indre. One Selina Chatters occurs in the Registrar-General's List; although this may be the same as Chatteris, from Chatteris co. Ely. See also CHARTER.

SHAVE. Mac Chave is a Gaelic surname. But see CALF and SHOVE.

SHAVEALL. See SAVEALL.

SHEAF. The same as Shelf. Ferguson derives Sheaf from Scef or Sceaf, according to the A. S. table of Woden's ancestry, the father of Scyld. He says Scef or Sceaf signifies " sheaf," and gives an anecdote in connection therewith.

SHEARGOLD, SHERGOLD. The same as Sherwood (by interchange of *g* and *w*) ; from Sherwood, a celebrated forest co. Nottingham, scene of the adventures of Robin Hood and his companions. Cf. the U. S. name Purgold.

SHEATH. See SHEET.

SHEEPSHANKS. According to some, this name may refer to badly-formed legs, and we certainly have the name Cruickshank, Cruikshanks, Crukshanks. Among other curious narrow lanes at Canterbury, however, was one called the Sheep Shank, which probably had its name from some tavern sign, signifying the Ship or Sheep Tavern ; from G. *schenke*, a drinking-house, ale-house. Cf. the surnames Schenck, Schenk, signifying a publican, vintner.

SHEET, SHEETS. U. S. names. We also find Shead, Sheard, Sheat, Sheath, and Sheed. Some derive the name Shead from a Gaelic word signifying a field, but there is no such word in that language. It might, however, be from *scadh*, strong. Sheat is a provincial (S.) word for a young hog ; the A. S. *sceard*, Eng. *sheard*, is a fragment; but these names, especially Sheat and Sheath, may translate a maker of sheaths or scabbards (Sheather is an English surname), from A. S. *sceath*, *scœthe*, a sheath.

SHELF. From Shelf, a township co. York, West Riding. The name Shelf has also been derived from the hero Scelf or Scylf, presumed founder of the Scylfingas, a Scandinavian tribe.

SHELL. From Shell, a hamlet in the parish of Himbledon, co. Worcester.

SHERRY. 1. For Sheridan, *i. e.* Jeridan ; from Jerry, *i. e.* Jeremiah. 2. Perhaps sometimes from Sheriff.

SHEW. From Chew Magna (Bishop-Chew), a parish co. Somerset. Cf. Chew.

SHEWCRAFT. See SHOECRAFT.

SHILLINGLAW. See LAW.

SHIN, SHINN. Same as Chin, *q. v.*

SHIP, SHIPP. The same as Skipp, Skyp. These names may mean a sailor, from A. S. *scif*, a ship, boat, whence *sciper*, and the surname Skipper. Ship, Shippe, Shippie, Shep, Skippon are found as U. S. names.

SHIPLAKE. See LEGG.

SHIPTON. See SHIPWASH.

SHIPWASH. A corruption of sheepwash, the place where sheep are cleansed before shearing. Cf. the names Shipton and Shipway.

SHIPWAY. See SHIPWASH.

SHIRT. Same as Shurt. Corrupted from Sherard, Sherrard. Mr. Bowditch, in his humorous work on Suffolk (American) sur-names, says Abraham Shurt, of Pemaquid (near Bristol, Me.), took an acknowledgment of an Indian deed in 1826, twenty years before any enactment on that subject ; and he dedicates his work " To the Memory of A. Shurt, the Father of American Convey-ancing, whose Name is associated alike with my Daily Toilet, and my Daily Occupation."

SHIRTCLIFF. Same as Shirtliff and Shurtleff, both found in the U. S. Derived from some local name, most probably Shortcliff.

SHOE, *i. q.* Chew and Shew, *q. v.*

SHOEBOTTOM. See BOTTOM.

SHOECRAFT. A name found at Buffalo, U. S. There is also a U. S. Shewcraft. These names are compounded of *croft*, a small field adjoining a dwellinghouse.

SHOOTER. The same as Shuter, Sutor, Suter, Sutler, Soutar, Souter, Soutter, Sowter ; from O. Eng. *souter*, a cobbler, shoe-maker, from A. S. *sutere*, L. *sutor*. Hence doubtless the U. S. name Shouter.

SHOTBOLT. From A. S. *bolt*, a dwelling. See BOTTLE.

SHOUT. The same as Shute ; from Shute, a parish co. Devon. Shout, Shut, Shutt, Shute, Shuts are found in Bowditch. Cf. Chute, from Chute in Wilts.

SHOUTER. See SHOOTER.

SHOVE. A corruption of the French name Chauve. See CALF and SHAVE.

SHOVEL. From Showell, a chapelry in the parish of Swerford, co. Oxford ; or from the surname Scovell (in H. R. De Scoville, De Scovile) ; from Escoville, now Ecoville, arrond. Caen, Normandy. Sir Cloudesley Shovel was the name of a gallant British admiral, born near Clay, in Norfolk, about 1650.

SHOW. A name occurring in the Registrar-General's List. There is also a U. S. Showe. The same as Chew, Shew, Shoe, *q. v.*

SHUFFLE, SHUFFELL. 1. From Sheffield co. York. 2. The same as Suffield ; from Suffield (south field), name of a parish of England, co. Norfolk, and of two townships of the U. S., the one Connecticut, the other Ohio. 3. Same as the U. S. names Shufelt, Shufeldt, compounded of G. *feld*, a field. See also BOTTOM.

SHUFFLEBOTTOM. See BOTTOM.

SHUFFLER. The same as Shoveller, a probable corruption of Chevalier (H. R. Le Chevaler), a knight or horseman (Fr.).

SHUN. Same as Shin, *q. v.*

SHUT, SHUTT. Same as Shout, *q. v.*

SICILY. An Edinburgh surname. A corruption of the female Christian name Cicely or Cœcilia.

SICKMAN. From root of Sugarman, *q. v.*

SIDE. According to Lower, *side* implies the side of a hill, stream, &c. Ferguson renders it a " possession " or " location ;" and if so it would seem to be from A. S. *sæt*, a sitting, station, &c. We have many names compounded of *side*, as Silverside, Silversides, Whiteside, Handyside, &c.

SIDEBOTHER. See SIDE.

SIDEBOTTOM. See BOTTOM.

SILENCE. From Saillans or Seillans, a comm. and market town of France, dep. Drôme.

SILK. From Silk-Willoughby, a parish co. Lincoln.

SILL. A nickname of Silas or Silvester.

SILLY, SILLEY. Properly Ceely. D. Gilbert says John Silly, gent., of St. Wenn, Cornwall, altered his name from Ceely to Silly, which Lower considers " a truly silly deed, especially for a lawyer, to have executed."

SILVERLOCK. See LEGG.

SILVERSIDE, SILVERSIDES.. See SIDE.

SILVERSTONE. From Silverston, a parish co. Northampton. But see SMALSTONE.

SIMMER. 1. Same as Seamer, Seymour ; from A. S. *seamere*, a tailor. 2. From Seamer, name of two parishes co. York ; or Semer co. Suffolk, on the Bret. Some derive the name Seymour from Roger de Sancto Mauro ; and Ferguson says Seamer, Seymour correspond with the G. Siemer, Simmer, from Sigimar. But see SKIMMER.

SIMPER. From St. Pierre, *i. e.* St. Peter. St. Pierre is the name of a parish co. Monmouth.

SIMPLE. From Simplicius. Ménage, in his Receuil de Noms de Saints, gives a St. Simples, corrupted from St. Simplicius. Simple may also sometimes be the same as Semple and Sample, from St. Paul. See SAMPLE.

SINFOOT. Compound of *ford*. See HAZLEFOOT.

SING. Found Singer, alias Synge (a singer in a church); from A. S. *singan*, to sing. Cf. the names Sang, Sangar, Sangster. The Indian name Sing, Singh is derived from the Sanscrit *sinh*, *sinha*, a lion.

SINGLEDAY. Persons named Monday, Munday, Thursday, Friday, Saturday, Sunday, G. Sontag, may have been so named from having been born on those days ; but whence such names as Doubleday, Otherday, Purday, Singleday, Twiceaday is doubtful. Meidinger, under *tag*, *tac*, splendour, glory, renown, fame (glanz, ruhm), gives the Alt D. names Alptac, Helmtac, Richdag, Tagafrid, the Alt S. Berndag, Hildidag, Liuddag, Wildag. But these names may sometimes be from *deo*, *diu*, confidant, servant; whence the Alt D. names Arndeo, Helmdeo, Irmindeo, Pirideo, Regindeo, &c. &c. Cf. also the English name Heritage, in H. R. Heritag.'

SINJOHN. A U. S. corruption of St. John. The name is also found written Sinjen.

SIP. From Sibert, a name occurring iu the genealogy of the kings of the East Angles, East Saxons, and West Saxons, corresponding with the G. name Siebert, an O. H. G. Sigiperaht, and a G. Sigibert; or from Sibbald, G. Sebald, Siebold, Sybelt, from Sigebald, name of a king of the East Saxons. Cf. the G. names Sibja, Sibo, Sivo, Siffo, O. G. Sepp, Seebe, Sybel, and the U. S. names Sibel, Sibell, Sibbs, Sip, Sipp, Sipps, Sipples, Sippel, Sipple, Sippet.

SIPPET. See SIP.

SIRGOOD. Same as Sargood, Sherwood, Shergold. See SHEARGOLD.

SITWELL. The same as Sidwell, for some local name compounded of *ville*. The name would also corrupt from the German name Sigiwald.

SIX. See SEX.

SIXSMITHS. A corruption of Sucksmith, *q. v.*

SIXTY. Perhaps the same as Sexty and Saxty; from Saxty, a parish co. Suffolk. Lower makes the name Sexty a corruption of *sacristy*.

SKIFF. A U. S. name. Perhaps from A. S. *scife*, *scyfe*, a precipice.

SKILL. Camden renders *skell* "a well, in the Northern English." Skyll and Skell are also found. But see SKULL.

SKILLET. Perhaps a diminutive of Skill, *q. v.*

H

SKIMMER. Same as the G. Sigimar ; from *sig-mar*, renowned for victory.

SKINLEY, *i. q.* SKINGLEY, SHENLEY, SHELLEY. From A. S. *scean-leag*, beautiful meadow. See LEGG.

SKINNING. Formed like Winning, *q. v.*

SKULL, SCULL. From Skull, in the Barony of Carbery, co. Cork.

SLACK. A name of local origin. The word *slack* signifies valley, a small shallow dell. "*Slack, slak, slake*, an opening in the higher part of a hill or mountain, where it becomes less steep, and forms a sort of pass ; a gap or narrow pass between two hills or mountains." (*Jamieson.*)

SLATE. From Sleat or Slate, in the Isle of Wight.

SLAUGHTER. From one of the two parishes so called co. Gloucester ; perhaps derived from the name of a river. There is a place called Slaughterford co. Wilts. Slaughter may also sometimes be the same as Slatter, which has been derived from the Dan. *slagter*, a butcher. Slaughter is the name of a butcher at Notting Hill, Middlesex.

SLEEP, SLEAP. From Sleep, a hamlet in the parish of St. Peter, at St. Albans, co. Herts.

SLEEPER. See SLIPPER.

SLEWMAN. Same as Slowman, *q. v.*

SLIM. The Boston Courier (4th June, 1859) mentions that Mr. Slim had a *narrow* escape from drowning. Slim is probably a corruption of Selim, a name which occurs twice in the Post-Office Directory.

SLIPPER. The same as Slyper. From the old word *sword-sleiper*, a sword-grinder ; from Teut. *schwerdt-schleiffer*. Slyper is the name of a diamond-cutter in London. Hence no doubt the surname Sleeper. The name Slipper has been connected with the Spanish name Zapata ; and *zapáta, zapáto* is a kind of half-boot. Mellado gives three Spaniards of the name of Zapata—Antonio Zapata de Cisneros, a cardinal, born at Madrid in 1550 ; Antonio or Lupian Zapata, born at Segorbe in the seventeenth century; and Antonio Zapata, born at Soria at the end of the seventeenth century. The latter was one of the most celebrated of the pupils of Antonio Palomino, and, among many others, painted a fine picture of St. Peter and St. Paul for the cathedral of Osma. The name is probably derived from locality. Zapata is the appellation of a district of Spain, prov. Avila; and of a place prov. Pontevedra. Zapateros is the name of a village prov. Córdoba; and there are places in Spain called Zapategui, Zapateira, Zapateiro, Zapatera, Zapateria, Zapatero, and Zapaton.

SLIPSHOE. See STEPTOE.

SLIT. Same as Slight, one thin and tall.

SLOCOCK. See COCK.

SLOW. This name was anciently written De la Slo, Ad le Slow, or De la Slou, and is the same as Slough; from *slough*, a place of deep mud or mire, from A. S. *slog*. Slough is the name of a place in Bucks. Slow, Slowe, Slowey, Slough, Sloog, Sloggett, Sluggett are found as surnames in Bowditch.

SLOWCOCK. See COCK.

SLOWLY, SLOWLEY. From some local name compounded of *ley*. See LEGG.

SLOWMAN. The same as Sloman, and the U. S. Slooman, Sluman, Sleuman, Slewman, Slyman; corrupted from the Hebrew name Solomon.

SLUMBER. A U. S. corruption of Lumber, Limber, *q. v.* It would even corrupt from St. Lambert, if there ever was such a saint or sinner.

SLYBODY. The same as Slytbody, which Lower says is found in Sussex in the thirteenth century, and four centuries after in the same county as Slybody. The name means thin and tall in body.

SLYMAN. The same as Sleeman, Slemmon, and Slowman, *q. v.* But see also SLYBODY.

SMALLAGE. See MARRIAGE.

SMALLBACK. From some local name compounded of G. *bach*, a brook.

SMALLBONE, SMALLBONES. From some local name compounded of *bourn*, a brook, A. S. *burn*. Hence Collarbone, Crackbone, Fulborn, Kneebone, Newbone, Newborne, Stubborne, Whalebone.

SMALLCOMB. See COMB.

SMALLEY. SEE SMILES.

SMALLPAGE, SMALPAGE. This name may mean the small village. Page (L. *pagus*) was an old English word for a village. But see PAGE.

SMALPENNY. See PENNY.

SMALSTONE. A name found in the U. S. From some local name compounded of *ton* (A. S. *tun*), an enclosure. Hence Silverstone, &c.

SMELT. 1. A diminutive of Small = to the names Little, Petit, Klein, &c. 2. From A. S. *smylt, smelt*, serene, gentle, placid, mild.

SMILES. Said to be derived from the name Smellie, probably from Smalley, a chapelry in the parish of Morley, co. Bucks; from A. S. *smeth-leag*, smooth pasture. Smalley, Smily, Smedley would seem to be the same name.

SMOKER. Mr. Ferguson thinks this name may be from the A. S. *smicere*, elegant, polished; but the Dan. form of the word, viz. *smuk* (fair, handsome, fine), would be nearer. Halliwell says, "At Preston, before the passing of the Reform Bill in 1832, every person who had a cottage with a chimney, and used the latter, had a vote, and was called a *smoker*." Smucker, Smock, Smoke are found as U. S. names.

SMUT. A name found in Lower's Appendix. The same as Smout, Smoot, Smoote, Smyth, Smythe, Smith. Cf. Smooth-man, which is doubtless a corruption of Smithyman or Smitherman. All these names, as well as Smither, Smyther, and Smithers, are found in Bowditch.

SNIPE. Same as Snape, Snepp; from Snape, name of a parish co. Suffolk, and of a township co. York, North Riding. The Devonshire word *snape* signifies a spring in arable ground. The names Snape, Snapp, Snipe, Snupe are found in the U. S.

SNIVELLY, SNIVELY, SNIVELEY. U. S. names. From some local name compounded of *ley*. See LEGG.

SNOOKS. The word snooks is often brought forward as the answer to an idle question, or as the perpetrator of a senseless joke. It was probably the name of a character in some modern play or song. The surname is a gross corruption of Sevenoaks; from Sevenoaks, Kent, the provincial pronunciation of which is Se'noaks. Sevenoaks is still a surname, and there was formerly a Sir William de Sevenoke. " Mr. Sevenoke," says Bowditch, " was an ancient Lord Mayor of London."

SNOWBALL. From some local name compounded of *bold* ; perhaps from *snaw-bold*, the snow dwelling. See BOTTLE.

SNOWHITE. Compounded of *thwaite*. See LILYWHITE.

SOAR. See SORE.

SOBER. The same as Seaber and Seubar in the Domesday of Lincolnshire; probably from Sibert, for Sigibert.

SOCKETT. Probably of local origin. According to Lower, Sockett is an alias for the parish of Playden co. Sussex.

SOFTLY, SOFTLEY. See LEGG.

SOLACE. Same as Solis ; from Sollies, a commune and town of France, dep. Var ; or from Soules, an ancient Scottish family that gave name to Soulestoun, now Saltoun, or Salton, in Scotland.

SOLE, SOUL. 1. From the Scripture name Saul. 2. From Saul, name of a parish of England, co. Gloucester, and of a parish of Ireland, co. Down. 3. From Soulle, a town of France, dep. La Manche. 4. The same as Seal, Seale ; from root of Counsell, *q. v.* Cf. Shrubsole, Plimsaul, Plimsoll; and see also SALE, SALES.

SOMANY. The same as Soman and Samand; from A. S.

sœ-man, *sœ-mann*, a seaman. Samand would also corrupt from St. Amant. St. Amant and Stamamant are found in Bowditch.

SOMEBORN. Bowditch mentions a Mr. Someborn of Philadelphia, who, he says, may feel assured that somebody was his father. Sombourn is the name of two parishes (King's and Little) co. Hants.

SON. The same as Sonne; perhaps from G. *sonne*, the sun. Son, Sonne, Sonna, and Sunrise are found in Bowditch, and Sunshine in Lower's Appendix.

SOPPETT, SOPPITT. A corruption of Sopwith, from Sopworth co. Wilts. But see SIP and SIPPET.

SORE. A Maria Sore and an Ellen Soar occur in the Registrar-General's List. They may be from Sore, a town of France, dep. Landes. They may also be the same as Shore and the U. S. Shower.

SORELY. A U. S. name. See LEGG.

SORTWELL. From some local name compounded of *ville*.

SOUL. See SOLE.

SOURWINE. See WINE.

SOUTHERLY. See LEGG.

SOUTHMAYD. The same as Southmead, both U. S. names. See LONGMAID.

SOY. A U. S. name. A corruption of Say; from Sąi, near Argentan, a town of France, dep. Orne; probably derived from *saxum*, a rock.

SPAN, SPANE. Same as Spain, Spayne, originally from Spain. See Morant's Essex.

SPANIEL. One from Spain or Hispaniola. See Charnock's Verba Nominalia.

SPAR. Same as Spurr, *q. v.*

SPEAK, SPEAKE. The same as Speke; from Branford Speke (found Speak in one map) co. Devon. Speke is also the name of a township co. Lancaster. Lower says the Spekes of Somersetshire descend from Richard le Espek, who lived in the

reign of Henry II., but that he is unable to explain Le Espek·
A correspondent of Notes and Queries thinks "Willi le Espec"
may be a misreading for " Willi le Espee "—that is, William the
Swordsman, or William of the Sword; another thinks *espec* may
mean a spicer, who was formerly something between a grocer
and a chemist, and he quotes Roquefort, " Especiaire, épicier,
droquiste, apothecaire; de *species, specierum.*" The O. Fr. *spec* is
an inspector.

SPEAR. Same as Spurr, *q. v.*

SPENCE. See EXPENCE.

SPENCER, SPENSER. From Fr. *dispensier*, a dispenser,
steward, literally one having the care of the spence or buttery.
The ancestor of the noble family of Spencer was Robert de
Spencer, steward, *i. e.* dispenser, to William the Conqueror.

SPENDLOVE. See LAW.

SPIDER. Properly Spinner. The name of the insect is properly spinner.

SPIER. See SPIRE.

SPILLARD. See HAZARD.

SPINNAGE. See MARRIAGE.

SPIRE, SPIRES. From Spires, G. Speyer, a city of Germany, cap. Rhenish Bavaria.

SPIRIT. A name found in the records of the Registrar-
General. It is probably the same as Spurrett, a diminutive
of Spurr, *q. v.* One Spiritus Presbyter, however, occurs in
a charter of Hardacnut, Cod. Dip. Ang. Sax., No. 762. Cf.
Ferguson.

SPIRT. Same as Spirit, *q. v.*

SPITTLE. Found Spittal, Spital, Spittel. Spital is the name
of two places in Austria, of a parish in South Wales, and of a
township co. Lincoln. It is a corruption of *hospital.*

SPOTTS. From Spott, a parish of Scotland, co. Haddington.

SPRATT. A probable corruption of Pratt, for Parratt, a
diminutive of the French Pierre.

SPRUCE. Like the adjective, probably derived from Prussia. But see Charnock's Verba Nominalia.

SPURAWAY. 1. Same as Spurway; from A. S. *speara, spearwa*, a sparrow. 2. From Spurway, the name of an estate co. Devon. Cf. Spar, Spear, Spurr.

SPURR. The same as Spar, Spear, and Sparrow, from A. S. *speara, spearwa*, Dan. *spurre*.

SQUIRREL. The same as the U. S. name Esquirell, and the Fr. Esquirol; or from the English surname Squirhill, derived from some local name ending in " hill."

STABB, STABBS. The same as Stubbs, from St. Aubyn, or from St. Ebbe's. There is however a U. S. name Staab, which would seem to be from Stab or Staab (Boh. Stoda), a market town of Bohemia.

STABLE, STABLES. Same as Staple, Staples, *q. v.*

STAGG, STAGGS. From St. Agg, St. Aggs, *i. e.* St. Agatha's,

STAIR. From Stair, a parish of Scotland, co. Ayr, which gives title to the Earl of Stair.

STALLION. Corrupted from some English local name, perhaps Stelling, a parish co. Kent. It may also be a French diminutive. Stall, Stallo, Stallion are found as surnames in the U. S.

STAIN. The same as Stein, Steinn, Steen, Stone; from G. *stein*, A. S. *stán*, O. N. *steinn*, a stone.

STAMMER, STAMMERS (U. S. Stamer, Stemmer, Stamers). This name might certainly be an English rendering of the Roman name Balbus, but it is more probably derived from a local name. It may be a corruption of the surname Starmer, perhaps from Sturmer, a parish co. Essex, or Stormere co. Leicester ; or from the surname Stanmer, from Stanmer, a parish co. Sussex. J. Stammers, Esq., barrister-at-law, considers his name to be of Dutch or German origin, and thinks that Stammensdorff, a local name mentioned in Alison's History, may give a clue. Stammers would easily corrupt from St. Audomarus (whence St. Omer), doubtless the same as Audomer or Aumer, from which Pont Audemer had its name.

STUBBORNE. See SMALLBONE.

STAMP, STAMPS. The same as Estampes. From Etampes, formerly Estampes, a commune and town of France, dep. Seine et Oise.

STANDFAST. See MATTERFACE.

STANDING. The same as Standin and Standen; from some local name ending in *den*, a valley.

STANDWELL. The same as Stanville and Stanwell; from Stanwell co. Middlesex, compounded of *ville*.

STAPLE, STAPLES. From Staple, name of parishes cos. Kent and Somerset. Hence the names Stable, Stables.

STAR, STARR. Star is found in H. R., and Ster and Sterr in Domesday; and there is a place named Star near Markinch, in Scotland. Ferguson thinks Starr may be from O. N. *starri*, a hawk, A. S. *stær*, a starling.

STARBOARD, STARBIRD. These names would easily corrupt from Tarbert, the name of places in Ireland and Scotland. If of Anglo-Saxon origin, they may be from *stor-beorht*, very distinguished, or excelling in greatness.

STARE. Same as Stair, *q. v.*

STARING. From some local name compounded of *ing*, a meadow.

STARKWEATHER. See MERRYWEATHER.

STARLING (in H. R. Starlyng, Sterlyng). From Stirling, Scotland.

START. Start Point is the name of a headland near the south extremity of co. Devon.

STARTUP. See HOPE.

STATE, STATES. From root of Steed, *q. v.* Hence the name Staight.

STAY. From root of Steed, *q. v.*

STEED. Same as Stead; from A. S. *sted*, a place (Dan. id.,
D. *stede*, G. *statt*). Stede or Stidd is the name of a chapelry co.
Lancaster.

STEDDY. A corruption of St. Edith.

STEP. From Stephen.

STEPTOE. From some local name compounded of *hoo, hoe,*
from G. *hohe*, height, elevation. Cf. the names Prudhoe, Sand-
hoe, Shafthoe, Slipshoe, Tudhoe.

STIFF. From Stephen. See TIFFANY.

STILLWAGON, STILLWAGEN. Perhaps from G. *stell-
wagner*, a maker of the vehicle called *stellwagen.*

STIRRUP. See HOPE. Stirrop is found in the Hist. Canterbury.

STOCK, STOCKS. From Stock, name of parishes cos. Essex,
Dorset, Somerset, Worcester, and York; from A. S. *stoc*, a
place.

STOCKING, STOCKINGS. From some local name compounded of A. S. *ing*, a meadow. Stocken is a surname, and De
Stocking is found in H. R. See STOCK.

STOKER. Same as Stocker (found in H. R.). In the West
of England a *stocker* is one employed to fell or grub up trees.

STONEHEART. Same as Stonhard, Stannard, Stennard,
Steinhard, Steinhardt, Steinhart; from G. *stein-hart*, as strong as
a stone.

STONELAKE. See LEGG.

STOPPARD. See HAZARD.

STORK, STORKS. A corruption of Stock, Stocks, *q. v.*

STORY. From A. S. and O. N. *stór*, great. Stori is a Scandinavian name, and we have the English names Storr and Store.

STRADLING. Corrupted from Estarling or Easterling, once
the popular name of certain German traders in England, *i. e.*
"people from the East," whose money was of the purest quality,
whence the term "sterling money."

STRANGEWAYS. There is a Major Hon. S. D. Strangeways

in the U. S. It is the same with the English names Strangwayes, Strangwish, Strangwich; corrupted from Strangwish, a place near Manchester, which was possessed by the family in the fourteenth century.

STRAW. The same as Straith; from Straith, a parish of Scotland, co. Inverness; from Sco. *strath*, Gael. *srath*, a valley, a mountain valley, bottom of a valley, a low-lying country through which a river rolls, the low inhabited part of a country, in contradistinction to its hilly ground, a dell. Cf. the surname Rackstraw.

STRAWMAT. Bowditch mentions a Dr. Strawmat who was punished by a mob. This name may be from some locality in Scotland compounded of *strath*. See STRAW.

STRAY. The same as Straw, *q. v.*

STURGEON. From an estate in Essex called Sturgeons, formerly Turges Cassus. Turges may be the same name as Turgesius, a celebrated Norwegian king, called by Irish writers Tuirghes, who established his power in Ireland for thirty years. Hence probably the names Sturch, Sturge, Sturges, Sturgess, Sturgis.

STUTTER. One who has to do with stots; or perhaps rather a corruption of the name Stotherd = stotherd. Stot is a northern provincialism for a young ox, and Chaucer uses the word *stot* for a horse. " Stot hors, *caballus* " (Pr. Parv., f. 165). Tyrwhitt thinks Chaucer uses the term *stot* for *stod*, a stallion. Stutgard, capital of Wurtemburg, had its name from the *stuts* or stallions, formerly kept there for war purposes, and the arms of the city are a mare suckling her colt. We may have this vocable in Studham, Studland, Studley, local names in England. The name Stotherd has become Stothurd, Stothert, Stothard, Stodhart, Stoddart, Stoddard, Stodart, Studart, Studdart, Studdert.

SUCH. Corrupted from the name Zouch, a baronial family that gave the suffix to Ashby-de-la-Zouch co. Leicester. The name is also found written Sutch, Souch, Zoche, Zuche, Zusch,

Zusche, and is said to be derived from A. S. *stoc,* a place, also the stem of a tree.

SUCK. Same as Such, *q. v.*

SUCKBITCH (U. S. Suxpitch). A corruption of Sokespic, a name probably of local origin. The A. S. *soc* is a soke, liberty, jurisdiction, *spic* is bacon, and the O. Fr. *spec* is an inspector. See SPEAK.

SUCKSMITH. From *sock,* a North of England word for a plough-share, from A. S. *sulg.* The first part of this name may also be from A. S. *seax, sex,* a knife, sword, dagger, plough-share.

SUDDEN. From Southdean, "southern valley," a parish of Scotland, co. Roxburgh. There is however the French surname Soudan, and two communes and villages of France named Soudan, one dep. Deux Sevres, the other dep. Loire-Inf.

SUE, SUES. Perhaps from the nickname for Susan.

SUET, SUETT. 1. The same as Sweet and the German name Süss. 2. A diminutive of Sue, *q. v.,* also Sweatman. Suet is found in the French Directory.

SUGAR. See SEGAR.

SUGARMAN. The same as Sigmundr, Sigemund, Sigismundus, Segimundus (filius Segestis apud Tacitum Annales, 1, 57); from G. *sig-mund,* vir victoriæ. Sugarman and Shugerman are found in Bowditch.

SUIT. Same as Suet, *q. v.*

SULLEN. From Soulaines, a commune and market town of France, dep. Aube, on the Soulaine. Lower, under Sellen, Sellens, says he can prove, by the evidence of parish registers, &c., in Sussex, that these names are corrupted from the ancient surname of Selwyn.

SULLY. 1. From Sully (*Solliaco*), name of two towns of France, one dep. Loiret, the other dep. Nievre. 2. From Sully, a parish of South Wales, co. Glamorgan.

SUMMERBEE. From Somerby, name of three parishes, one co. Leicester, and two co. Lincoln. But see BEE.

SUMMERBELL. A U. S. name. The same as the English names Somervell, Somervail; corrupted from Somerville.

SUMMERFIELD. The same as Somerfield, Somervail, Somervell, Summerwill, corrupted from Somerville.

SUMMERSETT. A corruption of Somerset.

SUMMERWILL. See SUMMERFIELD.

SUMMONS. Same as Summonds; a corruption of Symonds, Symons, Simmonds, Simmons; perhaps sometimes from Simon, but generally from Simund or Sigmund, or from Seman, Seaman.

SUPPLE. A corruption of Shuffle, q. v.

SURPLICE. This name is found in the Registrar-General's List. It is the same as the U. S. name Surpluss, and the French Supplice, doubtless corrupted from Sulpicius. Ménage gives St. Sulpice and St. Souplex, as corrupted down from Sulpicius. St. Sulpice is the name of numerous communes and villages of France.

SURPLUSS. See SURPLICE.

SWALLOW. From Swallow, a parish co. Lincoln. There is however the French name Hirondelle.

SWAN. The same as Swain, Swaine, Swayne, and the Scandinavian name Sweyn; from A. S. *swán*, a herdsman or pastoral servant.

SWEARING. Formed like Winning, q. v.

SWEAT. Same as Suet.

SWEATING, SWETTING. Same as Sweeten, q. v.

SWEATMAN. The same as Sweetman, and an ancient name Swetman, and the præ-Domesday name Suetman or Suetmannus. The name may mean strong or powerful man. The A. S. *swith*, *wyth* is strong, powerful, great; Fries. *swid*, strong, much, crafty, bad; Mœso-G. *swinths*, validus, robustus. Hence the Gothic proper name Suintila = Valentius; and Swintebold, which Wachter renders valide audax.

SWEETBUTTER. Name of an old family in the neighbourhood of Woodstock. See BUTTER.

SWEETEN. Same as Sweeting. A patronymic of the name Sweet; or compounded of *ing*, a meadow. See WILLING. Lower gives Sweeting as an old Anglo-Saxon personal name, and mentions the Domesday Sueting, Suetingus.

SWEETLAND. The same as the U. S. names Swetland and Sweedland; from Swethland, Sweedland, old names for Sweden, found in Dr. Bosworth's Anglo-Saxon Dictionary. The name might also be from Swithland, a parish of England, co. Leicester.

SWEETLOVE. See LAW.

SWEETMAN. See SWEATMAN.

SWEETSIR. Same as Sweetser, Sweetsur, Sweetzer, Sweitzer, Schweitzer, the German for a Swiss.

SWELL, SWELLS. From Swell, a parish co. Somerset ; or Swell, name of two parishes (Upper and Lower) co. Gloucester.

SWILLAWAY. From some local name compounded of *way*. Swillaway, Silloway, Silaway are found as surnames in the U. S.

SWILLING. From some local name compounded of *ing*, a meadow. But see WILLING.

SWINDLE. From Swindale, co. Westmoreland.

SWINDLER. A maker of swindles, a northern provincialism for *spindles*.

SWINE. 1. A corruption of Swain, Swaine, Swayne. See SWAN. 2. From Swine, a parish co. York, East Riding.

SWINESHEAD. From Swineshead, a market town and parish co. Lincoln ; also a parish co. Hunts.

SWING. Same as Swine ; or from some local name. Swingfield is the name of a parish co. Kent.

SWORD, SWORDS. From Swords, a town and parish of Ireland, co. Dublin.

SYNTAX. Perhaps a corruption of St. Agg's, *i. e.* Agatha's. See AGUE.

TAILBUSH. Same as Talboys, *q.v.*

T.

TALBOYS, TAILBOYS. From Fr. *taille bois*, cut-wood; or rather *qui taille le bois*, one who cuts wood, a wood-cutter. This name has been rendered in English Cutbush, which, by the bye, was formerly the name of a gardener at Highgate, Middlesex.

TAME. Not from Tame, a river cos. Stafford and Warwick; nor from the Tame which rises in Yorkshire; nor the Thame or Tame which falls into the Thames; but from Thame or Tame, a market town and parish co. Oxford, which takes its name from the latter river.

TANKARD. From O. G. Tanchard (ninth century), Thancred, from *dank-rat*, a willing counsellor; or perhaps rather from A. S. *thanc-red*, thoughtful counsellor. Cf. the O. G. names Thancheri, Thancrih, the It. Tancredi, Eng. Tanqueray, G. Danco, Eng. Danks.

TAPLADY. See TOPLADY.

TAPPING. A patronymic of Tapp; or compounded of *ing*, a meadow. See WILLING. Tapp, Tappan, Tapping, Tapps, Tappy are found as U. S. names.

TARBATH. From Tarbat, Tarbart, or Tarbert, in Scotland; or Tarbert, near Limerick, Ireland; from Gael. *tairbeart*, a peninsula.

TARBOTTOM. According to Lower, this name is a corruption of the surname Tarbotton, probably from Tarbolton, a parish in Ayrshire. But see BOTTOM.

TARBOX. The same as Torbock; from Torbock, an estate in Lancashire, held by a family of the name in early times.

TARGET, TARGETT. See THOROUGHGOOD.

TARRY. A corruption of Terry, like the French name Thierry, derived from Theodoric.

TART. A corruption of the surname Tarratt, for Tarrant;

from Tarrant, name of several parishes in co. Dorset, through one of which runs the small river of the same name.

TASSELL. The It. word *tásso* is a badger, also a yew-tree and an anvil ; but Tasso is said to be an O. G. name and there is the diminutive Tassilo, and the English name Tassell, and *tassel* is an O. Eng. word for a male hawk, from Fr. *tiercelet* (It. terzolo). Some make Tassilo and Tetzel diminutives of Tatto, Tasso, from O. G. *tatte*, pater, tutor, nutricius. Wachter doubts this, and thinks them rather abbreviated from Tadelbert, which he translates parentibus clarus, and he says Totila, the name of a king of the Ostrogoths, might be from the same root. All these names may be from the O. Fr. *tasse*, assemblage de quelques arbres, petit bois touffu, touffe d'arbres. Most of the following surnames are found in the French Directory — viz., Tasse, Tassus, Tassy, Tassel, Tassilly, Tassily, Tasset, Tassot, Taskin, Tassin, Tassain, Tasselin, Tassart, Tassaert.

TAUNT. The same as Daunt, both found in the Registrar-General's List, and the U. S. North America. Lower says Daunt is said to be the same as the Dauntre of the so-called Battel Abbey Roll. If so, it may be from Daventry co. Northampton.

TAYLECOATE. See COAT.

TAX. From Tack, Tacke, Tagg, Tagge ; perhaps from Tagert, Taggard, Taggart, Taggert.

TEACHOUT. A name found in the U. S. Compounded of the D. *would*, a wood ; or *hout*, wood. Cf. Turnhout, a town of Belgium, prov. East Antwerp.

TEAR. From the Gael. name MacTear ; from *mac-an-saoir*, son of the carpenter. Hence MacIntyre.

TEETH. From atte Heath, or at-the-heath, one living upon or near the heath.

TELFAIR. The same as Telfer, from the Norman name Taillefer = cut-iron. Lower says, "The exploits of the noble jonglere Taillefer at the battle of Hastings are well known. William, Count of Angouleme, in a battle against the Northmen, engaged their king, Storris, and with one stroke of his sword *Durissima,* forged by the great Wayland Smith, cut in two his body and cuirass. Hence he acquired the sobriquet of Taillefer, or '*cut iron.*'" In the sixteenth century the name in Scotland was written Tailzefer. Telfer, the celebrated engineer, not aware of the origin of his name, changed it to Telford. Hence no doubt Talford, Talfourd, Tolfrey, and Tolfree.

TELLING. Formed like Winning, *q. v.*

TENCH. Same as Dench. See DANCE.

TENDER. Halliwell says tender, in the eastern counties, signifies a waiter at an inn.

TENET. One Joseph Tenet occurs in the Registrar-General's List. It is doubtless corrupted from Thiennette, a French diminutive of Etienne, *i. e.* Stephen.

TENT. A corruption of Tenet, *q. v.*

THALER. See CASHDOLLAR.

THANKFUL. Corrupted from the Norman name Tankerville.

THICKNESSE. From some local name compounded of *ness,* a cape or headland; from A. S. *næsse, nésse, ness.* Cf. the local names Sheerness, Dungeness, Eastonness. It sometimes means an island, as in Foulness, Essex.

THICKPENNY. See PENNY.

THIMBLEBEE. From Thimbleby, a parish co. Lincoln.

THIN. The same as Thynne. The latter name is said to have originated with the ancient house of Botfield or Botevile. The alias is said to have originated with John de Botteville, who lived at the family house at Church-Stretton, who was familiarly known as *John o' th' Inne,* which abbreviated became Thynne, though John de la Inne de Botfelde was his usual appellation. It seems that the house in question was called "The Inn."

THING. A corruption of Thin, *q. v.*

THIRST. The same as Thurst; from Thursk co. York; or from *at-the-hurst* = at the wood or forest (A. S. *hyrst*). The A. S. *thrist* is bold, daring.

I

THISTLECOCK. See Cock.

THORNBACK. Not from the fish; but from some local name ending in *back*, a brook. See Newback and Smallback.

THOROUGHGOOD. The same as Thorowgood, the Essex Thurgar, the Dan. Thurgood, and the Domesday Turgod and Thurgot, name of the first bishop of Sweden. The name seems to come from the O. G. *thor*, bold, strong, fierce, perhaps the same as the W. *dewr*, brave, bold, valiant, stout; Gr. θούριος, θοῦρος, warlike, ardent, fierce, an epithet of Mars, and doubtless the origin of the name of the Scandinavian god Thor. Wachter thinks Thurgot may be rendered "trusting in God." He gives also from this root Thurovaro, Thorismodus, Thorisin, &c. From Thurgood, Turgod, Thurgot we may have the name Targett.

THROWER. One that twists or winds silk; from A. S. *thrawan*, to twist, turn, curl, throw, &c.

THRUSH. The same as Thirst, *q. v.*

TICKLE, TICKELL. From Tickhill, a parish and formerly a market town co. York, West Riding.

TICKLEPENNY. From Ticklepenny, a parish near Grimsby co. Lincoln. But see Penny.

TIDY. From Tadhg, the Irish form of Thady, *i. e.* Thaddeus. MacTaidhg or Teige, O'Taidhg or O'Teige (mentioned by O'Herin as chiefs of Ui Maile and of Ui Teigh) anglicised their name to Tighe. They derive their name from Ir. *tadhg*, a poet, philoophers.

TIDYMAN. The same as Tiddeman and Tidman. From some old German name, perhaps Theudmund or Theodmund; from O. G. *teut-mund*, which might translate both "a protector of man" and "a prince." I do not find such a name, but we have many names compounded of *teut*, as Theudorix, Theodoricus, Theudebert, Theudibaldus, &c.

TIFFANY, TIFFINY. From Stephen. Hence also Tiffin, Tiffen, and Stiff. Roquefort renders the O. Fr. *tiphaine, tiphagne, tiphaingue*, la fête de l'Épiphanie, le jour des Rois, du Grec. ἐπιφανεια.

TIFFIN. See TIFFANY.

TIGHT. A name found in the Registrar-General's List and also in the U. S. It is probably a corruption of Tite, the French form of Titus.

TILL. 1. The nickname for Matilda. 2. Said to be sometimes from William. Hence, as a diminutive, Tillet, by contraction Tilt.

TILT. A contraction of Tillet. See TILL.

TIMBER. [There is a U. S. Timbers.] Perhaps the same as Timbury; from Timsbury, parishes cos. Somerset and Southampton; or from Tenbury co. Worcester. There are places named Timberley co. Chester, Timberland co. Lincoln, and Timberscombe co. Somerset.

TIMBERLAKE. According to Mr. Talbot, from Timber-leg, a wounded soldier with a wooden leg. The last part of the name is from *ley*. See LEGG.

TIMES. A corruption of Timms, from Timothy.

TIMESLOW. An ancient name derived from some locality compounded of *law*, q. v.

TIMEWELL. From some local name compounded of *ville*. See FAREWELL.

TINDALE. Same as Tindal, Tindall; from Tindale-ward, the largest of the six wards of co. Northumberland, traversed by the Tyne.

TINGLE. The same as Tingley, compounded of *ley*, a pasture. See LEGG.

TIPLADY. See TOPLADY.

TIPLER, TIPPLER (in H. R. Tipeler). Formerly a seller of beer or strong drink. In the corporation archives of Warwick is preserved " the note of such Typlers and alehouse-kepers as the justices of pease have returned to me this Michilmas session. Thies underwriten were returnyd by Sir Thomas Lucy and Humphrey Peto, esquire, March 15, Eliz." See Halliwell's Life of Shakspeare.

TIPPET, TIPPETS. The same as Tippett, Tebbitt, Tebbutt, Tibbatt, Tibbutt, Tebutt, Turbot, Tibbats, Tibbets, Tibbetts, Tibbits, Twopotts; corrupted from Tibbald, for Theobald. Hence also the names Tubb (Tebbs, Tibbs), Tubbs, Tippins, Tipple, Tipkins, and sometimes Tubby.

TIPPING (anciently Typpynge). From a locality in the township of Clayton-le-Dale co. Lancaster.

TIPPLE. See TIPPET.

TITLE. 1. A diminutive of Titt, from some personal name. 2. Same as Tittle.

TITMOUSE. The same as Titmuss, Tidmas, Titchmarsh, Tidmarsh; from Tidmarsh co. Berks. The name would also easily corrupt from the ancient name Theodomerus (dux clarus), hodie Dietmar.

TITTLE. Same as Tittell; or perhaps from Titley, a parish co. Hereford. Tittel is the name of a village of Hungary.

TOADVINE. A U. S. name. Probably of German origin; from *theud-win*, which would translate both "war-leader" and "friend of the people." But see WINE and TITMOUSE.

TODDY. A U. S. name. From Todd, Tod, said to be from *tod*, a provincial word for a fox. It is more probably a nickname for Theodore or Thaddeus.

TOLEFREE. See TELFAIR.

TOLLER. Perhaps sometimes from Toller, name of two parishes co. Dorset.

TOMB, TOMBS, TOOMBS. 1. From Tom, Toms, from Thomas. 2. From Tim, Timm, Tims, Timms, Timbs, from Timothy.

TONE. See TUNE.

TONGUE (Tong, Tonge). From the parish of Tongue co. Sutherland, and perhaps sometimes from Tong or Tonge, parishes, &c., in cos. Kent, Lancaster, Leicester, Salop, and York. Tongue (originally Tung) co. Sutherland was named from a narrow neck of land; from Gaelic *teanga*.

TOOGOOD. The same as Towgood. From some local name compounded of "wood."

TOOL, TOOLE. Same as the Irish name O'Toole or O'Tuaghall. See TOTTLE.

TOP, TOPP. From some dwelling at the top of a hill; from A. S. *top*, vertex, fastigium. A comparison of names will show that we have fewer tops than bottoms.

TOOTHAKER. Bowditch mentions a " Dr. Toothaker, of Middlesex county, as a general practitioner, and not a dentist." Lower gives a Toothacker, which he derives from *todtenacker*, field of the dead, a burying ground, analogous to churchyard.

TOPCOAT. See COAT.

TOPLADY. This name, as well as Taplady and Tiplady, may be from some local name compounded of A. S. *lád*, a lode, canal; or more probably from the Irish name O'Dubhlaidhe (O'Dooley), from *dubhlaidh*, dark, wintry; or from *dubh-laoch*, a dark hero, champion, or soldier.

TOPLEAF, TOPLIFF. From Topcliff, a parish co. York, North Riding, where are to be seen the ruins of the " Maiden Bower," a former seat of the Percies, in which Charles I. was confined before his delivery to the Scots.

TORTOISE. A name found in the London Directory. See TORTOISESHELL.

TORTOISESHELL. A name found in Lower's Appendix. It is doubtless the same as Tattersall, Tattershall, Tattersill; from Tattershall co. Lincoln. The castle of Tattershall appears to have been built by Robert de Tateshall, whose son was created Baron Tateshall in 1295. It is quite possible also that from the name Tate, Tates, perhaps by corruption Tatters, we may have the surname Tortoise.

TORY. Same as Torrey and the Edinburgh name Torry; from Torry, name of places in Scotland, in cos. Kirkardine and Fife. Tory or Torry Island is the name of an island off the north-west coast of Ireland, co. Donegal. Torre is also found as a surname.

TOTTLE. 1. From Tothill, a parish co. Lincoln. "A tote-hill is an eminence from whence there is a good look-out." Cheshire, Archœol. xix., 39. 2. The same as Tootal, Tuttle, and the Irish name Tuathal. O'Reilly renders *tuathal* the left hand, and *tuathal, tuathallach,* awkward, ungainly, clownish, rustic, left-handed, undexterous.

TOUCH. From the French name Touche or De la Touche. Cf. the French surnames Destouches, Touche-Tréville, and Touchon may be a diminutive. There is the Manoir de la Tousche near Nantes, and Touches and Touchet are local names in France. La Touche is also the name of a river in North America. Cotgrave defines *touche,* "a hoult, a little thick grove or tuft of high trees, especially such a one as is neere a house, and serves to beautifie it, or as a marke for,it." The O. Fr. *touche, sousche* is rendered petit bois de haute futaie proche la maison d'un fief. At Metz *toc* is "un pied d'arbre," and *tocquée,* "une poignée d'herbes ou de fleurs avec leurs racines."

TOUCHARD. See TOUCH and HAZARD.

TOUCHSTONE. A modern surname. It is probably from Tuschetum, the Latinised form of Touchet, a parish, arrond. Mortain, Normandy, whence the Touchet family derived their name.

TOUGH. 1. From the parish of Tough co. Aberdeen, Scotland, which in Gaelic is said to mean " northern exposure ;" but the name was originally Tullyunch. 2. From Tough, name of two parishes of Ireland, Munster, co. Limerick.

TOW. Another orthography of Tough, *q. v.*

TOWELL. The same as Towill and perhaps Dobell, Dowell; from some local name compounded of *ville.*

TOY, TOYE. Perhaps from Towie, a parish of Scotland, co. Aberdeen. There are however the French names Toy, Doye; and perhaps, as diminutives, Toyot and Doyat, which may be from O. Fr. *doy,* a canal, from L. *ductus.* There are however the U. S. names Doy, Duy, Douai ; and they may all be from Douai or Douay, a town of France, dep. Nord.

TRACTION. According to Lower, this name, as well as Trackson, is corrupted from Threxton; from Threxton, a village of Norfolk.

TRAIL, TRAILL. This family claims to be of Norse extraction, and derives its name from Trolle or Troil, the devil. It is more probably the same with the French name Latreille = the vine arbour. It may even be of Cornish origin, perhaps from *tre-hale*, the dwelling on the moor. There is a place called Treal in Ruan Minor.

TRAVELLER. Same as the Cornish name Trevailor, from Trevailer, in Madderne; from *tre-vailer, vayler*, the workman's town.

TREADGOLD, TREDGOLD, THRIDGOULD. From some local name compounded of *wood*. See SHEARGOLD

TREASURE. Same as Tresahar, from Tresare, Cornwall; from Cornish *tre-sair*, the woodman's or carpenter's town.

TREBLE. A name probably of Cornish origin, from Trebel, the fair or fine place (*tre-bel*). Hence no doubt by corruption the surname Tremble.

TREMBLE. See TREBLE.

TRENCHARD. See HAZARD.

TRESS, TRESSE. The same as Tracey, Tracie; corrupted from Theresa. Hence Truss, and perhaps, as diminutives, Trussel, Trussell.

TRICK. A corruption of Derrick, Derick, from Theodoric.

TRICKER. In some parts of Cornwall *tricker* means a dancer, perhaps a corruption of *tripper*. Tricker may also be a corruption of the name Trigger, *q. v.*

TRIGGER. A corruption of the surname Tregeare, Tregear, Tregere, Tregare; from Tregeare in the parish of Crowan, where the family were resident as late as 1732; from *tre-geare*, the green or fruitful place.

TRILL. A corruption of Tyrrell, Tyrell, Tirrell. See TRUEFIT.

TRIM, TRIMM. From Trim, a market town and parish of Ireland, co. Leinster.

TRIMMER. Same as Tremeer, Tremere, Tremear; from Tremeer in Lantelos-by-Fowey, or Tremere in Lanivet, Cornwall; from *tre-mèr*, the great town. Hence doubtless the name Trummer.

TRIMMING, TRIMMINGS, *i. q.* **TRIMEN.** From Drymen, near Glasgow; or *i. q.* Tremain, Tremaine, from Tremaine in East Hundred, Cornwall; or from Tremáyn, Tremayne, from Tremayne in Crowan, from *tre-mean, mên,* the stone town.

TROLL. The same as Trull, from Trull, a parish co. Somerset. Ferguson thinks Troll to be from O. N. *tröll,* a giant or demon; and he says there was a Danish family named Trolle, of importance in the fifteenth or sixteenth centuries, who bore in their coat of arms a troll or dœmon, and that their name was acquired in a sort of *lucus a non lucendo* way from an exploit of their ancestor in killing a troll. He also gives Trolle as a modern German name.

TROLLOPE. See HOPE.

TROOP. Same as Troup; from Troup co. Perth, Scotland. Hence doubtless the name Droop.

TROTMAN. Same as Trottman, Tratman, and Trautman; from G. *traut-mund,* beloved protector.

TROUBLEFIELD. The name as Turbyfield, Turberville, and Turbervill (which was Latinised De Turbida Villa), supposed to be derived from some local name in Normandy. No such name is now to be found in that province, and it is more probably derived from Tubberville or Trubby in the barony of Deece co. Meath, Ireland. Cf. Tubbermore or Tobarmore co. Londonderry, and Tubber co. Wicklow. The word *tobar, tubber* in Irish names signifies a well, formed by a spring of water.

TROUT. Perhaps from Drought or its root. (See DROUGHT.) It would also corrupt from Tyrwhitt. See TRUEFITT.

TROWELL. From Trowell, a parish co. Nottingham.

TROY. From Troyes, a town of France, cap. dep. Aube. There was a French artist named Francis de Troy. Troy is the name of a city and of several townships and villages of the U. S. North America.

TRUANT. Same as Truan, and perhaps Treuan; a name probably of Cornish origin, and compounded of *tre*.

TRUCE. Same as Trouse; from Trowse, a parish of England, co. Norfolk.

TRUE. Same as Trew, and perhaps also Drew.

TRUEFITT. Same as the U. S. name Trufhitt, corrupted from Tyrwhitt, which, as well as Tyrrell, Tyrell, Tirrell, Tirrill, would seem to be diminutives formed from the Latin *turris*, a tower.

TRUEWORTHY. See WORTH, WORTHY.

TRULOCK. See LEGG.

TRUELOVE. Mr. Bowditch mentions a London bookseller of the name of Truelove who was found wanting in love to Louis Napoleon. See LAW.

TRULL. See TROLL.

TRULY. Truleigh or Truly is the name of a manor in the parish of Edburton, Sussex. See also LEGG.

TRUMAN. The same with Trueman, *i. q.* Tremain, Tremaine; from Tremaine in East Hundred, Cornwall; from tremean, the stone town. Tremayn, Tremayne are also Cornish names, from Tremayne in Crowan, said to mean the town on shore or sea coast.

TRUNDLE. Same as Trendle; from Trendle, parish of Pitminster, Somerset.

TRUSLOVE. See LAW.

TRUSS. Same as Tress, *q. v.*

TRUSSEL, TRUSSELL. There is a parish called Trusley co. Derby. But see TRESS.

TRUST. A probable corruption of Thirst, *q. v.*

TRY, TRYE. Said to be derived from some locality in Normandy.

TUB, TUBBS. 1. From Theobald. 2. Same as Tubby, sometimes a Cornish form of Thomas.

TUBMAN. Same as Tupman, a breeder of tups or rams.

TUCKER. A name of the same meaning as Fuller, one who fulls or mills cloth. Cf. the name Tuckerman.

TUFT. From Toft, name of parishes cos. Cambridge, Lincoln, and Norfolk.

TUFTS. From Tofts, a parish co. Norfolk, having an ancient church.

TUGWELL. This name, says Lower, is borne by dentists, shoemakers, &c. It is the same as the Tuckwell and Tuckfield, and is derived from some local name compounded of *ville*. Tugwell, Tuckwell, and Tuckfield are found as U. S. surnames.

TUNE. Probably the same as Toon, *i. q.* Town; from A. S. *tún*, an enclosure; or from *túna*, a townman. Tune and Tone are both found in the United States.

TURBOT. See Tippet.

TURK, variously Turke, Turck; from Mac Turk; Gael. Mac Torc, son of the boar.

TURNBULL. This name is said to be local, and that of Trumbull a corruption. It is also connected with an anecdote about a ferocious bull. The Biog. Univ., under Turnèbe, says his father, a Scottish gentleman, called himself Turnbull; that his name was replaced in French by that of Tournebœuf, and Tournbou, which in Latin became Turnebus, and in French .Turnèbe. If the original name was Trumbull, it was probably derived from some place in Scotland or Ireland, compounded of the Gaelic *druim, droma* (Ir. *druim*, W. *trwm*), the top of a hill, a ridge (Carlisle, *drum, drom*, a knoll, ridge, eminence), and A. S. *bold*, a dwelling. *Drum, drom* are very common in local names in Ireland, and there are *drums* as well as bagpipes in Scotland. It is however possible that the English name may be derived from the Continental name. In an article contained in the Mémoires of the Roy. Soc. of N. Antiquarians, entitled *Orthographie de juelques noms nordiques*, I find that Caldebekkr became *Caudebec*, Langibyr *Longbu*, and Tournebyr *Tournebu*. These names would seem to be from the Ice. *byr*, Su.-Goth. *bo*, a dwelling; and Tournebu might mean the 'tower-dwelling.' From this root we probably have many French names compounded of *beuf, bœuf*. Among others are Belbeuf, Belbœuf, Brébeuf, Chabeuf or Chabeu (Chabot?), Cordebœuf, De Marbœuf, Poinbœuf, Porcabœuf, Quilbœuf. Cf. the French local names Cordebœuf, Coulibœuf, Criquebœuf, Elbeuf, Elbœuf (L. Elbovium), and Quillebœuf, anciently Quilebeuf.

TURTLE. Same as Turtell, Thurtle, and Thyrtell, bishops of Hereford A. D. 688. Corrupted from Thurkle, Thorkell, Thorketell, Thorketil, Thurkettle, Thirkettle, O. N. Thorkell, Thorketill, and Thorketil, which Grimm thinks may be from the famous kettle which Thor captured from the giant Hymir for the gods to brew their beer in. Cf. the names Ashkettle, Asketell, O. N. Asketill, A. S. Oscytel.

TWADDLE. Bowditch says that in Philadelphia there are four families of Twaddell, and two of Twaddle. Doubtless a corruption of Tweedle, *q. v.*

TWEEDLE. A corruption of Tweedale, " dale of the Tweed."

TWICEADAY. See Singleday.

TWILIGHT, TWYLIGHT. From some local name componded of A. S. *leag*, a pasture. Cf. Fairlight, Hastings, properly Fairley or Farley = the sheep pasture.

TWINING. From Twining, a parish co. Gloucester.

TWOPENNY. See Halfpenny.

TWOPOTTS. Corrupted from Theobald. See Tippet.

U.

UGLY. From Ugley, a parish co. Essex, concerning which is the following proverb :—

> Ugley Church, Ugley Steeple,
> Ugley Parson, Ugley People.

But see LEGG.

UNCLE, UNCLES. Johannes le Uncle occurs in H. R.; but both these names may sometimes be derived from the Domesday Hunchil, and an O. G. Unculus, which are probably from G. *hunchild*, powerful warrior. See CHILD.

UNDERFINGER. This name, which is found in the U. S., is probably of German origin, and derived from locality. The A. S. *ing*, a meadow, among other forms in German, &c., is liable to become *ingen, ingr, ving, vingen, vingr, fing, fingen, fingr*. The termination *fingen* is very common in Southern Germany. Finger is found as a surname.

UNIT. See UNITE.

UNITE. The same as Unett, a family said to be of Norman Conquest origin. A Colonel Unett was killed at the assault of the Redan. Unett may be a diminutive of the name Hunn. Hun was a common name among the old Frisians (*Outzen, Gloss*) ; and Huna appears as the name of a manumitted serf in a chart, Cod. Dip. Ang.-Sax. Unn, Una, Hun, Hunn, Hunne, Unett, Unit, Unite are all found as U. S. names.

UNTHANK. From places so named in cos. Cumberland and Northumberland ; but perhaps originally from Unthank or Intack co. Elgin, which Carlisle translates " lonely," " solitary." There is however no such word in Gaelic. It may be from *uaigneach*, for *uaignidheach*, lonely, solitary, deserted ; or from *àite uaigneach*, a solitary place ; or perhaps from *innteach*, a way, road, gate.

. .

UPFILL. From Upwell, name of parishes cos. Norfolk and Cambridge, compounded of *ville*.

UPJOHN. From the Welsh name Apjohn, *i. e.* son of John. Hence, by further corruption, Applejohn.

URINE. The same as the Cornish name Euren, from Cornish *voren*, strange ; or a corruption of Uren, from the ancient personal name Urwyn, for Irvine ; from Irvine, a parish of Scotland, co. Ayr (formerly written Irwyn and Irwine), on the river Irvine. Urann, Urin are found as U. S. names.

UTTER. Same as Otter, *q. v.*

V.

VAST. From St. Vedast, Med. L. Vedastus, which is found corrupted to Vedasto, Vedaste, Vaast, Vast, and Waast. Vedast is Latinised from Foster, or from its root, the D. or Flem. *voedster*, a nurse, from *voeden*, to feed. In old deeds St. Vedast and Foster are synonymous ; and Butler, in his Lives of the Saints, says, "Our ancestors had a particular devotion to St. Vedast, whom they called St. Foster, as Camden takes notice in his Remains."

VENUS. As an English surname, doubtless the same as Veness, and the U. S. names Winas and Winaus ; perhaps from Venice. Under "Venus," Lower says, "De Venuse occurs as a surname, 31 Edw. I.—Step. de Venuse miles." Ferguson thinks Venus may be from the surname Venn and *house*, or *ness*, a promontory.

VERITY. This name and Varty are found both in England and the U. S. The original name was probably Varty, and is probably derived from some local name in France.

VERY, VERRY, VERREY. From Everard or Everhard ; from G. *eber-hard*, as strong as a boar (G. *eber*, A. S. *efor, efyr*, a boar). Hence the names Eber, Ever, Every. Again, from *ofor*, another A. S. form, we may sometimes have the name Over.

VESPER (U. S. Vesper, Vespre). The same as the Cornish name Vosper, Bosper (found Vospar, Vospur, Uspar); from Cornish *vos-ber*, the bare dwelling; or *bos-ver*, the great dwelling. There is a place called Trevosper near Launceston.

VESSEL, VESSELS. Same as Wessel, Wessell, Wessels; from Vesoul, a town of France, dep. H. Saône; or from Wesel, a town of Rhenish Prussia.

VEST. A corruption of Vast, *q. v.*

VICE. See VOICE.

VILE. From the name Viel; from O. Fr. *le viel*, the old. Lower says Vile is probably a corruption of the Fr. La Ville.

VINEGAR. The same as Winegar; from O. G. *win-ger*, very warlike; or the same as Weniger, from G. *weniger*, less. Wenige (G. *wenig*, little), Weniger, Winegar, Winger, and Vinegar are found in Bowditch.

VIPER (U. S. Wiper). This name is found in the New England Genealogical Register for April, 1845. Bowditch says "Mr. Bull Frog, not long since before the police-court, Cincinnati, probably adopted an alias for the occasion." Viper may be a corruption of Vibert, the Wibert of the Yorkshire Domesday, and the A. S. name Uibert (Cod. Dip. A. S., No. 523). It may also be from the French Vipont (Latinised De Veteri Ponte); from Vipont, near Lisieux, in Normandy. The names Viper, Vipond are found in Norfolk.

VIRGIL. Bowditch gives this as the name of a New York expressman. It is hardly from the classical name; but may be derived from Virgil, a township U. S., New York.

VIRTUE. From Vertus, in Champagne; or perhaps rather from Vertou, on the left bank of the Loire, nearly opposite to Nantes. Vertue is a French surname.

VOICE. The same as Voase, Voaz, Voce, Vos, Voss, Vossa, Voyce; from Cornish *vose*, a ditch, intrenchment, wall, fortification ; *vôz, vôza, foza, vose,* id.; *boza, bose,* an intrenchment ; *fôz, fôs,* a wall; from L. *fossa,* a ditch, moat, trench. Hence doubtless the name Vice.

VOWELL. Bowditch says of this name, " Our newspapers mention that a friend informed Dr. Barton that Mr. Vowell was dead. He said, ' Vowell dead? How glad I am that it is not *u* or *i* !' This anecdote is also mentioned by Lower, 1860. A Mr. Vowell was executed for a plot against Cromwell. His views were not *consonant* to those of the Protector." This name may be the same as Voel, Moel ; from root of Mole. Ferguson says Vowell, Vowles correspond with the G. and D. *vogel ;* and he derives Fuggel, Fuel, Fowell, Fowle from A. S. *fugel,* a fowl. But see FUEL.

VULGAR. The same as the U. S. Wulgar, our Woolgar, and the old name Wulfgar, which Ferguson connects with *wolf,* but which is rather from *ulf-ger,* very helping.

W.

WADDING. A probable patronymic of the name Wade. Waddingham, Waddington, and Waddingworth are found as local names in England ; and Waddington is also a surname.

WADDLE. The same as Waddell, a corruption of Wardell, Wardill, Wardle ; from Wardle or Wardhall co. Chester; or Wuerdale (Weardale) co. Lancaster.

WADLING. From some local name ending in *ing,* a meadow.

WAFER. The same as Wefer, Wiffer, Weber, Veber, Webber, Wheaver, Weever, Weaver (in H. R. Textor).

WAGER. " Wageoure is used by the Scotch poet Barbour for a mercenary soldier—one who fights for a ' wage ' or hire. Hence also Wageman " (Lower). Both Wager and Wagir are found as U. S. names, and Wager is the name of a large estuary or inlet of British North America.

WAGSTAFF, WAGSTAFFE (H. R. Waggestaff, Wagestaf).
The last syllable of this name is the A. S. *stede*, a place, station
(*locus, situs, statio, spatium*). Cf. the names Bickerstaff, Bickerstaffe, Eavestaff, Hackstaff, Halstaff, Halstead, Halsted, Hardstaff, Langstaffe, Longstaff.

WAIL. The same as Wale and De Wale, found in the ancient
records of Ireland. It may be derived from locality. But see
WHALE.

WAILING. A corruption of Waylen, Weland ; from the old
name Wayland, and Weland, the Vulcan of the North, which
Grimm thinks from O. N. *vél*, A. S. *wtl*, Eng. "wile," in the sense
of skill. Wayland is the appellation of a hundred in Norfolk.

WAINSCOAT. See COAT.

WAIST. See VAST.

WAIT, WAITE (H. R. Le Wayte) = watchman. See
Prompt. Parv.

WAKE. Found Wac and Le Wake. Archbishop Wake
thinks the name Le Wake, or the watchful, a title given to Hereward, who flourished under the Confessor, to describe his character as a skilful military commander. The name doubtless
means " the watchman." Cf. the surname Wakeman ; from A. S.
wœc-man, a watchman ; also Notes and Queries, 2nd S. vi. Wake
is the name of a country of the U. S., North America, in the
centre of North Carolina.

WALK. A corruption of the name Wallack.

WALKINGHAME. From some local name compounded of
ham, a dwelling. It was doubtless originally Walkingham.
Walkington is the name of a parish co. York, East Riding. Cf.
the surnames Allingham, Allengame ; Burlingham, Burlingame ;
from Burlingham, name of three parishes co. Norfolk. This may
account for the surname Game.

WALKLATE. A corruption of some local name compounded
of *ley*. Cf. Twilight.

WALKUP, WALKUPE. See HOPE.]

WALLET. 1. The same as Waylett. 2. A corruption of Willet. See QUILL, QUILT.

WALLFREE. A corruption of Walfrid; from G. *wal-frid*, powerful protector. Walfridus was the name of a saint, and also of a Count of Lombardy.

WALLOP. From Wallop, name of two parishes (Nether and Over) co. Hants; so called, says Camden, from Well-hop, that is, a pretty well in the side of a hill. But see HOPE.

WALNUT. A U. S. corruption of Woolnoth and the old name Wulfnoth, probably from *ulf-neid*, zealous in help; or *ulf-noth*, needing help. See NOTHARD.

WALTZ, WALZ. 1. Corrupted from Wallace, Walsh, or Walls. [Walls is the name of parishes of Scotland, cos. Orkney and Shetland.] 2. From Wallis or Valais, a canton of Switzerland. 3. From Wilz or Wiltz, a town of Dutch Luxemburg, on the Wilz. Waltz, Walz, Voltz are found in Bowditch.

WAND. From G. *wand*, a wall.

WANDER. See WONDER.

WANE. This name may be the same as Vane, Fane; from the Gael. *beagan*, little, W. *bechan*, *bychan*, Armor. *bihan*, Corn. *vean*. Cf. the Cornish names Vian, Veen.

WANT. In Essex a provincial word for a cross-road. Want, Wants, and Wantman are found in Bowditch.

WANTON. A Robertus Lascivus occurs in Domesday; but this name is rather corrupted from some local name ending in *ton*.

WARBOYS. Same as Worboys and the U. S. Worbose (which may some day become Verbose); from Verbois, near Rouen. See BOYS.

WARCUP. From Warcup, a parish in Westmoreland, perhaps compounded of A. S. *cop*, the head.

WARDLAW. From Wardlaw, an ancient parish of Scotland, co. Inverness. See LAW.

WARDROBE. The same as Wardrop, Wardroper, the keeper

K

of the wardrobe, an important office in royal and noble house-holds. Thom' de la Warderobe occurs in H. R. See Lower.

WARE. From Ware, a market town and parish co. Herts.

WARMAN. A corruption of Wermund, an ancient name which occurs in the Genealogy of the Kings of Mercia, another orthography of Garman. See GARMENT.

WARMER. A U. S. corruption of Walmer co. Kent.

WARN. The same as Warne, Wearne; from Cornish *guernen,* an alder-tree. According to Lower, Warne is a curt pronuncia-tion of Warren.

WARNING. There is a Mount Warning in New South Wales, East Australia; but this name is doubtless a patronymic of Warn. See WILLING.

WART. See WORTH.

WASTE. See VAST.

WATER, WATERS. Corrupted from the name Walter, Walters. It may also sometimes be from *at-the-water.*

WATERHAIR. The same name as Whithair and Whiter Jamieson renders the word whiter "one who whittles." Ash translates the old verb to whittle, "to make white by cutting, t‹ edge, to sharpen," and says it is retained in the Scotch dialect. The name Waterer may be the same as Waterhair.

WATERLOW. See LAW.

WAX. Same as Wex and Wix; from Wix, a parish co. Essex.

WAYGOOD. From some local name compounded of *wood.*

WEAK. Same as Week, *q. v.*

WEALTHY. A name found in Lower's Patronymica Bri-tannica; perhaps the same as the name Walthew, the last syllabl‹ of which may be from *deo, diu,* a confidant, servant. See SINGLE-DAY.

WEATHERWAX, WITHERWAX. A corruption o‹ Witherick's. See WHITEBREAD.

WEAVING. Formed like Winning, *q. v.*

WEBB, WEBBE (H. R. Le Webbe). From A. S. *webba*, a weaver. Hence Whip. Cf. the names Whipp, Whippy, Whippey, Whippo, Whipple, Whippell, Whippen, Whipping, Wipkin; the O. G. Wippo, Wippa, Wibi, Wivikin, Wipilo, and the Mod. G. Webe and Wibel.

WEDD. Same as Weed, *q. v.*

WEDLAKE. The last syllable is from *leag*, a meadow (See LEGG). Ferguson however gives an O. G. Widolaic, which he derives from *lác*, sport.

WEDLOCK. The same as Wedlake.

WEED. There is a Friesic Wéda; but Weed is more probably the same as Wade, in H. R. De Wade and De la Wade, and = Ford.

WEEK, WEEKES, WEEKS. From Week, name of parishes cos. Cornwall, Hants, and Somerset.

WEEKLY. See LEGG.

WEINGOTT. The same as the U. S. name Wingood, the inverse of Goodwin or Godwin.

WELFARE. Corrupted from the old name Wulpher, a personal name in Domesday. Cf. the names Wulfhard, Wulfhere, Wulfred. Wulfhard signifies strong in help (*ulf-hardt*).

WELFITT. This name would corrupt from Wolfhead. It may also be from the German name Wulfhard or Welfhard. See WELFITT.

WELLBORN, WELBORN, WELLBOURNE, WILLBOURN. From Welbourn co. Norfolk, Welbourne co. Lincoln, or Welburn co. York (see SMALLBONE). There is however an Old German Wilbern.

WELLDONE. The same as Weldon; from Weldon, name of a parish co. Northampton, and of a hamlet in the same parish.

WELLHOP. A corruption of Wallop, *q. v.*

WESTCOAT, variously Westcott, Wescott, Waiscott. From Westcote, a parish co. Gloucester. But see COAT.

WESTFALL. The same as Westfield; from Westfield, name

of parishes cos. Norfolk and Sussex; and also of several townships of the U. S., North America. Westfall and Westfield are both found in Bowditch.

WHALE. The same as the O. G. names Walo, Wala, O. N. Vali; from G. *wale*, A. S. *weal*, *walh*, a stranger; O. N. *vali*, id. The name Wale is traced in Irish records to the fourteenth century.

WHALEBONE. From some local name ending in *bourn* (See SMALLBONE). Lower says the hundred of Whalesbone co. Sussex is a corruption of Wellsbourne, which had its name from a stream which formerly traversed it.

WHARF, WHARFF, WHORF. Not from Wharf or Wharfe, the Yorkshire river; but the same as Waugh (sometimes pronounced Wharf), a Scottish orthography of *wall*. It appears that the Waughs held lands at Heip co. Roxburgh from the thirteenth to the seventeenth century.

WHARM. Same as Wharram; from Wharram, name of two parishes co. York, East Riding.

WHATMORE. The same as Watmore, Whitmore, Whittemore; from Whitmore or Whittimere, a parish co. Stafford.

WHEAL. Not from *wheal*, a pustule; but from Cornish *wheal* (*huel*), a work, *i. e.* a mine. It may also sometimes be the same as Weale, Weall; or Veal, Veale, in O. R. Le Veal, "the calf" (O. Fr.)

WHEAT. The word *wheat* is found in composition of several local names. As a surname it may be a corruption of White, or perhaps the same as Witt.

WHEATSHEAF. From some local name compounded of *shelf*, a sand-bank in the sea, or a rock, or ledge of rocks, rendering the water shallow and dangerous to ships.

WHEATSTONE. See WHETSTONE.

WHEEL. The same as Wheal.

WHEELOCK. 1. From Wheelock, name of townships co. Chester, and in Vermont, N. E. Montpelier. 2. Same as Whellock, Whelock, Wellock, Willock; from Will, William.

WHELPS, WELP. From Guelf, a German corruption of Wolf, Wulf; from *wolf*, a wolf.

WHERRY. Probably another orthography of Very, *q. v.*

WHETHER. Bowditch says, among the arrivals in Boston October 19th, 1860, is that of Mr. Whether, of Haverhill. A corruption of the name Wether, found in Wethersfield or Wetherfield, a parish co. Essex. See MERRYWEATHER.

WHETSTONE. From Whetstone, name of places in cos. Derby, Leicester, and Middlesex. Hence, by corruption, Wheatstone. See SMALSTONE.

WHILE. From While, a parish of England, co. Hereford.

WHIMPER. Same as the U. S. Whymper and Winpress, and the English names Wimperis, Winepress; from Winibert, Winiberts = illustrious in war.

WHIP. See WEBB.

WHIPPING. See WEBB.

WHIRLPENNY. See PENNY.

WHISKER. The same as Wiskar, Wisker, the ancient names Wisgar, Wiscar, and O. G. Wiscard, Viscard; corrupted from Visigardus, which Wachter renders hortus belli Ducum. Visigardus was the name of a daughter of Theodebert, king of the Franks, wife of Gregory of Tours.

WHIST. This name may be the same as Wish, Whish, which Ferguson makes to correspond with the O. N. Osk, and the G. Wunsch. He says Osk, Wunsch, and Wish represent respectively the Scandinavian, the H. G., and the L. G. forms of Oski, a title of Odin. It is however more probably a corruption of the name West. Cf. the local names Wiston, Wistow, Whiston, Whistons, Whistley, in all which the first syllable is doubtless derived from "west."

WHITE. This name may not always be from fairness of complexion (A. S. *hwit*); but, as Mr. Akerman suggests, it may sometimes be from A. S. *hwita*, a sharpener, swordsmith, or armourer. White is the name of several counties of the U. S., North America.

WHITEBOON. Same as Whitbourne; from Whitbourne, a parish co. Hereford; Whitburn, a parish co. Durham; or Whitburn or Whiteburn, a parish of Scotland, co Linlithgow.

WHITEBREAD. The same as Whitbread; corrupted from the ancient name Whitberht, which might translate "very distinguished."

WHITECAR. Same as Whitaker or Whittaker; from Whitacre, name of two parishes co. Warwick; or same as Wihtgar, name of the nephew of Cerdic, king of the West Saxons, which Ferguson derives from *wiht*, a man or a warrior.

WHITEFOOT. Same as Whiteford (and perhaps Whitford), said to be from Whitefoord co. Renfrew, Scotland. Whiteford is the name of a parish of North Wales, co. Flint. But see HAZLE-FOOT.

WHITEGIFT. Same as Whitgift; from Whitgift, a parish co. York, West Riding.

WHITEHEAT. A U. S. corruption of Whitehead.

WHITEHORSE. Corrupted from Whitehouse; from Whitehouse, a village in the parish of Tough, co. Aberdeen. There is also Whitehouse Abbey, a village of Ireland, Ulster.

WHITEKIND. The name of one of the principal chiefs of the Saxons in their war against Charlemagne. Some render it "white child;" but it was originally written Witikindus, which would translate, "very celebrated or known." We have still a Wittekind.

WHITELAW. See WHITLOW.

WHITELEGG. The same as Whiteley, Whitely, Whittley, Whitlie, Whitley; from Whitley, name of places in cos. Berks, Chester, Northumberland, Salop, Somerset, and York; from A. S. *hwit-leag*, the white meadow. But see LEGG.

WHITELOCK, variously Whitelocke, Whitlock. See LEGG.

WHITELY. See WHITELEGG and LEGG.

WHITEROD. See WHITETHREAD.

WHITESIDE. See SIDE.

WHITETHREAD. A name found in Lower's Appendix. Same as Whiterod, from some such O. G. name as Withred ; from *weit-rat*, distinguished counsellor. Cf. the name Witherick, and the O G. Widerich.

WHITING. From A. S. *hwít-ing*, the white meadow. But see WILLING.

WHITLOW, WHITELOW. From A. S. *hwít-hlaw*, the white heap, barrow, or small hill. See LAW. The inflammation called whitlow is said to be derived from *hwít-low*, a white flame.

WHITTLE, WITTLE. Not from the small pocket-knife (A. S. *hwitel, hwitle*); but from Whittle, name of several townships of England, in cos. Derby, Lancaster, and Northumberland; corrupted from Whitley. See WHITELEGG.

WHY. A name found in the Registrar-General's List. It seems to be corrupted from Wy, Gui, Guy (whence Wyat, Wyatt, Wyot, Wiatt, Guyot, Guiot, Wyon, Guyon, Wiart) ; formed from William.

WICK. From Wick, name of places cos. Caithness, Gloucester, and Somerset ; from *wic, wick*, a village, from A. S. *wic, wyc*. Wick, Wicke, Wickes, Wicks, are found as surnames.

WICKWIRE. A U. S. name. Same as the English name Wickwar; from Wickwar co. Gloucester.

WIDOWS. Same as Widowson; from the O. G. name Widow. Lower renders Widowson, the son of Guido or Wido, a Norman personal name; and he says that at the time of the great Survey, William Filius Widonis, literally " William Wido's son," was a tenant-in-chief in the counties of Wilts, Gloucester, and Somerset.

WIFE, WIFFE. Same as Wiffer, Wefer, Wafer, all found in Bowditch. See WAFER.

WIG. See WIGG.

WIGFALL. From some local name ending in *ville*.

WIGG, WIGGS. 1. From O. G. *wig*, strong, warlike, a soldier, &c. ; A. S. *wig* war, *wiga* warrior ; O. N. *vig* war, *vigr* warlike. Wig, says Lower, occurs in the ancestry of Cerdic, king of the West Saxons; and Wiga is found in the Domesday of Yorkshire. 2. Same as Wick, Wicks, *q. v.*

WILDBORE. Same as Wilboar, Wilbor, Wilbur, Wilber, Wilbar, all found as U. S. names; from Wilbert = very illustrious.

WILDGOOSE. The same as Wilgoss, Willgoss, the O. G. Willigis and Wilgis, and the A. S. Wilgis, a name which occurs in the genealogy of the Northumbrian kings. It might translate very warlike, or very strong, from *fil*, much, full; *gais*, a spear; from the Gael. *gais*, *geis*, a weapon peculiar to the old Gauls, whence the L. *gæsum*, Gr. γαισος, a weapon; Gael. *gaisge*, valor; *gaisgeach*, a hero.

WILKS. From Wilkins, a patronymic of Will, for William.

WILKSHIRE. A corruption of Wiltshire.

WILL. From William.

WILLING. 1. A corruption of Willan, a diminutive of Will, for William. 2. A patronymic of Will, or compounded of *ing*, a meadow. Cf. the names Bedding, Billing, Browning, Bunting, Chatting, Cutting, Dining, Dowsing, Dunning, Fanning, Hemming, Living, Manning, Spilling, Tapping, Tilling, Topping, Whiting. See also WINNING.

WILT. A corruption of Willet. See QUILT.

WILY. From Wily, a parish co. Wilts. Wiley, Wilye, Wyllie, Wyleigh are found as surnames.

WIMBLE. Perhaps the same as Whimple, from Whimple, a parish co. Devon; or a corruption of the name Winibald. Cf. the local names Wimbledon and Wimpole.

WINBOLT. From some local name compounded of *bolt*. See BOTTLE.

WINCH. 1. From Vincent. Hence doubtless the name Finch. 2. From Winch, name of two parishes (East and West) co. Norfolk.

WINDARD. See HAZARD.

WINDOW, WINDOWE. Ferguson gives an O. G. Windó, which Förstemann refers to the name of the people, the Wends.

These names may however be from locality, perhaps from some such name as Windhaugh or Windhow. There is a place in Russia called Windau or Vindau.

WINDUST. For Windus; perhaps originally Windhurst. Cf. Lindus, from Lyndhurst.

WINE. From O. G. *win*, which signifies not only a friend and beloved, but also war. Wachter renders Winipreht, "amicus clarus;" Winfridus, "defensor amicorum;" Truotwin, "fidelis amicus." Hence the names Sauerwein, Sourwine, Lightwine, Winehart, Winegar. See VINEGAR.

WINEHART. See WINE.

WINEMAN. The same as Winmen and Winemen, Cod. Dip. No. 853; from O. G. *win-mund*, which would translate both a protector in war and a warrior.

WINEPRESS. See WHIMPER.

WINFARTHING. From Winfarthing co. Norfolk.

WING. From WING or Winge, a parish co. Bucks; or Wing, a parish co. Rutland.

WINGOOD. The same as Winwood; from some local name compounded of *wood*.

WINKLE. The same as Wincle; from Wincle, a township and chapelry co. Chester; or from Winkel in the Duchy of Nassau; from A. S. *wincel*, G. *winkle*, a corner (D. *winkel*, a shop, workshop, or laboratory). Cf. the surnames Wincles, Aldwincle, Bullwincle, Dallwinkle, Gansewinkel (goose), Schöpwinkel.

WINLOCK. From Wenlock co. Salop. See LEGG.

WINNING. From some local name ending in *ing*, a meadow. Cf. the names Goring, Grayling, Healing, Jutting, Nutting, Salting, Selling, Shilling, Spiking, Stebbing, Tarring, Tinkling, Tipping, Turning. See also WILLING.

WINPENNY. See PENNY.

WINSHIP. The termination *ship* in many names is a corruption of *lordship*.

WINSHOT. From some local name compounded of *holt*, or the D. *hout* (see RUSHOUT). Winschoten is the name of a town of the Netherlands.

WINSLOW. From Winslow, a parish and market town co. Bucks; or Winslow, a township co. Hereford. But see ONSLOW and LAW.

WINTER. Winter was the name of one of the companions of the Anglo-Saxon Hereward, and Winter and Sommer are both German and modern Danish names. Ferguson thinks Summer and Winter derived from the personification of these seasons in Northern mythology. Others derive Summer and Winter from Sumner and Vintner, and there is the name Vinter.

WINTERBORN, WINTERBOURNE. From Winterbourn, name of many places in cos. Dorset, Gloucester, and Wilts.

WINTERBOTTOM. See BOTTOM

WIPER. See VIPER.

WIRE, WIRES. The same as Weir, said to be the same as De Vere, considered to be of Norman origin; from the parish and château of Ver, dep. La Manche; by others thought from Veer, a town of the Netherlands, prov. Zeeland, on the coast of the island Walcheren.

WISDOM. From Wisdom in the parish of Cornwood co. Devon. "Matthew Hele, of Holwell co. Devon, was high sheriff of the county the year of Charles the Second's Restoration, 1660, and so numerous and influential were the family that he was enabled to assemble a grand jury *all of his own name and blood*, gentlemen of estate and quality, which made the judge observe, when he heard Hele of Wisdom, Esq., called—a gentill seat in the parish of Cornwood—'that he thought they must all be descended from Wisdom, in that they had acquired such considerable fortunes.' "—Burke's Ext. Barts.

WITCH. A corruption of the name Wich, Wiche, Wyche. It has been considered that, as the vocable *wich* enters into composition of names of places where salt is found, as in Droitwich,

Nantwich, Northwich, that it must mean a salt-mine. It comes from *wic*, *wick*, a village. See WICK.

WITCRAFT. Same as Whitcraft, Withcraft, Wheatcroft, which explains itself. But see CRAFT.

WITH. According to some, *with* signifies a forest or wood, from O. N. *vidr*, Goth. *vidus;* according to others it is corrupted from *worth*, q. v. *With*, *wath* are often met with in composition of local names, as Langwith, Darwath. Whit. Craven (422) renders *with*, *wath*, a fold. The W. *gwydd* is trees, and *gwyth* a channel, drain. Ferguson gives With as a Mod. G. name, which he connects with an O. G. Wido.

WITHCRAFT. See WITCRAFT.

WITT. The Domesday Wit, Uuit, Uite. The same as White.

WITTY, WHITTY. Ferguson considers Whitty as a diminutive of White. Lower says in ancient times witty meant clever, sagacious. Vitte, Vitté are found as French surnames.

WONDER. This and Wunder and Wander are found in Bowditch, and Wonders occurs in the Registrar-General's List. These names are probably of German origin. Wandersleben is the appellation of a market town in Prussian Saxony, and is also a surname; and Wander is the name of a celebrated German author. There is also a village and commune of Belgium, prov. Liége, named Wandre.

WOODCOCK. See COCK.

WOODCRAFT. Same as Woodcroft. See CRAFT.

WOODEN, WOODIN. This name has been connected with Odin or Woden. It is more probably derived from Wooden, in the parish of Kelso, co. Roxburgh.

WOODFALL. From Woodfall, a hamlet in South Wilts; a corruption of Woodville. See GOODWILL.

WOODFINE. Same as the Lincolnshire name Woodbine; or a corruption of Goodwine, Goodwin, *q. v.*

WOODFULL. Same as Woodfall, *q. v.*

WOODHÉAD. From Woodhead, a chapelry co. Chester.

WOODNOT. Probably from some local name compounded of *knot*, a cluster.

WOODNUTT. The same as Woodnot, *q. v.*

WOODROUGH. The same as Woodroff, Woodroffe, Woodrooffe, Woodroofs, Woodruff, Woodruffe, Woodriff, Woodrove, Woodrow; from wood-reeve, *i. e.* a wood or forest bailiff.

WOODROVE. See WOODROUGH.

WOOF. A corruption of Wolf, Wolff, Woolf, Woolfe; or from the O. G. Uffo, Offo, and Uffa or Wuffa, name of a king of East Anglia. Hence no doubt the name Hoof.

WOOL, WOOLL. 1. A corruption of Will, for William. 2. From Wool, a parish of England, co. Dorset. "About Langport, co. Somerset, are persons of the labouring class who are commonly called Wooll, but they say that their real old name is Attwooll, probably a corruption of At-Wold. Inform. W. B. Paul, Esq." (Lower).

WOOLARD, WOOLLARD. See HAZARD.

WOOLCOCK. See COCK.

WOOLFORD. From Woolford, a parish and a township co. Warwick, doubtless named from some stream called the Wool; from *ol*, *al*, frequently found in local names, and signifying "water." Woolford may also sometimes be corrupted from the old German name Waldfrid.

WOOLY. The same as Wooley, Woolley; from Wooley, a chapelry in the parish of Royston co. York, North Riding; or Woolley, a parish co. Huntingdon. Lower says Woolley, Wooley was anciently written Wolflege and Wolveley, *i. e.* Anglo-Saxonicè '*wulfes-leag*,' a district abounding in wolves, the name of many localities in Saxon times. See also LEGG.

WORD, WORDE. From Worth or Word, a parish co. Kent.

WORKNOT. Derived like Woodnot, *q. v.*

WORLD. Corrupted from the O. G. name Worald; from *wer-alt*, which will translate both "noble man" and "noble in battle." Worldham is the name of two parishes co. Hants.

WORM. Perhaps the same as Wharm, *q. v.*

WORMS. This name has been derived from A. S. *wurm*, Eng. *worm*, a serpent; O. N. *ormr*, Dan. *orm*, whence it is said we have Orme. It is rather from Worms, the celebrated German city.

WORN. Perhaps the same as Warn, *q. v.*

WORST, WURST. Most probably the same as the D. name Van Voorst; from *vorst*, a prince; or from Vorst, a village of Rhenish Prussia.

WORT. See WORTH.

WORTH, WORTHY. These names are from A. S. *worth*, *worthig*, *weorthig*, *wurthig*, a field, portion of land, a farm, manor, an estate, also a street, public way (vicus, platea). Wort is the name of parishes cos. Kent and Dorset. Hence doubtless the names Wart, Wort, Warts, Worts, and the compound names Foxworth, Larkworthy, &c.

WORTHMAN, WORTMAN. This name may mean the keeper of a farm or manor. See WORTH.

WORTHY. See WORTH.

WORTHYLAKE. From Wortley, name of a township and of a chapelry co. York, West Riding. See LEGG.

WOULD. Same as the name Wold, which Lower renders an unwooded hill.

WOULDHAVE. The name of a boat-builder on the banks of the Tyne in 1790 (Lond. Quar. Rev., July, 1858). This name is also found written Woodhave, and is doubtless from some local name compounded of *wood* and *haw*, *haugh*, enclosed land, a small field; in Chaucer, a dale; from A. S. *haga*, *hagen*, a hay, hedge, meadow. Woodhay is the name of parishes cos. Berks and Hants.

WREN. From Rheims or Reims, a city of France, dep. Marne; or Rennes dep. Ille-et-Vilaine. But see RAIN.

WRENCH. This name is said to be a corruption of Olerenshaw, which first became Renshaw, and then Rench and Wrench. See Lower, quoting Rev. J. Eastwood. It may sometimes be from a different source, being found in H. R. without prefix.

WRINKLE. From some local name (perhaps Ringley co. Lancaster) ending in *ley*. Cf. Acle for Acley, "oak ley," &c.

WRITE. Same as Wright.

WYNDEBEARD. A Dr. Wyndebeard was buried in Westminster Abbey. This name is without doubt a corruption of the O. G. Winbert; from *win-bert,* illustrious warrior. Cf. the names Winibald, Winiram, &c.

Y.

YEA. The same as the ancient Devonshire family Yeo, which C. S. Gilbert derives from Tre-yeo, in the parish of Lancells. Yeo is probably corrupted from Hugh. See You.

YEARLY. From some local name compounded of *ley*. See Legg.

YELL. Perhaps from Yell, name of one of the Shetland Isles.

YELLOW. This name is probably the same as Jolley, Jolly, Joly, Jelley, Jelly, Jelliff, Joliffe, Jolliffe, Jolliff, Iliff, Iliffe, Eylif, Jelf, Yelf, Ayliffe, Ayliff, Auliffe, Ayloffe, Aylove, Aloph, Aloof; all doubtless corrupted from Adolphus. I am confirmed in this last by Wright (in his History of Essex, vol. ii. 443, note), who says, "The ancient Saxon family of Ayloffe was seated in Bocton or Boughton parish, hundred of Eythorne, near the Wye, in Kent, of which town´ they were possessors in the time of Henry the Third. The name Aloph was given to this town from having been anciently under the jurisdiction of Adolphus."

YESTERDAY. See SINGLEDAY. Yester is found as the name of a parish co. Haddington.

YIELDING, YEILDING. From Yielden, a parish co. Beds.

YOU. A corruption of Hugh; from the D. *hoog*, tall. Hence probably the names Yoh, Yoe, Yeo, Yew, Yaw.

YOUNGLOVE. See LAW.

YOUNGMAY. See MAY.

Z.

ZEAL. From Zeal-Monachorum, a parish co. Devon; from L. *cella*, Gael. *cill*, a burying-ground, cell, chapel, grave; in local names in Ireland and Scotland, *kill*, *kil*.

A SELECT LIST

OF

PECULIAR SURNAMES.*

A.

Able.
Ablewhite.
About.
Ace.
Achates.
Ache.
Achilles.
Acorn.
Addlehead.
Adwers.
Agate.
Ages.
Agent.
Agin.
Ague.
Agutter.
Ahem.
Ailman.
Air.
Airy.
Akid.
Akin.
Akyng.
Alabaster.
Aldwine.
Ale.

Alecock.
Alefounder.
Alehouse.
Aleman.
Ales.
Alfoot.
Allbee.
Allblaster.
Allbones.
Allbright.
Allcard.
Allcock.
Allcorn.
Allengame.
Alley.
Allfree.
Allgood.
Allman.
Allnut.
Allpenny.
Allport.
Allpress.
Allso.
Allsupt.
Alltrew.
Allward.
Allwater.
Allwright.
Alm.

Alman.
Almond.
Alms.
Aloe.
Alone.
Aloof.
Alp.
Alpenny.
Alpha.
Alshop.
Alsobrook.
Alsop.
Alter.
Alway.
Always.
Alwell.
Alwin.
Amber.
Ambers.
Ambleman.
Ambler.
Ambush.
Amen.
Amend.
Amiss.
Ammon.
Amor.
Amour.
Ampleman.

Anchor.
And.
Anders.
Angel.
Anger.
Angle.
Anguish.
Annis.
Anser.
Antcliffe.
Ante.
Antill.
Antler.
Anvil.
Ape.
Apedaile.
Apple.
Applebee.
Applegate.
Applejohn.
Appleman.
Apostles.
Aram.
Arblaster.
Arbuckle.
Arch.
Archbold.
Archever.
Ardent.

---

* Compiled from the Registrar-General's List, Bowditch's Suffolk (America) Surnames, Lower's Patronymica Britannica, &c. &c.

L

Areskin.	Aub.	Bagley.	Barebones.
Argue.	Auger.	Bagshaw.	Barefoot.
Argument.	Augur.	Bagwell.	Barehard.
Aries.	Augurs.	Bail.	Barehead.
Arm.	Avant,	Baird.	Barge.
Arms.	Avis.	Bairnsfather.	Bargy.
Armour.	Awe.	Bakanas.	Bark.
Arrand.	Awkward.	Bake.	Barker.
Arrow.	Awl.	Bakeover.	Barley.
Art.	Axe.	Bakewell.	Barlicorn.
Artery.	Axel.	Balaam.	Barnacle.
Artist.	Axman.	Bald.	Barndollar.
Asbone.	Axup.	Baldhead. `	Barnfather.
Ascough.	Ayde.	Baldry.	Bar-quarrel.
Ash.		Baldgrave.	Barrable.
Ashbee.		Bale.	Barrell.
Ashbolt.	**B.**	Bales.	Barren.
Ashenbottom.		Balk.	Barringdollar.
Ashconner.		Balkwill.	Barrow.
Ashcraft.	Baa.	Ball.	Barrows.
Ashes.	Bab.	Ballance.	Barter.
Ashforth.	Babb.	Ballasty.	Barters.
Ashman.	Babcock.	Ballingall.	Barwig.
Ashpart.	Babel.	Ballman.	Base.
Ashplant.	Babler.	Balls.	Basin.
Ashpole.	Baby.	Balm.	Bask.
Ashport.	Bacchus.	Balsam.	Basket.
Ashwin.	Back.	Baltic.	Bastard.
Ask.	Backer.	Banchor.	Batch.
Asker.	Backerman.	Band.	Batchelor.
Askew.	Backman.	Bandy.	Bate.
Askin.	Backoff.	Bane.	Bathcake.
Ashkettle.	Backshell.	Banes.	Batman.
Aslock.	Backup.	Bang.	Bathomeal.
Asp.	Bacon.	Banger.	Batt.
Aspen.	Bad.	Bangs.	Batten.
Aspland.	Badcock.	Banish.	Batter.
Ass.	Badgent.	Banner.	Batterbury.
Assman.	Badger.	Bans.	Batterman.
Astrap.	Badham.	Bantam.	Batterton.
Astray.	Badlam.	Bar.	Battery.
Atcock.	Badland.	Barbary.	Batting.
Atkey.	Badman.	Barcave.	Battle.
Atkiss.	Bag.	Barclay.	Battles.
Attack.	Baggs.	Bard.	Bawler.
Atwill.	Bagless.	Bare.	Baxtux.

Bay.	Bibbler.	Blaze.	Bolster.
Beach.	Bible.	Bleach.	Bolt.
Beacon.	Bidder.	Bleak.	Bolter.
Beadle.	Biddy.	Blear.	Bond.
Beads.	Bidwell.	Bless.	Bone.
Beagle.	Biffin.	Blest.	Bones.
Beak.	Biggerstaff.	Blew.	Bonfellow.
Beam.'	Bigod.	Blight.	Bonnechose.
Beams.	Bigot.	Blind.	Bonnemot.
Bean.	Bilke.	Blinker.	Bonnet.
Bear.	Bill.	Bliss.	Bonny.
Bearblock.	Billet.	Blithe.	Bonus.
Beard.	Billiard.	Block.	Boobyer.
Beardman.	Billman.	Blood.	Boocock.
Beatman.	Billow.	Bloodgood.	Book.
Beau.	Bills.	Bloodworth.	Booker.
Beaver.	Bin.	Bloom.	Bookstore.
Bedbug.	Binder.	Bloomer.	Boom.
Bedgood.	Bindloose.	Bloomy.	Boon.
Bedlock.	Birchard.	Blossom.	Boor.
Bedwell.	Bird.	Blot.	Boot.
Bee.	Birds.	Blow.	Bootman.
Beech.	Birdseye.	Blower.	Boots.
Been.	Births.	Blue.	Booty.
Beer.	Bishop.	Blues.	Bore.
Beet.	Bitch.	Blueman.	Born.
Beetle.	Bitter.	Blunder.	Borrow.
Begin.	Bitters.	Blunt.	Bos.
Belch.	Bitterwolf.	Blush.	Bosh.
Bell.	Blackadder.	Board.	Bosom.
Bellaw.	Blackamore.	Boardwine.	Bosquet.
Bellows.	Blackbird.	Boat.	Boss.
Belt.	Blacklaw.	Boatman.	Botfish.
Benbow.	Blackleak.	Bobbin.	Both.
Bench.	Blacklock.	Bobby.	Bottle.
Bend.	Blackman.	Bocock.	Bottles.
Bender.	Blackmonster.	Bodfish.	Bottom.
Bending.	Blackstaff.	Bodily.	Boucock.
Benison.	Blade.	Bodkin.	Bough.
Bentwright.	Blague.	Body.	Boughtwhore.
Besom.	Blank.	Bogg.	Boulder.
Best.	Blankenship.	Bogy.	Bouncer.
Betty.	Blanket.	Boil.	Bound.
Bias.	Blankman.	Boils.	Bounty.
Bibb.	Blare.	Boisson.	Bouquet.
Bibber.	Blast.	Bold.	Bow.

Bowel.
Bowels.
Bower.
Bowl.
Bowling.
Box.
Boxer.
Boy.
Boys.
Brace.
Bragg.
Braid.
Brain.
Brains.
Brake.
Bramble.
Bran.
Branch.
Branchflower.
Brand.
Brandish.
Brandy.
Brass.
Brassbridge.
Bratt.
Bravo.
Brawn.
Bray.
Bread.
Breake.
Breaker.
Breakspear.
Breakwell.
Bream.
Bredcake.
Breed.
Breeding.
Breeze.
Briars.
Brick.
Bridal.
Bride.
Bridecake.
Bridle.
Bright.
Brightman.

Brim.
Brimmer.
Brine.
Brink.
Brisk.
Brittle.
Broach.
Broadbelt.
Broadfoot.
Broadhead.
Broom.
Brother.
Brow.
Brownbill.
Brownjohn.
Brownsword.
Bruin.
Bruise.
Brunt.
Brush.
Bub.
Buck.
Buckett.
Buckle.
Buckles.
Buckthought.
Bud.
Budge.
Buff.
Buffet.
Bugbee.
Bugbird.
Bugg.
Buggin.
Buggy.
Buglehorne.
Bulcock.
Bulflower.
Bulk.
Bulky.
Bull.
Bulled.
Bullet.
Bulley.
Bullock.
Bullpit.

Bullwinkle.
Bultitude.
Bumside.
Bun.
Bunch.
Bundle.
Bunflower.
Burden.
Burke.
Burlingame.
Burn.
Burnish.
Bush.
Bushel.
Buskin.
Buss.
Butt.
Butter.
Butterfield.
Butterfly.
Butters.
Buttery.
Button.
Buzzard.
Buzzy.
By.
Bye.
Bygod.

C.

Cabbage.
Cable.
Cad.
Caddy.
Caffre.
Cage.
Cain.
Cake.
Cakebread.
Calf.
Call.
Callard.
Callman.

Calvary.
Came.
Camel.
Camomile.
Can.
Candell.
Candor.
Cannon.
Cannot.
Cant.
Canter.
Cantwell.
Cap.
Cape.
Capes.
Capon.
Capp.
Caps.
Capstick.
Caravan.
Card.
Care.
Careless.
Caress.
Caret.
Cargo.
Carp.
Carriage.
Carrier.
Carrott.
Cart.
Carve.
Carver.
Case.
Cash.
Cashdollar.
Cashman.
Cashmere.
Cast.
Castor.
Cat.
Catchaside.
Catchasides.
Catchlove.
Catchpole.
Cate.

Cates.	Cheers.	Clay.	Comer.
Catharine.	Chess.	Claypole.	Comet.
Cato.	Cheese.	Clean.	Comfort.
Cats.	Cheeseman.	Clear.	Comly.
Cattle.	Cheesewright.	Cleave.	Commander.
Caudle.	Chequer.	Cleverly.	Common.
Caught.	Cherry.	Cliff.	Commons.
Caul.	Cherryman.	Clink.	Concete.
Caulk.	Chesnut.	Clinker.	Conduit.
Caulking.	Chessman.	Clipp.	Cone.
Cause.	Chest.	Clitter.	Congo.
Cavalier.	Chew.	Cloak.	Conn.
Cave.	Chick.	Clock.	Conquest.
Caw.	Chicken.	Clodd.	Conscience.
Caws.	Chicks.	Clogg.	Constance.
Cease.	Child.	Close.	Constant.
Ceider.	Children.	Clothier.	Content.
Cent.	Chillman.	Cloud.	Convey.
Center.	Chin.	Clout.	Convoy.
Centlivre.	Chine.	Clover.	Coo.
Centre.	Chip.	Club.	Cook.
Chace.	Chipchase.	Clutterbuck.	Cookworthy.
Chafer.	Chipman.	Coal.	Cool.
Chaff.	Chisel.	Coalman.	Coon.
Chalice.	Chisels.	Coat.	Coop.
Chalk.	Choice.	Cobb.	Coot.
Challenger.	Christ.	Cobbledick.	Cop.
Challice.	Christian.	Cockeye.	Cope.
Chance.	Christmas.	Cockle.	Copper.
Chant.	Chub.	Codd.	Copperwheat.
Chap.	Chuck.	Code.	Cord.
Chaplain.	Church.	Codex.	Corderoy.
Charge.	Churchyard.	Codling.	Cork.
Charity.	Circuit.	Coffee.	Corn.
Charley.	Citizen.	Coffin.	Corner.
Chart.	City.	Coil.	Corns.
Chase.	Civil.	Coke.	Corpse.
Chataway.	Clack.	Cold.	Cost.
Chatfish.	Clad.	Coldman.	Cosey.
Chatt.	Clam.	Colepepper.	Costard.
Chaunter.	Clan.	Collar.	Cot.
Cheap.	Clap.	Collarbone.	Cotton.
Check.	Clapper.	Collick.	Couch.
Cheek.	Claret.	Colt.	Councillor.
Cheeks.	Clash.	Comb.	Counsell.
Cheer.	Clasp.	Combs.	Couplet.

Courage.
Course.
Courtier.
Cousin.
Cover.
Coward.
Cow.
Cowhorn.
Cowl.
Cowstick.
Coy.
Crab.
Crabtree.
Crack.
Crackbone.
Crackles.
Cracklin.
Cracknell.
Craft.
Cram.
Cramp.
Crane.
Crank.
Craven.
Craw.
Craze.
Creak.
Cream.
Creed.
Creeper.
Cress.
Cribb.
Crickett.
Crier.
Crime.
Crimp.
Crisp.
Crispin.
Croak.
Crochet.
Crone.
Crook.
Crop.
Cross.
Crosscup.
Crossman.

Crotch.
Crow.
Crowd.
Crowfoot.
Crown.
Crucifix.
Crude.
Cruikshanks.
Cruise.
Crumb.
Crumpler.
Crush.
Crust.
Crutch.
Cryer.
Cube.
Cuckoo.
Cud.
Cuddy.
Cuff.
Cull.
Culpepper.
Cumber.
Cupper.
Curd.
Cure.
Curius.
Curl.
Curly.
Curr.
Currant.
Cursin.
Curtain.
Cushion.
Cuss.
Custard.
Cutbill.
Cute.
Cutforth.
Cutlove.
Cutmutton.
Cutright.
Cutting.
Cuttle.
Cutts.

D.

Dab.
Dabbs.
Dace.
Dadd.
Daft.
Dagger.
Daily.
Dainty.
Dairy.
Dais.
Daisy.
Dally.
Dam.
Dame.
Damon.
Damp.
Damper.
Damson.
Dance.
Dancer.
Dandy.
Danger.
Dare.
Dark.
Darling.
Dart.
Dash.
Date.
Dates.
Daub.
Daughters.
Daunt.
Daw.
Dawber.
Dawn.
Day.
Daybell.
Dayfoot.
Dayman.
Deadman.
Dearman.
Deal.

Dealing.
Dealchamber.
Dear.
Dearlove.
Dearth.
Death.
Decent.
Deck.
Deed.
Deeds.
Deer.
Deeprose.
Delf.
Delves.
Demon.
Deo.
Desert.
Desire.
Dessert.
Deuce.
Devil.
Dew.
Dial.
Dialogue.
Diamond.
Diaper.
Dibble.
Dieu.
Diggory.
Digweed.
Dike.
Dilly.
Dine.
Dines.
Dingy.
Dining.
Dinn.
Dinning.
Diprose.
Dirk.
Distill.
Ditch.
Dito.
Divan.
Diver.
Dives.

Dobbin.
Dodge.
Doe.
Doer.
Dole.
Doll.
Dollar.
Dolphin.
Dolt.
Dominey.
Don.
Done.
Doo.
Doolittle.
Dott.
Dotts.
Double.
Doubleday.
Doublet.
Doubt.
Doubtfire.
Douce.
Dough.
Dove.
Dowdy.
Dower.
Down.
Downwards.
Downy.
Dowse.
Doxey.
Doze.
Dozy.
Drabble.
Dragon.
Drain.
Drake.
Dram.
Drape.
Drawbridge.
Drawwater.
Dray.
Dredge.
Dresser.
Drewmilk.
Drink.

Drinkard.
Drinkdregs.
Drinker.
Drinkmilk.
Drinkwater.
Dripps.
Droop.
Drought.
Drown.
Drudge.
Drum.
Dry.
Ducat.
Duck.
Duckling.
Dudgeon.
Dulhumphry.
Dull.
Dullard.
Dulled.
Duly.
Dumbell.
Duel.
Dun.
Duncalf.
Dunnakin.
Dunner.
Dunning.
Duns.
Dupe.
Dust.
Duty.
Dye.

E.

Eager.
Eagle.
Early.
Earth.
Earthy.
Earwaker.
Earwhisper.
Earwig.

Earwiger.
Easy.
Eatwell.
Eddy.
Eels.
Egg.
Eggbeer.
Eggs.
Ego.
Eighteen.
Element.
Ell.
Elms.
Emblem.
Emmet.
End.
Enough.
Ermine.
Err.
Esse.
Essence.
Eve.
Even.
Eveness.
Everhard.
Every.
Evil.
Ewe.
Excell.
Expence.
Eye.
Eyes.

F.

Fable.
Face.
Facer.
Faddy.
Fagg.
Fail.
Fain.
Faint.
Fair.

Fairbairn.
Fairbeard.
Fairbones.
Fairborn.
Fairchild.
Faircloth.
Fairest.
Fairfeather.
Fairfield.
Fairfoot.
Fairfoul.
Fairhead.
Fairlamb.
Fairly.
Fairman.
Fairmanners.
Fairplay.
Fairs.
Fairservice.
Fairtitle.
Fairweather.
Fairwheater.
Fairy.
Faith.
Faithful.
Fall.
Fallow.
Fame.
Fancy.
Fanning.
Fardle.
Fare.
Farewell.
Farman.
Farming.
Farthing.
Fast.
Fasting.
Fatal.
Fatherly
Fathers.
Fatt.
Fatty.
Faultless.
Fawn.
Fay.

Fear.
Fearman.
Fearweather.
Feast.
Feather.
Feathers.
Fee.
Fees.
Fell.
Felon.
Felony.
Fender.
Fern.
Ferret.
Ferry.
Ferryman.
Fetter.
Fetters.
Fever.
Fevers.
Feveryear.
Few.
Fibbs.
Fidler.
Fife.
Figg.
Filbert.
File.
Filer.
Fill.
Fillpot.
Fines.
Finger.
Finis.
Finny.
Fippenny.
Firebrass.
Firkin.
Fish.
Fisher.
Fishline.
Fist.
Fitt.
Fitter.
Fix.
Fizard.

Flagg.
Flake.
Flame.
Flaming.
Flare.
Flashman.
Flat.
Flatman.
Flatter.
Flatters.
Flaws.
Flay.
Flea.
Fleet.
Flesh.
Fleshman.
Flick.
Flight.
Fling.
Flint.
Flitt.
Float.
Flock.
Flood.
Flora.
Flounders.
Flowerday.
Flue.
Flum.
Flush.
Fluter.
Flux.
Fly.
Foale.
Fodder.
Fog.
Fogey.
Fold.
Folk.
Folly.
Foot.
Footman.
Fop.
Fopless.
Force.
Forecast.

Forcer.
Forfait.
Forehead.
Forge.
Forget.
Forke.
Forks.
Fort.
Forte.
Fortune.
Forty.
Fortyman.
Forward.
Foulfoot.
Foully.
Foulweather.
Found.
Foundling.
Fouracre.
Fourapenny.
Fourname.
Fowl.
Fowls.
Fox.
Foxcraft.
Foxworthy.
Foyster.
Frail.
Frain.
Frame.
Franc.
Frank.
Frater.
Fray.
Freak.
Free.
Freed.
Freeguard.
Freelove.
Freely.
Freeman.
Freeze.
French.
Fresh.
Freshfield.
Freshwater.

Fretwell.
Friday.
Friend.
Friendly.
Friendship.
Fright.
Frill.
Frip.
Frizzle.
Frog.
From.
Frost.
Fry.
Fryman.
Fudge.
Fuel.
Fuge.
Fugit.
Full.
Fullborn.
Fullalove.
Fullbridge.
Fulsom.
Funk.
Funnell.
Furlong.
Furnace.
Furnish.
Furr.
Furrow.
Fury.
Furze.
Fussey.
Fye.

G.

Gab.
Gable.
Gaby.
Gaffer.
Gage.
Gagg.
Gaily.

Gain.	Gerken.	Goeth.	Goodwill.
Gainer.	Gherken.	Gofirst.	Goodwine.
Gait.	Ghost.	Going.	Goodwright.
Gaiter.	Giblett.	Goings.	Goody.
Gala.	Giddy.	Gold.	Goodyear.
Gale.	Gift.	Golden.	Goose.
Gall.	Gig.	Goldfinch.	Gooseman.
Gallant.	Gildersleeves.	Goldham.	Goosey.
Gallantry.	Gilding.	Goldhawk.	Gore.
Gallery.	Gill.	Goldman.	Gorebrown.
Galley.	Gimlet.	Goldsack.	Gory.
Galliard.	Gin.	Goldwater.	Gosling.
Gallon.	Ginever.	Golightly.	Gospel.
Gallop.	Ginger.	Gollop.	Gotobed.
Gallows.	Gingle.	Good.	Gouger.
Galt.	Ginner.	Goodacre.	Gout.
Gamble.	Girl.	Goodair.	Gown.
Gambling.	Girth.	Goodale.	Grabby.
Game.	Gist.	Goodbairn.	Grace.
Gammon.	Given.	Goodbeer.	Grain.
Gander.	Glad.	Goodbehere.	Grammar.
Ganderton.	Gladden.	Goodbody.	Grand.
Gapp.	Gladman.	Goodborn.	Grapes.
Garden.	Gladson.	Goodboys.	Grass.
Garland.	Glass.	Goodby.	Grates.
Garlick.	Glasscock.	Goodchap.	Grave.
Garment.	Glasspool.	Goodcheap.	Gravel.
Garnish.	Glazard.	Goodchild.	Gravelly.
Garret.	Glide.	Goodenough.	Graves.
Gash.	Glister.	Goodfellow.	Gray.
Gate.	Gloss.	Goodgroom.	Graygoose.
Gatehouse.	Glue.	Goodhand.	Greathead.
Gathergood.	Goad.	Goodhead.	Greedy.
Gaudy.	Goat.	Goodheart.	Greenberry.
Gaul.	Goater.	Goodhind.	Greengrass.
Gaunt.	Goatman.	Goodlad.	Greengrow
Gauntlett.	Goblet.	Goodlake.	Greenhalf.
Gay.	God.	Goodluck.	Greenhead.
Gaze.	Godbehere.	Goodman.	Greenish.
Gear.	Godlip.	Goodram.	Greenman.
Gem.	Godly.	Goodrum.	Greensides.
Gender.	Godman.	Goodsheep.	Greensword.
Genders.	Godson.	Goodship.	Grew.
Gent.	Godspenny.	Goodsir.	Grice.
Gentle.	Godward.	Goodson.	Grief.
Gentry.	Goes.	Goodway.	Grieve.

Griffin.
Griffinhoofe.
Grill.
Grim.
Grindall.
Grist.
Gritt.
Groat.
Groom.
Gross.
Ground.
Groundsell.
Grouse.
Grow.
Growing.
Grubb.
Grumble.
Gudgeon.
Guess.
Guessard.
Guest.
Guile.
Guily.
Guise.
Gull.
Gullet.
Gulley.
Gum.
Gumboil.
Gump.
Gun.
Gunner.
Gush.
Gut.
Gutter.
Guy.

H.

Hack.
Hackblock.
Hackstaff.
Haddock.
Hagg.

Haggard.
Hail.
Hailstone.
Hailstones.
Hair.
Hairs.
Hake.
Hale.
Halfacre.
Halfhead.
Halfnight.
Halfpenny.
Halfyard.
Halstaff.
Halt.
Halter. ·
Ham.
Hammer.
Hamock.
Hamper.
Hamrogue.
Hand.
Handforth.
Hands.
Handsomebody.
Handy.
Handyside.
Hanger.
Hanks.
Hannibal.
Happy.
Harbird.
Harbour.
Hard.
Hardbottle.
Hardedge.
Hardgraft.
Hardman.
Hardstaff.
Hardware.
Hardy.
Hardyman.
Hare.
Harefoot.
Hark.
Harken.

Harlot.
Harm.
Harmony.
Harness.
Harper.
Harras.
Harrow.
Hart.
Hartfull.
Hartshorn.
Hash.
Hasluck.
Hasmore.
Haste.
Hat.
Hatfull.
Hatoff.
Hatred.
Hatter.
Haven.
Havens.
Hawke.
Hawker.
Hawking.
Hawthorn.
Hay.
Hayball.
Haycock.
Hayday.
Hazard.
Hazel.
Hazlefoot.
Head.
Headache.
Heady.
Heal.
Heath.
Heap.
Heaps.
Heard.
Hearing.
Hearsay.
Hearse.
Heart.
Heartfree.
Hearty.

Heater.
Heath.
Heather.
Heathman.
Heats.
Heaven.
Heavens.
Heaver.
Heaviside.
Heavy.
Heavyeye.
Hector.
Hedge.
Hedgecock.
Hedger.
Hedges.
Heel.
Heifer.
Height.
Held.
Hell.
Hellhouse.
Helm.
Helpusgod.
Hemp.
Hen.
Herd.
Herdsman.
Heriot.
Heritage.
Hero.
Herod.
Herring.
Hidden.
Hide.
Hider.
Higginbottom.
Highcock.
Highman.
Highway.
Hilt.
Hinder.
Hinderwell.
Hinge.
Hip.
Hiscock.

Hist.
Hitch.
Hitchcock.
Hives.
Hoar.
Hoard.
Hobby.
Hodd.
Hoe.
Hog.
Hogger.
Hogmire.
Hogsflesh.
Hogsmouth.
Hold.
Holdback.
Holdcroft.
Holder.
Hole.
Hollow.
Holly.
Holy.
Holyday.
Holyland.
Holyoak.
Home.
Homer.
Hone.
Honey.
Honeyball.
Honeybone.
Honeybum.
Honeybun.
Honeyman.
Honour.
Honywill.
Hood.
Hoodless.
Hoof.
Hook.
Hookaway.
Hooker.
Hop.
Hope.
Hopeless.
Hopewell.

Hopper.
Horn.
Hornblower.
Horner.
Hornet.
Horsecraft.
Horsefall.
Horseman.
Horsenail.
Hose.
Hospital.
Hotham.
Hour.
Hours.
House.
Household.
Houseman.
Hovell.
How.
Howl.
Howlong.
Hoy.
Hue.
Hug.
Hull.
Hum.
Human.
Humble.
Hunger.
Hunting.
Hurdle.
Hurll.
Hurt.
Husband.
Hush.
Husk.
Hussey.
Hutch.
Hutt.

I.

Icemonger.
Idle.

Idol.
Image.
In.
Incarnation.
Inch.
Inches.
Ingold.
Ingrain.
Inkpen.
Innocent.
Instance.
Iris.
Iron.
Irons.
Isles.
Ivory.
Ivy.
Ivyleaf.

J.

Jack.
Jacket.
Jane.
January.
Jar.
Jay.
Jealous.
Jelly.
Jerusalem.
Jester.
Jew.
Jewell.
Job.
Joint.
Jolly.
Joy.
Judge.
July.
Jump.
Jumper.
June.
Juniper.
Jury.

Just.
Justice.
Jutting.

K.

Keel.
Keen.
Keep.
Keeping
Kettle.
Key.
Keylock
Keys.
Kick.
Kid.
Kilboy.
Kilbride.
Kill.
Killard.
Killer.'
Killman.
Killmartin.
Killmaster.
Killmister.
Kilmany.
Kilpatrick.
Kilt.
Kind.
Kinder.
Kindred.
Kine.
Kinsman.
Kiss.
Kitcat.
Kitchen.
Kitchenman.
Kite.
Kitten.
Kitty.
Klinghammer.
Klingheart.
Knee.
Kneebone.

Knell.
Knife.
Knitt.
Knock.
Knocker.
Knower.

L.

Lace.
Lack.
Ladd.
Ladle.
Lady.
Ladyman.
Laimbeer.
Lake.
Lamb.
Lambkin.
Lambshead.
Lame.
Lamp.
Lamprey.
Lance.
Lancet.
Land.
Landless.
Large.
Lark.
Larking.
Lash.
Lassy.
Last.
Late.
Later.
Lathe.
Lavender.
Law.
Lawless.
Lawman.
Lawn.
Lax.
Lay.
Leach.

Leaf.
Leak.
Lean.
Leaning.
Leaper.
Lear.
Leary.
Leather.
Leatherbarrow.
Ledger.
Leech.
Leftwitch.
Leg.
Legless.
Lemon.
Lent.
Leopard.
Letter.
Letters.
Lettice.
Light.
Liberty.
Licence.
Linch.
Life.
Lightbody.
Lightfoot.
Lightly.
Lightning.
Lightwine.
Likely.
Lillywhite.
Lily.
Limb.
Limber.
Limebeer.
Line.
Ling.
Link.
Liquorice.
Liquorish.
Lions.
List.
Little.
Littleboy.
Littleboys.

Littlechild.
Littlefair.
Littlefear.
Littlehead.
Littlejohn.
Littlepage.
Littleproud.
Lively.
Liver.
Livery.
Living.
Lo.
Loach.
Loads.
Loan.
Lob.
Lock.
Locker.
Locket.
Locock.
Lofty.
Lollard.
Lone.
Long.
Longbottom.
Longcake.
Longden.
Longest.
Longfellow.
Longmaid.
Longman.
Longmate.
Longshanks.
Longstaff.
Look.
Loom.
Loop.
Loose.
Loosely.
Losecamp.
Lots.
Love.
Lovecock.
Loveday.
Lovejoy.
Lovekin.

Lovelady.
Loveless.
Lovelock.
Loveluck.
Lovely.
Lover.
Loving.
Low.
Luce.
Luck.
Lucky.
Lucy.
Lull.
Lumber.
Lumpy.
Lung.
Lush.
Lute.
Lye.
Lyes.
Lyon.

M.

Mabb.
Mabee.
Mace.
Mackerell.
Made.
Madder.
Maggot.
Maggs.
Maid.
Maiden.
Maidman.
Maids.
Mail.
Mails.
Main.
Mainland.
Mainprize.
Maize.
Maker.
Makin.
Malady

Malay.
Male.
Mall.
Mallard.
Mallet.
Malt.
Mandrake.
Man.
Manage.
Manger.
Mangles.
Mangy.
Manhood.
Manifold.
Manlove.
Manlover.
Manly.
Manners.
Mansard.
Mansion.
Mantle.
Many.
Manypenny.
Maple.
Maples.
Mapp.
Maps.
Marble.
March.
Mare.
Marjoram.
Marklove.
Markquick.
Markthaler.
Marlock.
Marriage.
Marry.
Mars.
Martyr.
Marvel.
Mash.
Matterface.
Mattock.
Matts.
Maudlin.
Maw.

Maxim.
May.
Maybee.
Maycock.
Maydenhead.
Maypowder.
Maze.
M'Quirk.
M'Turk.
Mead.
Meal.
Mealy.
Mean.
Means.
Meanwell.
Measure.
Meats.
Mecca.
Meddle.
Medlar.
Medley.
Meek.
Mellow.
Melon.
Mention.
Merry.
Merryman.
Merrymouth.
Merryweather.
Mess.
Metcalf.
Mew.
Middlecoat.
Middlemast.
Middleweek.
Mildmay.
Midwinter.
Milady.
Mile.
Milk.
Milksop.
Mill.
Million.
Minnow.
Mires.
Missing.

Mist.
Mite.
Moat.
Mock.
Mode.
Moist.
Mole.
Moll.
Molten.
Monarch.
Monday.
Money.
Moneypenny.
Monkey.
Monument.
Moon.
Mooney.
Morcock.
Morehen.
Morrow.
Mort.
Mortar.
Moss.
Most.
Mote.
Moth.
Motley.
Mouse.
Mouth.
Much.
Muchmore.
Muckle.
Mudd.
Muddle.
Muff.
Muffin.
Mug.
Mulberry.
Mule.
Mull.
Mullet.
Mumbler.
Mumm.
Mummery.
Mummy.
Munch.

Murther.
Muse.
Muses.
Musick.
Musk.
Musket.
Muspratt.
Mussel.
Mustard.
Muster.
Musty.
Mutter.
Mutton.
Mycock.
Myrtle.
Muzzy.

N.

Nabb.
Nack.
Naggs.
Nail.
Nap.
Napkin.
Napper.
Narrowcoat.
Nave.
Navy.
Nation.
Nay.
Near.
Neat.
Neck.
Need.
Needle.
Needs.
Negus.
Neighbour.
Neithermill.
Nero.
Nest.
Nethersole.
Nettle.

Nettleship.
New.|
Newback.
Newbegin.
Newbirth.
Newbold.
Newbolt.
Newbone.
Newborn.
Newcomb.
Newgate.
Newlove.
Newmarch.
Newts.
Nibbs.
Nice.
Nick.
Nicks.
Niger.
Nigh.
Night.
Nightingale.
Nihill.
Nile.
Nine.
Nipper.
Nix.
Noah.
Nobbs.
Noddle.
Nodes.
Nogget.
Noise.
Noodle.
Noon.
Northeast.
Nose.
Noser.
Nosworthy.
Not.
Notcutt.
Nothing.
Nothard.
Notman.
Now.
Nox.

Null.
Nun.
Nurse.
Nut.
Nutbean.
Nutman.
Nutbrown.
Nutting.
Nutty.

O.

Oak.
Oakenbottom.
Oaks.
Oakleaf.
Oar.
Oat.
Oaten.
Oats.
Odium.
Off.
Offer.
Office.
Officer.
Ogg.
Ogle.
Oill.
Old.
Oldacre.
Oldcorn.
Oldman.
Olyfather.
Omega.
Omen.
Omit.
Omnibus.
Once.
One.
Onion.
Onions.
Only.
Onslow.
Onyx.

Orange.
Orchard.
Orders.
Organ.
Ormduel.
Orphan.
Ostler.
Ostrich.
Other.
Otherday.
Otherman.
Otter.
Ought.
Ouldbief.
Our.
Outcry.
Outlaw.
Outpin.
Oven.
Over.
Overall.
Overmire.
Ovid.
Owings.
Owner.
Oyster.

P.

Pace.
Pacer.
Pack.
Packet.
Packman.
Paddock.
Paddy.
Pagan.
Page.
Pail.
Pain.
Painter.
Painting.
Pair.
Palfrey.

Paling.
Pallace.
Pallas.
Pallet.
Palm.
Palsy.
Pamphlet.
Pan.
Pander.
Pane.
Pannel.
Pannier.
Panter.
Panther.
Panting.
Pantry.
Papa.
Paquet.
Par.
Paradise.
Paragon.
Paramour.
Parcel.
Parcells.
Pardon.
Pare.
Parent.
Paring.
Parish.
Park.
Parlour.
Parrot.
Parshall.
Parsley.
Parson.
Part.
Partner.
Partridge.
Passenger.
Past.
Patch.
Pate.
Pater.
Path.
Patience.
Patient.

Paunch.	Pennycuick.	Pillage.	Plume.
Pause.	Pennyfather.	Pillar.	Plumtree.
Paviour.	Pennyfeather.	Pillow.	Poacher.
Paw.	Pennymaker.	Pimple.	Pock.
Pay.	Pennyman.	Pinch.	Pocket.
Payment.	Pennymore.	Pinchard.	Podd.
Pax.	Pennypacker.	Pinchback.	Poet.
Pea.	Pentecost.	Pinchbeck.	Poignard.
Peace.	Pepper.	Pindar.	Point.
Peaceable.	Peppercorn.	Pine.	Pointer.
Peach.	Perch.	Pinfound.	Poke.
Peachy.	Perfect.	Pinion.	Pole.
Peacock.	Perk.	Pink.	Polk.
Peak.	Perry.	Pinn.	Poll.
Peal.	Person.	Pipe.	Polly.
Peanot.	Pert.	Pissard.	Pond.
Pear.	Pescod.	Pisse.	Ponder.
Pearl.	Pester.	Pish.	Poodle.
Pearly.	Pestle.	Piso.	Pool.
Peas.	Pett.	Pistol.	Poor.
Pease.	Pettibone.	Pit.	Pop.
Peasoup.	Pettycoat.	Pitchbottom.	Pope.
Peat.	Pew.	Pitcher.	Popoff.
Pebble.	Pharoah.	Pitchford.	Poppy.
Peck.	Pharrisee.	Pitchfork.	Porch.
Pecker.	Pheasant.	Place.	Port.
Peckit.	Phœnix.	Plaice.	Portal.
Peckover.	Physick.	Plain.	Porter.
Peddle.	Pick.	Plane.	Portwine.
Pedigree.	Picker.	Plank.	Poser.
Pedlar.	Pickle.	Plant.	Post.
Peed.	Pickles.	Plaster.	Pothecary.
Peep.	Pickup.	Play.	Potiphar.
Peer.	Pickwoad.	Playfair.	Pot.
Peerless.	Piddle.	Please.	Pottage.
Peg.	Pie.	Pleasent.	Pottle.
Pelisse.	Pierce.	Pledge.	Pounce.
Pellet.	Pig.	Pledger.	Pound.
Pelter.	Pigeon.	Plenty.	Pout.
Pen.	Pigfat.	Plot.	Powder.
Pence.	Pighog.	Ploughman.	Praise.
Penfound.	Pike.	Pluck.	Prance.
Penhole.	Pilchard.	Plug.	Pray.
Pennebaker.	Pile.	Plum.	Precious.
Penny.	Pilgrim.	Plumb.	Prentice.
Pennycook.	Pill.	Plumber.	Presence.

Press.
Prestige.
Pretty.
Priam.
Price.
Pride.
Priest.
Priestly.
Prigg.
Prime.
Primrose.
Prince.
Prior.
Prizeman.
Proctor.
Profit.
Prong.
Prophet.
Proud.
Proudfit.
Proudfoot.
Proudlock.
Proudlove.
Proudman.
Prudence.
Prudent.
Puddifoot.
Puddle.
Puff.
Puffer.
Pull.
Pulley.
Pulse.
Punch.
Punchard.
Puncheon.
Purchase.
Purely.
Purge.
Purple.
Purr.
Purse.
Pursglove.
Purslove.
Pushing.
Pussy.

Putt.
Putts.

Q.

Quail.
Quaint.
Quaintance.
Quare.
Quarrel.
Quarrels.
Quarry.
Quart.
Quarterly.
Quarterman.
Quarters.
Quash.
Quear.
Queen.
Quell.
Quere.
Quest.
Question.
Quhitelaw.
Quick.
Quicklove.
Quickly.
Quill.
Quilt.
Quilter.
Quince.
Quintal.
Quire.
Quirk.

R.

Rabbit.
Race.
Rack.
Raffle.
Raffles.

Rafter.
Ragg.
Ragless.
Raiment.
Rain.
Rainbird.
Rainbow.
Raisin.
Rake.
Rally.
Ram.
Ramard.
Rambelow.
Ramsbottom.
Range.
Ranger.
Rank.
Ransom.
Rant.
Rap.
Rape.
Rash.
Rasp.
Rat.
Rate.
Rathbone.
Rather.
Rattle.
Raven.
Raw.
Rawbone.
Ray.
Reach.
Reader.
Readless.
Ready.
Real.
Ream.
Rear.
Reason.
Reckless.
Record.
Red.
Redcock.
Reddish.
Redfoot.

Redhouse.
Redman.
Redmile.
Redpath.
Reed.
Register.
Render.
Renew.
Rescue.
Rest.
Restcome.
Revel.
Rex.
Reynard.
Ribbons.
Rice.
Rich.
Richbell.
Richer.
Riches.
Rick.
Rickets.
Ricks.
Riddle.
Ride.
Rideout.
Rider.
Ridge.
Riding.
Ridings.
Right.
Rightly.
Ring.
Ringgold.
Ringlet.
Rings.
Ringwell.
Rino.
Rip.
Risband.
Rise.
Rising.
Risk.
Rivet.
Roach.
Road.

Roak.	Ruff.	Saunter.	Sentance.
Roan.	Ruffle.	Saveall.	Sequin.
Roarer.	Rufus.	Savory.	Service.
Roast.	Rugg.	Saw.	Sessions.
Rob.	Rugs.	Saws.	Setter.
Robe.	Rule.	Saxon.	Settle.
Robin.	Rum.	Sayman.	Seton.
Rock.	Rumage.	Saywell.	Sex.
Rocket.	Rumball.	Scaffold.	Sexty.
Rod.	Rumbell.	Scamp.	Shade.
Roe.	Rumbellow.	Scarce.	Shaddock.
Roebuck.	Rumble.	Scaredevil.	Shakeshaft.
Roll.	Rummer.	Scattergood.	Shakspeare.
Rolls.	Rump.	Scholar.	Shallow.
Roman.	Ruse.	Schoolcraft.	Shally.
Rome.	Rush.	Schooling.	Shamely.
Rood.	Rushbrook.	Scipio.	Shark.
Roof.	Rushout.	Scolding.	Sharkey.
Rook.	Rust.	Score.	Sharpless.
Rooker.	Rye.	Scragg.	Sharpley.
Room.		Screech.	Shatter.
Roost.		Screen.	Shatterfoot.
Root.	**S.**	Scroggs.	Shave.
Rope.		Scrubbs.	Shaveall.
Roper.	Sack.	Scuffle.	Shaves.
Ropeyarn.	Sacks.	Scurry.	Sheaf.
Rose.	Safe.	Scutcheon.	Sheargold.
Rosebottom.	Sage.	Seaborn.	Shears.
Rosewell.	Sail.	Seabright.	Sheath.
Rosewharm.	Saint.	Seacock.	Shed.
Rotten.	Sale.	Seacole.	Sheepwash.
Rough.	Sales.	Seafart.	Sheepshanks.
Roughead.	Sall.	Seagood.	Sheet.
Roughly.	Salmon.	Seal.	Sheets.
Round.	Salt.	Seaquill.	Shelf.
Roundtree.	Same.	Search.	Shell.
Rout.	Sample.	Searchwell.	Shergold.
Row.	Sanctuary.	Seas.	Sherry.
Rowbottom.	Sand.	Seasongood.	Shew.
Rowell.	Sandal.	See.	Shewcraft.
Royal.	Sandell.	Seedsman.	Shield.
Ruby.	Sandman.	Segar.	Shilling.
Ruck.	Sands.	Self.	Shillinglaw.
Rudder.	Sandy.	Send.	Shin.
Ruddy.	Sattenshall.	Sendall.	Ship.
Rue.	Saul.	Sendfirst.	Shiplake.

M

Shipperbottom.	Silks.	Smoothy.	Spilling.
Shipping.	Sill.	Snare.	Spiltimber.
Shipwash.	Silly.	Sneezum.	Spindle.
Shipway.	Silver.	Snipes.	Spine.
Shirt.	Silverlock.	Snooks.	Spinnage.
Shirtcliff.	Silverside.	Snow.	Spinning.
Shoe.	Silversides.	Snowball.	Spire.
Shoebottom.	Silverstone.	Snugg.	Spires.
Shoecraft.	Simmer.	Sockett.	Spirit.
Shoesmith.	Simper.	Soda.	Spirt.
Shooter.	Simple.	Sofa.	Spite.
Shorthose.	Sinfoot.	Softly.	Spittle.
Shortland.	Sinew.	Sole.	Spittlehouse.
Shotbolt.	Sing.	Sop.	Spleen.
Shott.	Skill.	Sore.	Splint.
Shout.	Skillet.	Sorely.	Spokes.
Shouter.	Skin.	Soul.	Spoon.
Shove.	Skip.	Sour.	Spooney.
Shovel.	Skipper.	Sourbuts.	Spose.
Show.	Slack.	Sourmilk.	Spotts.
Shrub.	Slate.	Sourwine.	Sprat.
Shuffle.	Slaughter.	Sours.	Sprawling.
Shufflebottom.	Slaymaker.	Southcoat.	Spray.
Shuffler.	Sleep.	Soy.	Spread.
Shun.	Slender.	Spade.	Sprigg.
Shutter.	Slewman.	Span.	Spriggs.
Shuttle.	Slide.	Spar.	Spring.
Sicily.	Slight.	Spare.	Sprout.
Sickman.	Slinger.	Spark.	Spruce.
Side.	Slipper.	Sparks.	Spry.
Sidebother.	Slow.	Sparrow.	Spurr.
Sidebottom.	Slowman.	Spavin.	Square.
Singleday.	Sly.	Speak.	Squib.
Sink.	Small.	Spear.	Squirrel.
Sinker.	Smallbone.	Spearpoint.	Stabb.
Sirr.	Smallbyhynd.	Speck.	Stable.
Sitwell.	Smaller.	Speed.	Stack.
Six.	Smallman.	Spell.	Staff.
Sixty.	Smallpage.	Speller.	Stage.
Sixsmith.	Smallpiece.	Spellin.	Stagg.
Size.	Smart.	Spender.	Staggers.
Sketcher.	Smelt.	Spendlove.	Stain.
Sides.	Smiles.	Spice.	Stair.
Sign.	Smirke.	Spike.	Stairbird.
Silence.	Smitten.	Spiles.	Stairman.
Silk.	Smoker.	Spillard.	Stairs.

Stake.	Still.	Strip.	Surpluss.
Staker.	Stillaway.	Stripe.	Suttle.
Stall.	Stillman.	Stripling.	Swab.
Stallion.	Stillwagon.	Strode.	Swadling.
Stammer.	Sting.	Strong i' th' arm.	Swallow.
Stammers.	Stirrup.	Strongman.	Swan.
Stamp.	Stitch.	Struck.	Swap.
Stanback.	Stiver.	Struggles.	Swarm.
Standever.	Stivers.	Strutt.	Sweeper.
Standfast.	Stocking.	Stubblefield.	Sweet.
Stangroom.	Stockings.	Stuck.	Sweetapple.
Staple.	Stocks.	Studd.	Sweetlove.
Staples.	Stoker.	Studman.	Sweetman.
Star.	Stones.	Stuffins.	Swift.
Starbird.	Stoneystreet.	Stumbles.	Swigg.
Starboard.	Stopfull.	Stump.	Swindle.
Starbuck.	Stopher.	Stun.	Swindler.
Stare.	Stopp.	Sturdy.	Sword.
Stares.	Stops.	Sturgeon.	Sworder.
Stark.	Stork.	Style.	Swords.
Starkweather.	Storm.	Styman.	Sworn.
Starling.	Storms.	Styx.	Sycamore.
Start.	Story.	Such.	Synge.
Startup.	Stout.	Suck.	Sythe.
State.	Stove.	Suckbitch.	
States.	Stow.	Sucker.	
Station.	Strain.	Suckling.	**T.**
Stay.	Straight.	Sudden.	
Stead.	Strait.	Sudds.	
Stealin.	Strand.	Sue.	Tabernacle.
Steddy.	Strange.	Suet.	Tack.
Steed.	Strap.	Sugar.	Tackle.
Steel.	Straw.	Sugarman.	Tag.
Steeple.	Strawmat.	Sugars.	Talk.
Steer.	Stray.	Suit.	Talker.
Stem.	Strayline.	Sulkie.	Talks.
Stemfly.	Stream.	Sum.	Tall.
Step.	Streamer.	Summerbell.	Tallboy.
Steptoe.	Streams	Summersett.	Tally.
Stern.	Streek.	Summit.	Tame.
Stew.	Stretch.	Summons.	Tank.
Stick.	Stride.	Sunken.	Tann.
Stickle.	Strider.	Sunshine.	Tape.
Stickler.	Strike.	Super.	Taphouse.
Stiff.	String.	Surety.	Tapp.
Stilgoe.	Stringfellow.	Surplice.	Tapper.

Tarbottom.	Tether.	Timber.	Topcoat.
Tarbox.	Thaler.	Timberlake.	Tope.
Tarbuck.	Thane.	Timbers.	Topless.
Tardy.	Thaw.	Times.	Topp.
Tares.	Thew.	Timeslow.	Topper.
Target.	Thick.	Timewell.	Tout.
Tarr.	Thickbroom.	Tingle.	Tow.
Tarry.	Thin.	Tink.	Towell.
Tart.	Thing.	Tinker.	Toy.
Tassel.	Third.	Tinkling.	Trail.
Tatler.	Thirkettle.	Tinline.	Train.
Tatlock.	Thirst.	Tinn.	Trainer.
Tatt.	Thistle.	Tiplady.	Trapp.
Tatters.	Thorn.	Tipler.	Travel.
Tattle.	Thorns.	Tipp.	Tray.
Taunt.	Thorogall.	Tippet.	Trayfoot.
Taw.	Thoroughgood.	Tipple.	Treadgold.
Tawney.	Thousandpound	Title.	Treasure.
Tayles.	Thrash.	Titmouse.	Treble.
Tea.	Thrasher.	Titter.	Tree.
Teachem.	Threader.	Tittle.	Tremble.
Teal.	Threadgold.	Toad.	Tres.
Tear.	Threeneedle.	Toadwine.	Tribe.
Tears.	Thresher.	Toby.	Tribute.
Teas.	Thrift.	Toddy.	Trice.
Teat.	Thrush.	Todhunter.	Trick.
Teats.	Thrustout.	Toe.	Tricker.
Tee.	Thurkettle.	Toes.	Trickey.
Teeth.	Thunder.	Toewater.	Trim.
Telfair.	Thursday.	Tolefree.	Trimmer.
Tell.	Thus.	Toll.	Trinkle.
Telling.	Tick.	Tolls.	Trip.
Tempest.	Tickle.	Tolman.	Triplett.
Ten.	Ticklepenny.	Torn.	Trist.
Tenant.	Tidy.	Tombs.	Trivett.
Tench.	Tidyman.	Tommy.	Trodden.
Tendrill.	Tie.	Tone.	Trollop.
Tenet.	Tier.	Tongs.	Troop.
Tennis.	Tiff.	Tongue.	Trope.
Tense.	Tiffany.	Toogood.	Trotman.
Tent.	Tiffin.	Took.	Trott.
Tentimes.	Tiger.	Tool.	Trotter.
Terrier.	Tight.	Toombs.	Trout.
Test.	Till.	Toot.	Trow.
Tester.	Tilt.	Tooth.	Trowell.
Testimony.	Tiltman.	Toothaker.	Troy.

Truant.
Truck.
True.
Truebody.
Truefit.
Truelove.
Trull.
Truly.
Truman.
Truss.
Trust.
Trusty.
Try.
Tryon.
Tub.
Tubman.
Tuck.
Tucker.
Tuft.
Tufts.
Tulip.
Tune.
Tunn.
Tunnell.
Tunney.
Turning.
Turk.
Turns.
Turtle.
Twa.
Twaddle.
Tweedle.
Twelve.
Twelves.
Twelvetrees.
Twentyman.
Twice.
Twiceaday.
Twig.
Twilight.
Twin.
Twine.
Twist.
Two.
Twopenny.
Twopotts.

Tye.
Type.

U.

Ugly.
Uncle.
Uncles.
Under.
Unit.
Unite.
Unthank.
Upjohn.
Upward.
Urin.

V.

Vail.
Vain.
Valiant.
Value.
Van.
Vast.
Veal.
Venus.
Verge.
Verity.
Vert.
Very.
Vesper.
Vessel.
Vessels.
Vest.
Vestal.
Vial.
Vice.
Victory.
Vigor.
Vigors.
Vile.
Vine.
Vinegar.

Vineyard.
Violet.
Viper.
Virgin.
Virgo.
Virtue.
Voice.
Vowel.
Vox.
Vulgar.

W.

Waddilove.
Wade.
Waddle.
Wafer.
Wager.
Wagg.
Wagless.
Wail.
Wailes.
Wain.
Wainscoat.
Waiscot.
Wait.
Wake.
Waker.
Walk.
Wall.
Wallduck.
Wallet.
Wallower.
Wand.
Wane.
Want.
Wanton.
Wapper.
Warble.
Ward.
Wardlaw.
Wardrobe.
Ware.
Waredraper.

Wares.
Wardrobe.
Warn.
Warr.
Warrior.
Wart.
Wash.
Washer.
Wasp.
Waste.
Watch.
Watchman.
Water.
Waterfall.
Waterhair.
Watering.
Waterman.
Waterguard.
Wattle.
Wax.
Way.
Waygood.
Wayman.
Weak.
Weal.
Wean.
Wear.
Weatherbee.
Weatherhead.
Weatherhog.
Weatherspoon.
Weatherstone.
Weatherwax.
Webb.
Wedd.
Wedge.
Wedgewood.
Wedlock.
Weed.
Week.
Weeks.
Weekly.
Weeks.
Weight.
Weightman.
Welfare.

Welfill.
Well.
Welladvice.
Wellbeloved.
Wellborn.
Wellcome.
Wellhop.
Wells.
Welp.
Wench.
Went.
West.
Westcoat.
Westland.
Westwood.
Whale.
Whalebelly.
Whalebone.
Wharf.
Wheat.
Wheatcroft.
Wheel.
Wheeler.
Whelps.
Wherry.
While.
Whip.
Whippy.
Whirlpenny.
Whisker.
Whistler.
Whist.
Whiteboon.
Whitebread.
Whitefoot.
Whitehair.
Whitehand.
Whitehead.
Whiteheat.
Whitehorse.
Whiteland.
Whitelegg,
Whitelock.
Whiteside.
Whitethread.

Whitlow.
Whittle.
Why.
Whymark.
Wick.
Wicker.
Widdow.
Wide.
Widows.
Wife.
Wig.
Wight.
Wild.
Wildblood.
Wildboar.
Wildgoose.
Wildish.
Wildman.
Wildsmith.
Wile.
Wilks.
Will.
Willing.
Wily.
Winch.
Wind.
Windard.
Winder.
Windmill.
Window.
Windows.
Windybank.
Wine.
Winegar.
Wines.
Winfarthing.
Wing.
Wink.
Winker.
Winks.
Winner.
Winpenny.
Winter.
Winterflood.
Winterhalter.

Wintermute.
Wintersmith.
Wiper.
Wire.
Wires.
Wisdom.
Wise.
Wisecup.
Wiseman.
Wish.
Wisher.
Wit.
Witch.
Witcraft.
With.
Withcraft.
Witty.
Woad.
Wolf.
Wonder.
Wonders.
Woodbine.
Woodcock.
Woodfall.
Woodfork.
Woodhead.
Woodman.
Woodnot.
Woodthrift.
Woodyard.
Woof.
Wool.
Woollen.
Woolly.
Word.
World.
Worm.
Worms.
Worn.
Worry.
Worship.
Wort.
Worth.
Worthy.
Wouldhave.

Wrapp.
Wrath.
Wren.
Wrench.
Wrinkle.
Write.
Wroth.
Wry.
Wulgar.
Wunder.
Wunderly.
Wunders.
Wurst.

Y.

Yalowhaire.
Yam.
Yard.
Yaw.
Yea.
Yearly.
Yell.
Yellow.
Yeoman.
Yew.
You.
Youngblood.
Younghusband.
Youngjohns.
Younglove.
Youngman.
Youngmay.
Yule.

Z.

Zeal.
Zigzag.
Zink.